YESTERDAY'S PAPERS

Martin Edwards

Andrews UK Limited

Note from the author: In writing this book, I have been grateful for the help of friends and colleagues expert on the Liverpool and legal scenes. Nevertheless, this is a work of fiction and all the characters, firms, organisations and incidents described are wholly imaginary. So far as I know, they do not resemble any counterparts in the real world; in the unlikely event that any similarity does exist, it is an unintended coincidence.

Contents

Dedicated to Catherine

Where mystery begins, justice ends.

– Edmund Burke, A Vindication of Natural Society

Introduction

Like each of the Harry Devlin series, *Yesterday's Papers* is a title based on a song, from a 1967 album by the Rolling Stones. And like each of the others, it is an inspired choice. No other title would be so right for a story that rests on the legal documents filed away from a case of thirty years ago. Typically, too, there are more echoes of the title in the fact that from the beginning Devlin is offered assistance by a crime reporter from the local press. Moreover, the music business is central to the plot. The victim was the girlfriend of a pop singer at the heart of the Mersey Sound.

Layer upon layer. Martin Edwards knows the music scene of the sixties as if he worked for the Melody Maker. His Merseybeat stars, Ray Brill, Clive Doxey and Benny Frederick, co-exist in these pages with the Beatles, Cilla Black, Gene Pitney and John Barry. How appropriate that Liverpool solicitors store their old files in a disused pier ballroom known to Devlin as the Land of the Dead – and how pleasing that his visit there is heralded by a mangled saxophone rendition of A Hard Day's Night that would have John Coltrane turning in his grave, to say nothing of John Lennon. A wonderful concept, grippingly created.

Another rich seam is criminology. When I discovered the magic of reading, the first grown-up book I tackled at the age of nine (don't ask) was *The Life of Sir Edward Marshall Hall*, by Edward Marjoribanks, a colourful account of the cases this great barrister was involved in. I'm sure it influenced me to become a crime writer. How pleasing, then, to find my boyhood hero Marshall Hall mentioned in these pages. He died too soon to have featured in Liverpool's classic Wallace Case which is summarised in chapter two – but he would surely have secured an acquittal. The fictional crimes in the book get an extra cachet from references to the real murders studied by the odious Ernest Miller, the amateur criminologist who first approaches Devlin. As well as Wallace, other killers from Florence Maybrick to Myra Hindley lurk within the text, reminding the reader that even in a story rich in humour, horrors may be expected, too.

Then there is Liverpool itself. Martin Edwards was the first crime writer to think of setting a series here. Thanks largely to the Beatles, we all have some grasp of the unique character of the city and its witty people, but it takes a long-term association for a writer to convey it in totality, as he has through this engaging series of books. It's a mark of his care for authenticity that he was once asked by an interviewer if he could name any gaffe he had made and he admitted to writing in *Yesterday's Papers* about a set of railings in Sefton Park that don't , after all, exist. *A set of railings?* I mention this because the confession is typical of the author's thoroughness. The descriptions of the city aren't set pieces. They are little more than glimpses – of the ferry terminal, the pierhead, the pubs, the courts where Harry earns his keep – yet they pinpoint the vitality of the place as well as its seediness.

I've almost done. If I go on much longer I'll be revealing secrets from the plot, which is brilliant, producing surprise upon surprise, like a master magician. But I can't finish without mentioning my favourite example of the author's inventiveness – a policeman called Wedding Cake. Read on and find out why.

Peter Lovesey

Chapter One

I killed her many years ago

'**M**r Devlin, I would like to talk to you about a murder.'
Harry Devlin stopped in his tracks on his way out of
the law courts. For a fantastic moment he thought the man who
had hurried to catch him up and lay a hand on his shoulder was an
arresting officer.

Twisting his neck to see his assailant, Harry found himself
staring not at one of Liverpool's finest but at a scrawny old man
in a soup-stained bow tie and a shiny blue suit. Although he was
wheezing with the exertion, his bony grip was surprisingly fierce, as
if he feared Harry was about to take flight. The thick lenses of his
spectacles magnified the shape and size of his eyes and made them
seem not quite human.

Harry guessed the fellow was one of the city's courthouse
cranks who sat in the public galleries each morning and
afternoon, watching scenes from other people's lives distorted by
the fairground mirrors of litigation. Most lawyers disdained the
spectators as voyeurs, brushing by them in the corridors and on the
stairs, but sometimes Harry would pause in passing to exchange
a casual word. He could not resist feeling sympathy for anyone
whose life was so barren that this place became a second home.

'Want to make a confession?' he asked and gestured towards
a man in an overcoat striding past them towards the exit. 'The
detective sergeant there specialises in them. Don't worry, he doesn't
need much. Just give him your name and he'll invent the rest.'

The man released his hold and bared crooked teeth in a
conspiratorial smile. His shoulders were stooped, his wrinkled skin
the colour of parchment. In one claw-like hand he was carrying a

battered black document case and his breath seemed to Harry to have the whiff of mildewed books.

'It is your help I need, Mr Devlin. No-one else will do.'

He enunciated each syllable with pedantic care, as if English was not his native tongue. But it was the urgency of his tone that quickened Harry's interest.

'Are you in some kind of trouble?'

'No, no. You misunderstand. The murder I am speaking of occurred almost thirty years ago. Nonetheless, I believe you are able - if you will pardon the phrase - to assist me with my enquiries.'

'Thirty years ago?' Harry shook his head. 'I sometimes screamed blue murder as a babe in arms, but I never committed it. Sorry I can't help, Mr...'

'Miller, my name is Ernest Miller. Let me explain. I am looking into one of this city's most notorious crimes. You will have heard of the case, I'm sure. The newspapers, in their melodramatic way, dubbed it the Sefton Park Strangling.'

'It rings a bell.' Harry sifted through old memories. 'Wasn't it a young girl who was killed, the daughter of a well-known man?'

'Yes, the case attracted a great deal of publicity in its day. Carole Jeffries, the victim, was only sixteen years old. More importantly, to secure her lasting fame in death, she was a pretty girl with a good figure and a taste for short skirts.'

'And I seem to remember the murderer was a neighbour of hers?'

'A young man named Edwin Smith who lived nearby was arrested, it is true. Before long he confessed to having strangled Carole, but twenty-four hours before his trial was due to open, he tried to anticipate his fate by hanging himself. In that, as in so much else during his short life, he failed. A warder arrived in time to cut him down and save him for the gallows. Even so, the day of reckoning was postponed. Although the court proceedings were expected to be a formality, the authorities were reluctant to hang a man with an injured neck.'

'The executioner preferred more of a challenge?'

'I see you indulge in black humour, Mr Devlin. The best kind, I quite agree. But I think you miss the point. In those days - we are talking of 1964, you will recall - the campaign to abolish capital punishment was intensifying. The establishment dreaded a newsworthy incident.'

'Such as?'

Miller's tongue appeared between his teeth. 'They feared that a mistake might be made. If undue pressure were applied on the scaffold, there was a risk that the neck might snap and Smith would lose his head. Imagine, Mr Devlin, how the media would have feasted on that.'

Miller's eyes sparkled as he spoke, causing Harry to feel as cold as if he had stepped naked into the wintry streets outside, but something made him ask, 'So what happened?'

'The trial took place at the end of November and Smith was duly sentenced to death. However, as you will know, the law required three Sundays to pass before such a verdict could be carried out - and in the meantime the House of Commons voted to abolish capital punishment. As it happened, no hangings took place after the August of that year. Smith could certainly have expected a reprieve.'

'A lucky man.'

'Not so lucky as you may think,' said Ernest Miller. 'Having escaped the noose, Smith finally managed to kill himself in jail. Once again the authorities were careless - as they so often seem to be. He slashed his own throat on a jag of glass one night and severed the jugular vein.'

Harry bit his lip. His imagination was vivid - he had never quite decided whether that was an asset in a solicitor, or a fatal flaw - and Miller's words made his skin prickle. He could not help seeing in his mind's eye the sickening scene: the blood-soaked remains of a human being stretched across the concrete floor of a silent and unforgiving prison cell.

Gritting his teeth, he said, 'So where do I come in?'

'Smith's solicitor was Cyril Tweats.'

No wonder he was found guilty, Harry said to himself, the thought easing his tension. But all he said aloud was, 'I see.'

'You begin to appreciate my interest? I gather Mr Tweats retired recently and your firm took over his practice. Which is why I wanted to take a little of your time to talk about Carole's killing.'

'I don't quite...'

'I wonder,' said Miller. 'Your case has been adjourned until tomorrow morning. Perhaps you might allow me to buy you a drink and give you an idea of the information I am seeking. And if, at the end of half an hour, you decide I am wasting your time, well, no hard feelings. What do you say?'

Harry hesitated. He knew how much work in the office awaited his return; if he missed the last post, the following morning the sight of a mound of unsigned correspondence would reproach him like the grubby face of a neglected child. Besides, he had been repelled by the impression of pleasure Miller had given in lingering over the phrase *He slashed his own throat on a jag of glass one night and severed the jugular vein.* It was easy to visualise him salivating as he waited for a judge to don the black cap.

He glanced back over his shoulder towards the ground-floor lobby. The judicial roulette wheel had stopped spinning for the day, leaving losers to sulk in their cells whilst winners walked free to celebrate in style. His clients, Kevin and Jeannie Walter, had already disappeared, whisked off to the city's priciest restaurant by minders from the newspaper which had spent so much money to buy their story. He had last seen their barrister, Patrick Vaulkhard, in the robing room, taunting his opposite number about cover-ups and corruption. One of the bent coppers in the case was hanging around at the bottom of the open-tread staircase, waiting for his colleagues. With his hands in his pockets and his eyes fixed on the floor, he seemed deep in thought. If he had any sense, he was making plans for an early retirement.

Harry found himself recoiling from the prospect of ending the day back behind his desk. He was not by nature indolent, but a long afternoon in court had left him in a Philip Larkin mood: why should he let the toad of work squat on *his* life? The letters could wait: a drink would do him good. In any case, surely no harm could come from a brief conversation, however unappealing his companion?

He began to move towards the revolving door. 'Why not?'

'Splendid. I am most grateful for your co-operation.'

Outside a raw wind nipped at Harry's cheeks and knuckles. On the far side of Derby Square, harsh lights from the office blocks burned in the dirty darkness. Queuing commuters stamped their feet and tried to keep warm as they waited at bus stops for the procession of maroon double-deckers with bronchitic engines moving in sombre ritual along James Street. The snow of early morning had turned to slush, treacherous underfoot. Harry's shoes slid as he crossed the road at speed, trying to dodge the spray thrown up by a passing juggernaut.

At the corner of North John Street he waited for his companion to catch up. When at last he made it through the traffic to the safety of the pavement, Miller bent his head. 'Not - not as young as I was,' he panted.

'None of us are.'

Miller's breath was coming in shallow gasps and he seemed unsteady on his feet. The legacy, Harry guessed, of too many days, weeks and months spent in cramped surroundings, poring over faded type and living life at second hand.

He gave him a minute to recover before asking, 'So what is your interest in the Sefton Park murder?'

'I live on my own, Mr Devlin. My wife died ten years ago; I have no family and few outside interests. Since finishing work, I find I have a lot of time on my hands, and I need to occupy myself somehow. Crime has always fascinated me. Now I like to indulge my curiosity. The Sefton case is a superb example of its kind. It has all the classic ingredients.'

Miller lowered his voice, as if afraid that homeward bound shoppers might overhear, and ticked the items off on his fingers. 'A good-looking girl, forward for her years. A famous father and a pop musician boyfriend. A sudden brutal slaying - and a mystery. Police investigations carried out under the remorseless spotlight of the press and television. A suspect hounded without pity and brusquely condemned. And, above all, a grave injustice.'

His eyes gleamed and Harry again felt a chill of distaste. But he could not resist putting the question for which, he had no doubt, Miller was waiting.

'Who suffered the injustice?'

Miller studied Harry's expression before nodding, as if satisfied by what he found there.

'I spent much of today listening to your case from the back of the court. You must be happy with the progress your counsel made. The judge made it plain he is unsympathetic to the police, and no wonder. Your client, Mr Walter, was convicted of a crime he did not commit. He must be hoping for massive compensation.'

'We'll have to wait and see.'

'From all I have heard, you care about justice, Mr Devlin.'

If there was a hint of irony in the words, Harry was content to ignore it. Life as a lawyer in Liverpool had taught him to grow a thick skin. 'It's a rare commodity,' he agreed. 'Worth seeking out.'

'Forgive me for saying so, but I suspect most lawyers care more about their fees. However, let that pass. I would value your co-operation, since you have access to the files of Edwin Smith's solicitor. It is too late for Smith, but you may yet help me to prove he suffered a grievous wrong.'

'Did he protest his innocence at the trial?'

'On the contrary, he pleaded guilty.'

'Yet you're suggesting the confession was false?'

Miller cleared his throat. The strange shining eyes belied his deliberate manner. He was like a small boy, Harry thought, brimming with private knowledge and unable to restrain his excitement at making a disclosure.

'I am. And that is, for me, the fascination of the murder of Carole Jeffries. I do not pretend to have embarked on any moral crusade. I cannot even claim to share your devotion to seeing justice done. But I find murder irresistible - and perfect murder most of all.'

'No-one ever described the Sefton Park Strangling as a perfect murder.'

'You miss the point, Mr Devlin. If you accept that Smith was innocent, the conclusion is unavoidable.'

Miller showed his crooked teeth again.

'The true culprit escaped scot-free.'

Chapter Two

but I shall never forget the day of her death,

'Shall we drink to crime?' asked Miller as he returned to the table they had found in a pub called the Wallace. He handed Harry a pint in a dripping glass and, breathing heavily, squeezed past him into a corner seat designed for an agile midget.

Harry lifted his glass. 'The perfect toast for this place. The architect should have been blacklisted by the Health and Safety Executive.'

The Wallace's design and decor combined elements of the Liverpool Bridewell and an ersatz Gothic crypt. Half a dozen tables were crammed into a space no bigger than a police cell and the tiny stained-glass fanlights and dark carved wood panelling were enough to give a church mouse claustrophobia. The pub was squashed between a bank and a building society and the furniture had not been screwed to the floor - a sure sign that the landlord's sights were set on the white-collar trade. Harry was back to back with a balding executive who puffed at a fat cigar while pouring rum and blacks down his secretary's throat. There was less risk of death through passive smoking than of suffocating from an excess of duty-free aftershave and discount store perfume.

'Is this not one of your regular haunts, Mr Devlin? Well, I cannot blame you, although the beer, as you are about to discover, is excellent. But since we are speaking of miscarriages of justice, I thought it a suitable setting for our discussion.'

Harry gestured towards the mahogany-framed sheets of yellow newsprint which hung from the picture moulding. 'Because it takes its name from the Wallace case?'

'Do you know the story?' The question seemed to be rhetorical, for Miller continued without waiting for a reply. 'In 1931, an insurance agent called James Wallace was sentenced to death for the brutal murder of his wife with a poker. The judged summed up in Wallace's favour, as you will note from the trial report above your head, but the jury took a harsher view. Although the conviction was quashed on appeal, Wallace only lived for another couple of years. For once the cliché was correct - he died a broken man.'

Harry stretched in his chair. The beer was as good as Miller had predicted and he was starting to relax. 'One evening,' he said, 'Wallace was playing chess in a cafeteria not fifty yards from where we're sitting. A man who gave the name Qualtrough telephoned and asked him to call the next day at a fictitious address in Mossley Hill. When Wallace gave up the wild-goose chase and made his way home, he found his wife's battered corpse lying in the parlour.'

Miller beamed. 'It is good to talk to a knowledgeable man. So often people seem unaware of Liverpool's remarkable murderous heritage.'

'You can't blame the tourist board for concentrating on its Beatles trail and the Albert Dock.'

'Yet it is so easy to forget, Mr Devlin. There are lessons to be learned from the Wallace case. The ambiguous nature of circumstantial evidence, the ruthless tunnel vision of investigating policemen, the unpredictability of juries. It is far too tempting to believe that certain facts admit of only one explanation. I call it the Sherlock Holmes fallacy, a vice which detective fiction encourages. I do not know whether you have ever heard what Raymond Chandler said of the Wallace case...'

'He described it as unbeatable.'

'Again, I am impressed. You are well read.'

'A misspent youth. And adulthood, come to that.'

'But Chandler was wrong, was he not?' Miller leaned across the table, stabbing his forefinger at Harry to emphasise the point. 'Fifty years later, the Wallace case was solved.'

'Although the guilty man escaped justice.'

'My point entirely. So much of the fascination of these mysteries lies in the fact that one person killed another - and lived on for many years thereafter, untouched by the law, untroubled even by the clammy breath of suspicion.'

'And you believe that to be so with the strangling of Carole Jeffries?'

'I do. The first person I spoke to about the case was Edwin Smith's mother. She was widowed more than forty years ago and her son died by his own hand in circumstances she must have considered to be of the utmost shame. Yet she is still alive, although very frail. I visited her in Woolton, in the residential home where she has spent the last eighteen months. She is eighty-five but for the past thirty years she has clung to the notion that a terrible mistake occurred. She accepts that her son was weak; she told me that he always craved the limelight. That, she believes, is why he confessed to the crime. Yet she is adamant that for all his faults, he was no murderer.'

'Wouldn't any mother say the same?'

'I can understand your scepticism. Yet I believe she is right.'

'Why?'

'Please forgive me, Mr Devlin, if I do not put all my cards on the table in this first conversation. Besides I am still at the stage of piecing the facts together.' He opened his document case and slid from it a thin red file. Fanning out a sheaf of papers, cuttings and handwritten notes, he said, 'As you can see, I have already collected a good deal of material concerning the case, but I have yet to begin the rigorous analysis that a solicitor would consider appropriate.'

Depends on the solicitor, reflected Harry, thinking of Cyril Tweats. Aloud, he said, 'What's your objective? Do you plan to write a book?'

Miller's laugh reminded him of a seagull's keening. 'Dear me, I have no literary ambitions at all. Although I have written - well, one or two little personal things - I can assure you I have no ambition whatsoever to see them published. I leave creative fiction to second-rate CID men with an imperfect grasp of the Police and Criminal Evidence Act. My research is conducted out of interest, nothing more.'

'How long have you been working on this project?'

As if to give himself a few seconds to frame his reply, Miller put the papers back in their wallet, which he carefully replaced in the shabby case. 'Oh, a short time only. I - I had been casting round for a suitable subject for my enquiries. Of course, I hoped for something local, as I do not care to travel far afield. And nothing mundane would do, it had to be out of the ordinary. But even though, quite apart from Wallace, Liverpool is not lacking in murder stories, I discovered that most of the best had been - if you will excuse my choice of words - done to death.'

'So you hit on the killing of Carole Jeffries?'

'As I said, it boasts many appealing features.'

If Miller felt his adjective unfortunate, he gave no indication of it and Harry did not doubt that he was in the presence of a ghoul. Yet the man's deliberate and excessively formal way of speaking had a hypnotic quality and Harry found himself hungering to know more. 'Refresh my memory.'

'Guy Jeffries,' said Miller, with pedagogic gravity, 'seemed in 1964 to be a man who had everything. He was handsome and knew it, his wife Kathleen was a tall, striking brunette and their only daughter, Carole, was extremely pretty. They were a close family. Kathleen had been a brilliant undergraduate at the time she met Jeffries, but after marrying and starting a family, she gave up any thoughts of a career and dedicated herself to looking after Carole and supporting Guy as his reputation grew. Guy, for his part, although universally regarded as a charmer, does not seem to have looked at another woman after his marriage. Everyone was aware that he doted on Carole. They were, then, that rare thing - the perfect family.'

Miller permitted himself the glimmer of a smile. 'Yet as we are all too painfully aware, life is never perfect. On a bleak February night, Carole was murdered and the happy family destroyed forever.'

'About Guy,' said Harry. 'Wasn't he a writer?'

'Yes, your memory is excellent. He wrote a couple of seminal works on socialism in the sixties, although by profession he was a lecturer. His subject, political philosophy, might sound dull to you and me, but he had the gift of making it come alive for both students and readers. Shortly before the tragedy occurred, the University was buzzing with rumours that a new Chair was to be endowed by a charitable foundation and that Guy Jeffries would be the first to occupy it.'

'How old was he?'

'He had recently celebrated his fortieth birthday. The appointment would have made him one of the youngest professors in the University's distinguished history.'

'It didn't happen then?'

'No. So much in Jeffries' life came to an end when his daughter was killed.'

'Is he still alive?'

Miller shook his head. 'He died in 1979, by his own hand. It is said that he never recovered from his distress at Carole's death. I looked up his obituary in *The Times:* reading between the lines, he must have had a nervous breakdown and I gather he later turned to drink to drown his sorrows. Extraordinary, is it not, how one act of shocking violence can change so many lives?'

Harry remembered the death of his own wife, Liz. She too had been murdered and there had been times during the past two years when he had felt as though he would never recover from the loss of her - even though they had been living apart before she was killed. Friends meaning to be helpful would tell him that life must go on, and they were right, although their homilies made him grind his teeth in silent rage. All the same, he could imagine the horror Guy Jeffries must have felt, could understand how the death of his child might rob any man of the love for life.

Brusquely, he said, 'It was February, you say, and therefore as cold as hell, if the weather was anything like it is now. What was Carole doing in the park?'

'She had told her father she wanted to go for a short walk there. It had been a misty and miserable day and she wanted to blow away the cobwebs.'

'You sound unconvinced.'

'The picture I have of Carole does not suggest to me a fresh-air fanatic. It was already dark: of course, the clocks had not yet gone forward. I find the idea of a health-giving stroll implausible. But Guy Jeffries seems to have had no hesitation in believing what his daughter told him.'

'When was her body found?'

'Close on midnight. Jeffries was working in his study when Carole left the house and Kathleen was out, attending a seminar in Manchester. There had been one caller at the house earlier in the day, another upwardly mobile man of the people by the name of Clive Doxey.'

Harry raised his eyebrows. He had not been aware that a celebrity of the present day was involved in the story. 'Nowadays Sir Clive?'

'Yes, another doughty campaigner against injustice.' Miller smiled slightly. 'Doxey left before Carole went for her walk, however, and Jeffries failed to realise she was still missing until his wife returned. At first they assumed Carole must have decided to visit a friend, possibly a girl called Shirley with whom she worked. And there was her boyfriend, a pop star of the day whom she had met through her job at Benny Frederick's photographic studio and shop in Victoria Street.'

'And that's the same...?'

'Yes, today Benny Frederick runs a thriving business specialising, I believe, in the field of corporate videos. You may have come across it yourself. But thirty years ago he had taken over his father's old firm and started making a name for himself with his portraits of many of the stars of - ah - the Swinging Sixties.'

Miller was unable to disguise the mockery in his voice. He spoke as though he was describing a risible alien culture. 'Nevertheless,' he added, 'Guy would have expected Carole at least to leave a message. He and Kathleen rang around her friends and, drawing a blank, became alarmed. The girl had mentioned herself that the boyfriend would be out of town that night and so there was no question of her having sloped off with him. Finally Kathleen called the police. The Jeffries were an influential couple and their concern was taken seriously. A constable came round and his first thought was to check the park.'

'Hadn't Guy already done so?'

'Only in a cursory way, it seems. In any event, looking methodically under every thicket, the policeman soon discovered her corpse.'

'Was it hidden?'

'The killer - presumably - had pulled it into the bushes, but made little attempt at camouflage. The young policeman must have had an eagle's eyes to discover poor Carole in darkness, but her body would have been found the next morning in any event.'

'And the ligature? Was that left on the scene?'

'Carole's own scarf was knotted around her throat. The murderer seems to have made no attempt to remove it. As you may know, that is not uncommon in strangulation cases. One can guess that she was no longer a pretty sight. "Purple lips and ears, froth and blood-staining about the mouth, the tongue forced outward, the hands clenched" - *these are the typical signs of asphyxia.* I quote, of course, from that eminent pathologist, Sir Sydney Smith.'

Even at thirty years' remove, Harry found himself repelled by the picture Miller was sketching and by the relish with which he was sketching it. *Murder fascinates everyone,* Harry thought, *because of the hints it gives of the darkest recesses of the human soul.* But the act of killing and its physical consequences seemed to him obscene, and to exult in them, he felt, was akin to drooling over a pornographic film.

He drained his glass. His earlier mood of cautious tolerance towards Miller was evaporating. Yet he felt impelled to satisfy his curiosity. 'How long did it take the police to fasten on to Edwin Smith?'

'They picked him up within twenty-four hours.'

'And the boyfriend, what about him?'

Miller pursed his lips in disapproval. 'Ray Brill - that was what he called himself. Perhaps it was a pseudonym, I am not sure.'

Harry reached back into his memory and his treasury of pop music trivia. 'Of the Brill Brothers? Is that the man?'

'Again you are well informed. Yes, that was the name of his - ah - duo.'

'Was he ever a suspect?'

'A good question. In the press reports which I have seen, he expresses shock and horror at the outrage. Yet one would expect nothing less from a cruel and ruthless killer - if such he was.'

'And Smith hired Cyril Tweats?'

'His mother did, yes. The family had money and I gather that Tweats was a popular defence solicitor of the time, but if I may be blunt, the choice of representative was not a happy one.' Again he spoke in a knowing way that gave the impression he had something else up his sleeve.

Sharply, Harry said, 'And what made you approach me?'

'When I discovered that the firm of Tweats and Company no longer exists, I called at the office of the local law society. They told me Mr Tweats had sold his practice shortly before Christmas to you and your partner, Mr Crusoe.'

'Have you spoken to Cyril himself?'

'As yet, no, for two reasons. First, when I asked about you and your firm, I was told you have something of a name for digging into cases where the truth has yet to come out. I gather you have a weakness for a mystery, but people seem to think you are a man who strives to see the right thing done. Frankly, I hoped you would sympathise with my own instinct to investigate and be willing to offer a little practical assistance.'

'Flattery won't necessarily get you everywhere. What was the second reason?'

'Any approach I may make to Mr Tweats will need to be judged with delicacy. I have to say - I trust I do not offend you - it seems possible that, if Edwin Smith pleaded guilty, he did so as a result of receiving less than the best advice.'

'I won't pretend Cyril was a latter-day Marshall Hall, but I'm not clear about exactly what you're looking for.'

'I have taken pains to trace the present whereabouts of the main surviving actors in the drama. Guy is dead, of course, and so is Edwin Smith's barrister. The detective who headed the inquiry is a sick man, by all accounts, and Carole's mother a semi-recluse. But I plan to talk to as many people as I can over the course of the next few days. I hope to hear from Smith's former girlfriend, and perhaps I'll catch up with the young man Carole was courting at the time of her death. Meanwhile, I have gone as far as I can in researching the case through paperwork available to the public. I cannot hope to gain access to the police records. But there will, I expect, still be an office file somewhere in your archives. I would be interested to see it. There is just a faint possibility that it may contain information which helps me in my quest.'

'To decide whether Smith was innocent?'

'And, if he was, perhaps to gain a clearer idea of who might have been guilty.'

'You'll be lucky.'

'Indeed I may,' said Miller. His teeth glinted in the harsh yellow light as he added, 'Think of it, Mr Devlin. To discover the truth now, after all these years, wouldn't that be a prize? Think of old Mrs Smith and what it would mean to have her son exculpated at long last. And that is not all. Who knows, one might even have the opportunity to identify the person who took advantage of Smith's scapegoat role and succeeded - yes! - in getting away with murder.'

The man was *enjoying* himself, Harry felt sure. Never mind the convicted man's mother: he was treating his enquiries as a game. And in that moment, Harry made up his mind about Ernest Miller. He was too shrewd to be dismissed as a meddlesome old fool with a bee in his bonnet; there was nothing blind or self-deceiving about his confidence that Smith had not committed the crime. Yet Harry sensed he was a man who, for all his bookish air, would like to take his pleasure recklessly. A man who might relish it all the more if the game he was playing became dangerous.

Chapter Three

when I broke forever with the past

'I'm making no promises,' Harry said to Miller as they stood on the doorstep of the Wallace.

'I would not expect them. After all, you are a lawyer.' Miller gave a thin smile. 'I hope only that I have said enough to tantalise you, to make you anxious to know rather more about the killing of Carole Jeffries, even after thirty years.'

'I can't even be sure we'll still have the original papers. And if we do...'

'Naturally, I understand there is the question of professional confidentiality, although on this occasion, since the client has long been in his grave, I anticipate no practical objection. However, you may have other qualms about making any disclosures to me. As successor in practice to Cyril Tweats, you may be conscious of the risk of being tarnished by potential criticism of the way he handled Edwin Smith's defence.'

Harry shrugged. 'I'm not worried about that. But even if we do have the old file, it may cast no light on the case.'

Miller bowed. 'Of course. But if you do discover any relevant information and feel able to share it with me, you have my address and telephone number. I hope to hear from you. In the meantime, *au revoir*, Mr Devlin, and thank you for listening.'

Harry watched him walk away in the direction of the taxi rank, a frail old man with a taste for death. He found Miller easy to dislike, but not so easy to ignore. What exactly caused him to doubt Smith's guilt? It must be more than an old woman's blind faith in her son's innocence. Was it a snatch of gossip founded on fancy, or something more substantial, something a court might accept as evidence? Harry felt sure Miller did know more about the case than he was yet prepared to reveal and, almost to his dismay, he found himself itching to learn what it was.

'Penny for 'em,' said a voice in his ear.

Turning to face the man who had spoken, Harry said, 'Whatever makes you believe my thoughts could be published in a family newspaper?'

Ken Cafferty smiled broadly, as he often did. He was chief crime reporter on one of the city's local papers and his cherubic appearance and amiable manner often induced indiscretions from people who had meant to keep their mouths shut and soon had cause to wish they had done so.

'I'm always more interested in the bits we leave out of our stories than in those we print. Not so much the stuff that's libellous, but all the true stories the man in the street simply couldn't bring himself to believe.'

'Headlines we never see, like "Low Pay Unit Demands Higher Fees For Lawyers"?'

'Now I don't mind a little invention, but I draw the line at outright fantasy. Anyway, I can sniff an exclusive already. I've caught Harry Devlin standing outside a pub with no apparent intention of going inside.'

'I staggered to the exit after I ran out of oxygen.'

'I'd have thought after a few pints you wouldn't bother about that kind of thing. Personally, I don't mind the Wallace. I like anywhere so cramped that there's no alternative but to eavesdrop. Anyway, what were you up to, celebrating the Kevin Walter verdict in advance?'

Harry shook his head. 'I'm not counting my chickens. No, someone's been bending my ear about a trial that dates back to the sixties.'

'Don't tell me they've finally decided to appeal?'

'It's an old murder case, dead and buried in more ways than one. There's a suggestion that the wrong man may have been found guilty.'

'I sometimes wonder how any crimes are ever committed, given the number of innocents around who are unlucky enough to keep being convicted. But let that pass. A miscarriage story always sells papers. Who did the system stitch up this time?'

Harry wondered how much he should tell the journalist. He could see no harm in selective disclosure. Miller had not sworn him to secrecy and Ken might have ideas of his own about the case. His encyclopaedic knowledge of Liverpudlian crime was all the more impressive in view of the sheer volume of the subject matter. He claimed his years in the job had brought him face to face with more villains than Her Majesty's Inspector of Prisons ever saw.

'A young girl called Carole Jeffries was killed.'

'The Sefton Park Strangling,' said Ken promptly.

'Ten out of ten. You know the case?'

'Before my time, of course, but I've heard about it. Every now and then we dig something up from the archives to fill a few paragraphs on a slack day. If there's a mugger roaming round that part of the city, say, or we're doing a feature on famous Liverpool murders. Lazy journalism, admittedly.' He winked and added, 'I do it a lot.'

'Any chance I might have a look at the material you have?'

Ken clicked his tongue. 'Strictly classified, you should realise that. More than my job's worth, and all that.'

'You mean it will cost me?'

'With such a cynical mind, you should have become a reporter. As a matter of fact, I'm starving. I've spent the day on the trail of a crooked builder at a property developers' conference. It would have been easier to hunt for a particular twig in Delamere Forest. Buy me a meal and I may force myself to overcome my professional scruples. I should say this kind of information must be worth a table for two at the Ensenada.'

'I had a burger and chips in mind.'

'My old dad used to work for *The Sun*, and he taught me everything I ever learned about media ethics,' said Ken sadly. 'He must be spinning in his grave at the thought of my selling my soul - for less than the price of a Chateaubriand with champagne, that is. He knew his worth and we always lived well on it. But the traditional values are dead, I suppose. I'll settle for the junk food, you old skinflint.'

As they headed towards the city centre, Harry asked, 'Ever heard of any doubt that the right man was caught in the Sefton Park case?'

'Never. Wasn't there a guilty plea? As I recall, there was no mystery. All the excitement lay in the fact that a gorgeous young girl had died and her father was famous. The main thrust of the coverage was that the bastard who killed the little girl should have swung for it.'

'A distinct absence of liberal hand-wringing about whether all the niceties of procedure had been observed in persuading him to cough?'

'We're talking about the days when people thought *Dixon Of Dock Green* was a documentary. Are you suggesting - perish the thought - that the police beat a false confession out of whatshisname?'

'Edwin Smith. No, at this stage I simply don't know.'

'So what's your interest?'

'Smith died in jail, but one or two questions have been raised about whether the verdict was right.'

'Who's been bending your ear?'

'Sorry,' said Harry with relish. 'I'm not able to name my sources. You of all people will understand that.'

The orange neon of the welcome sign above the burger bar made a vivid splash in the evening darkness. The place was packed with people queuing for service from youngsters wearing paper kepis and badges emblazoned with smiley faces. The air was thick with the smell of fat and the sound of catarrhal Scouse voices chanting carefully rehearsed phrases like 'Hi, how may I help you?', 'Two triple whammies with fries!' and 'Have a nice night!'.

Harry bought the food and drink, then slid a hot polystyrene package across the formica surface of the table Ken had chosen. 'Thicken your arteries with that.'

Ken poured brown sauce over his burger with as much delicacy as if he were coating strawberries with cream. 'So what information are you looking for?'

'I'm keen to know more about the people in the case. I hadn't realised how many of Merseyside's great and good were involved, although I was vaguely aware that Guy Jeffries was a big name at the time.'

'We headed his obituary "Socialism's Nearly Man", as I recall, though I can think of scores of contenders for that particular epitaph. He topped himself the day Margaret Thatcher came into power, you know.'

One or two jokes rose to the tip of Harry's tongue, but he resisted temptation. 'How did he do it?'

'Overdose of sleeping pills. By all accounts, he'd followed the Iron Lady's career in opposition with mounting alarm and I suppose he realised that once the Tories regained power, they wouldn't let anyone prise it out of their claws in a hurry. Needless to say, with all the political excitement, his passing barely made the stop press. Of course, by then his time had gone. He was sitting on the sidelines of public life.'

'I gather he lost his way after the death of his daughter. Not like his pal, Clive Doxey.'

'Oh yes, Sir Clive's done well for himself. Trust a lawyer. Do you know him?'

'Hardly. We move in different circles.'

'You mean you act for the criminal classes, he simply talks about them?'

Harry grinned. Although Clive Doxey had qualified as a barrister many years ago, he had never practised, preferring a career in academe. In his early days as an angry young don, he had courted controversy by railing in lectures and in print against the cosy assumptions of the legal establishment. His ceaseless campaigning for justice for all had made him a household name and earned him a knighthood when his friend Harold Wilson left Downing Street for the last time. Nowadays, he had a weekly column in *The Guardian* and was married to a blonde less than half his age whose main claim to fame was a spell as a TV weather girl. Inevitably, his success had encouraged sniping and his detractors claimed that, amongst political turncoats, he made the Vicar of Bray look like a model of constancy. Commie Clive, the romantically hotheaded student from the London School of Economics, had matured into a man faithful for twenty years to the Labour Party before flirting with social democracy in the eighties and ultimately finishing up in bed with the Liberals. But he took all the criticism in his stride and continued to fight for what he believed in. Nowadays, no national debate - whether over the wearing of wigs in court or the need to tackle the causes of crime - was complete without a soundbite from Sir Clive.

'Did you know he called at the Jeffries' house on the day young Carole died?'

'No?' Ken's eyebrows rose. 'I must say, he's managed to keep that quiet over the years.'

'I might,' said Harry on impulse, 'like to talk to him about his memories of the case. See if he thinks Smith was innocent.'

'Why not? He seems to reckon most convicted killers are. A miscarriage story would be right up his street.'

'Maybe I'll get in touch with him. Not that he is the only well-known character connected with the case. Benny Frederick is another. Carole worked for him and she was a good-looking young girl, after all. He's bound to have taken an interest in her.'

'Don't let your imagination roam too far. One thing's for sure, if anyone would have been immune to the charms of a Liverpudlian Lolita, Benny's the man. Now if you'd been talking about a pretty schoolboy, things would have been different.'

'I didn't know Benny Frederick was gay.'

'For God's sake, I thought you fancied yourself as a detective, a student of your fellow human beings. Benny's preferences are common knowledge. Mind, he's a decent enough chap. I had a few words with him only the other day at the Bluecoat Gallery. They're exhibiting photographs he took in the sixties.'

'You think he'd be happy to talk to me?'

Benny Frederick had been among the first to see the marketing potential of the pop promotion video and later he had turned his hand to producing business tapes intended to aid the development of management skills. Harry's partner, Jim Crusoe, had even talked about investing in Frederick's best-selling *Guide to Client Care and Public Relations*. Hitherto, Harry had resisted the idea but now, he thought, the time might have come to climb aboard the PR bandwagon.

'I'm sure he wouldn't mind giving you a bit of back-ground.'

'What about Ray Brill?'

Chewing hard, Ken said in a muffled tone, 'The name sounds familiar, but I can't place it.'

'He was Carole's boyfriend. Surely you remember the Brill Brothers?'

'Oh, the pop group?'

'Just a duo - and I don't think they were brothers in real life.'

Ken's brow furrowed. 'Weren't they mixed up with some other murder case?'

'No idea.'

Ken thought for a moment, then shook his head. 'It's gone. I'll let you know when the story comes back to me. But I can't say I remember much about them - or any of their songs. Truth is, I'm tone deaf. Can't tell the difference between Beethoven and Bruce Springsteen. They both sound the same to me and it's not a sound I care for. As far as I'm concerned, the written word's the thing. The pen is mightier than the skiffle board.' He laid down his plastic knife and fork. 'So those are the *dramatis personae*?'

'The ones I know about. A mixed bag, don't you think?'

'I'll be interested to hear how they react to your view that the police's neat solution to the Sefton Park case may not have been correct.'

'It's not my view. But I don't believe in neat solutions.'

'You're simply embarrassed by your repeated failures with our quick crossword.' Ken wiped his mouth on a paper napkin bearing the ubiquitous smiley face. 'That filled a corner. Give my compliments to the chef, even though he did go a little too easy on the gherkin.'

'So when can I expect you to delve into your files for a little more info?'

'I told you, it's strictly against company rules.'

'You'll enjoy the *frisson*.'

'Stop talking dirty. Look, I'll see what I can do - on the understanding that if there's a story in it at the end of the day, you'll make sure I'm the first to know.' He paused, then said, 'Preferably a true story.'

'You never used to be so fussy. Listen, I'll have a pint of best waiting for you in the Dock Brief tomorrow night. Six sharp?'

'I'll be there.' Ken flipped the empty burger carton into a wastepaper basket which again bore a smiley face. 'And thanks for your lavish hospitality.'

Harry set off home, the city was quiet, with the pubs full and the clubs yet to open. His route took him down Mathew Street, once the site of the old Victorian fruit warehouse which later became a club known as the Cavern. The Brill Brothers would certainly have played there. He was too young to remember what it had been like in Liverpool during the sixties, but people still talked about those golden days when the Beatles were on three times a week and a hat-check girl could change her name from Priscilla White to Cilla Black and suddenly find herself at number one in the charts. It had been a time of endless possibilities, when the world watched what went on in a dirty old port and when everyone believed that fame and fortune were waiting around the next corner.

The Cavern had been bulldozed when Harry was still a boy, but he had heard enough about it for images of the place to be etched in his mind. The stink of oranges and cabbage in the street outside, the sweaty atmosphere within as a crush of kids clutching precious membership cards swayed to the rhythms of the Mersey Sound. Now those of Merseybeat's pioneers who were left mostly propped up city centre bars, reminiscing about what might have been. John Lennon would never have dreamed he had so many bosom buddies or recognised the tat flogged as Beatles memorabilia by sixties survivors with an eye for a fast buck and a gullible punter.

Pausing beneath the wall sculpture which celebrated the Four Lads Who Shook The World, Harry wondered what Ray Brill was doing these days. Had he, like Guy Jeffries, had his life ruined by his girlfriend's savage murder? Was it somehow to blame for his own descent into obscurity? After Carole's death the Brill Brothers had split up and Ray's subsequent attempt at a solo career had failed to set the Mersey on fire. Harry could recall seeing his name halfway down the bill of a social club concert two or three years ago. A miserable comedown for a man who had once scaled the charts with a steeplejack's aplomb.

A tune came into his head and he started humming, trying to remember the words. Of course! It was 'Blue On Blue', the ballad with which the Brill Brothers had scored their last chart entry. Must have been around the time of the Sefton Park Strangling, Harry thought. The melody lingered as he walked towards his flat on the bank of the Mersey and when he arrived home he started searching through his record collection, sure that he had a copy of the song somewhere.

In the end he found it on a compilation of sixties pop. He put the record on the turntable, poured himself a glass of whisky and listened to the echo-laden voice of Ray Brill. The singer invested the simple lyric of heartache with a genuine anguish and as soon as the track came to an end, Harry played it again, and then again.

Could it be that, when he sang about the end of an affair, Ray was conveying pain he had felt in his own life after losing the girl he loved? By the time the needle reached a movie song from Gene Pitney on the next track, Harry was on his third drink and his eyelids were beginning to droop. He couldn't care less about the man who shot Liberty Valance. But for the sake not only of the truth but of an old woman in a Woolton home whom he had never met, he wanted to find out whether Edwin Smith was indeed the man who had strangled Carole Jeffries.

Chapter Four

and made my murderous dream come true.

That night Harry dreamed he was in the dock. Counsel for the prosecution recited his numberless crimes in a damning monotone. The judge's features had grown dark with contempt. A low murmur of hatred came from the people in the public seats and several of the jurors had started weeping at the horror of it all. Harry became aware of the aching of his limbs and suddenly realised he was handcuffed to the railings and wearing huge leg irons. He knew he was innocent, yet when he tried to speak, to explain the Crown's mistake, no words came. As the prosecutor droned on with his litany of lies, Harry could feel the noose cutting into the flesh of his neck. At last his own advocate stood up, seizing a final chance to plead for him. Harry strained with every muscle for a sight of the face beneath the wig, the face of the man who could save his life.

Oh God, no hope left. His defender was Cyril Tweats.

Fear woke him. He was shivering uncontrollably, but as it dawned on him that he was lying in his own bed in his own home, he almost cried out with joy. No wonder he felt frozen: in his restlessness he had cast the duvet to the floor, and on the coldest night of the year so far. Forcing his body into motion, he stumbled to the window and parted the curtains.

The black starless sky merged with the river. From his vantage point in the Empire Dock development he peered towards the lights of Wirral. Birkenhead itself was invisible. So were the dying yards where once so many ships had been built - *Ark Royal*, *Achilles* and *Prince of Wales* - and their incongruous neighbour, the ruined twelfth-century priory. On the water itself, nothing moved. Harry had heard talk lately of plans to bring new life to the river. The old

28

days of colonial trade had gone, never to return, but the country's jails were overflowing and some bright spark in Whitehall had dreamed up the idea of putting a prison ship on the Mersey. Harry suspected that if some of his clients went on board, it would make the mutiny on the *Bounty* seem like a squabble on Southport's boating lake.

Turning, he squinted at the harsh red digits of his bedside alarm. Five-twenty. Although he felt only half awake, he was sure he would never get back to sleep again. He swore at the memory of Ernest Miller's farrago about murderous injustice. If only he hadn't agreed to listen to the man and absorbed into his subconscious the nightmarish prospect of having his fate rest in the hands of Cyril Tweats.

Yet, looking at his hollow-eyed reflection in the bedroom mirror, he found himself unable to resist a smile. That incompetent old sod Cyril, who could give the kiss of death to the strongest case. How had he managed for so many years to escape professional disaster?

Then he reminded himself of the money Cyril had made out of the law and the comfortable life he now led in retirement. Perhaps he was not such a fool as he seemed. Even so, could Miller be right? Was it possible that if only - that phrase again! - Edwin Smith had chosen to be competently represented, he might not merely be alive today, but walking the city streets a free man?

As he made his way towards the bathroom, Harry reminded himself of the stern New Year's resolution he had made a couple of weeks before: no more 'if onlys'. The trouble was that he had a restless mind; he could never resist the temptation to speculate. And so his good intention had gone the way of so many other vows made during the dying hours of old years in an optimistic whisky haze.

The stinging heat of a shower began to revive him. Standing motionless under the sharp jet of water, he wondered whether to respond to Miller's request for help. He had promised nothing, saying merely that he would check to see whether the old file remained in existence amongst the lorry load of dusty documents that Crusoe and Devlin had inherited on acquiring Cyril Tweats' practice. Miller had not pressed him for a yes or no within a specified time, perhaps reckoning he would not be able to conquer the compulsive urge to involve himself with the Jeffries case.

And in that, he acknowledged with wry self-awareness, bloody Ernest Miller was spot on.

Within half an hour he was well wrapped against a cutting wind and walking the short distance to his office in Fenwick Court. The giant buildings on the waterfront towered above him in the early morning gloom and the Liver birds watched as the rest of the city began to stir. Milk floats and trucks full of groceries moved in stealth through the deserted streets and from time to time a police Rover slid past on its way back to headquarters at the end of the night shift.

At the last moment before unlocking the front door of New Commodities House he remembered to switch off the burglar alarm. A week before Christmas he had come here in the small hours to finish preparing an important case, only to risk a heart attack and permanent deafness on triggering the security system. Convincing the sceptical occupants of a passing panda car that he was not an opportunist thief had tested his persuasive skills to the limit. But as he had pointed out to a gum chewing constable, only a madman would bother to rob Crusoe and Devlin. Even the second-hand record shop in the basement offered richer pickings.

Once inside, he made rapid progress with the mound of papers on his desk. Lucy, his secretary, had left him a note complaining about his failure to sign his mail the previous evening. He tacked on a sentence authorising her to send the stuff first class and, cheekily virtuous, added the time of his arrival before taping it above her desk. Never mind the cost of the stamps, he thought, preparing himself for the heavenward glances of his cost-conscious partner. If Kevin Walter's compensation claim succeeded, Crusoe and Devlin would be quids in.

Hunger started to grind at his stomach and he hurried off in search of a plate piled high with bacon, sausage and eggs. His destination was at the bottom end of a passageway linking Lord Street with Derby Square: a cafeteria called The Condemned Man.

Within seconds of his sitting down, the massive bulk of Muriel, the proprietress, loomed over him. Her complexion and figure bore testimony to a lifetime devoted to fat and greasy food and she was wielding a pencil and pad like truncheons.

'In court this morning, Harry?'

He nodded. 'My client's Kevin Walter.'

Muriel's bosom gave a seismic heave. Harry had often marvelled that nylon overalls were made in her size and he feared that now the garment would finally burst.

'That's your case, is it? Wrongful imprisonment, so called? A little bird tells me the plaintiffs have briefed Paddy Vaulkhard.'

Muriel's business was geared to the morning trade and most of it was connected with the courts. Barristers, solicitors, ushers, transcript-takers, policemen, journalists - as well as the soon-to-be-convicted, stopping off here for their last hearty breakfast before sampling Walton Jail's cuisine. What Muriel did not know about law and order in Liverpool was not worth knowing. According to rumour, she was the Chief Constable's agony aunt.

'He's very good,' said Harry, a shade reluctantly.

'You don't care for him, eh?' demanded Muriel. 'Can't say as I blame you. All the same, if he gets his teeth into a witness anything like the way he tackles my fried bread, he'll take some stopping. Though all I can say is, the Walter family have been customers here for years and if Kevin really was innocent, my name's Myra Hindley.'

'Now be fair,' he said, though remonstrating with Muriel was like urging the merits of agnosticism on a hellfire preacher. 'The man spent years inside for a crime he didn't commit.'

She grunted. 'I'm a plain woman...'

He gave a cautious smile, but honesty triumphed over good manners and he did not argue with her.

'...and I speak plainly. But any road, I hear the busies are worried sick about the case. They wanted it settled out of court. Could be your lucky day.'

'I'm not counting any chickens yet.'

'Bullshit,' said Muriel, whose willingness to express an unequivocal opinion on the basis of slender data would have made her a first-class expert witness. 'Paddy Vaulkhard will love a case like that. And the fees you'll make won't do you any harm, either.'

She considered his ageing suit and loosely knotted tie; contrary as ever, he had resisted the temptation to dress to impress the television cameras he expected at court today. Her disfavour was suggestive of Judge Jeffreys presiding over the Bloody Assizes.

'Time you smartened yourself up a bit and started acting for a better class of criminal.'

'I'd love to, if only a few more drug-pushing peers of the realm or sleek insider traders beat a path to my door.'

She banged a mug of hot tea - good old English Breakfast, none of your Darjeeling muck for Muriel - on the fraying gingham tablecloth and lumbered off to exchange gossip about a kinky vicar case with a loose-tongued girl from the Crown Prosecution Service.

As he battled through the fried hillock on his plate, Harry wondered whether he should worry about having his appearance criticised by a woman for whom a duelling scar would have represented a cosmetic improvement. No point, he decided. There was always a core of truth at the heart of Muriel's exaggerations. He consoled himself with the thought that his clients might feel ill at ease with a solicitor who was a model of sartorial elegance. Dress code in the Liverpool Bridewell was not quite the same as in the Old Bailey.

By the time he had drained the last drop from his chipped mug, it was close on half eight. If he moved fast, he might be able to pick up the old file on Edwin Smith before meeting Vaulkhard to discuss battle plans. He paid the bill and flirted briefly with the pretty young cashier before setting off in the direction of the Pierhead.

The icy blast coming in from the river slowed his progress as he crossed the Strand and headed for Mann Island. He half-closed his eyes and, although he knew he should be preparing mentally for his day in court, found himself scraping the barrel of his memory for scraps of information he might have picked up over the years when reading about the Sefton Park Strangling.

The murder had never been a mystery, but rather a pointless act of brutality which had brought nothing except disaster for everyone concerned. Two loving parents had lost their only child and seen their own lives blighted forever. The same was equally true of Edwin Smith's mother. Smith had killed himself and so, fifteen years later, had his victim's father - although to all intents and purposes, Guy's life had ended on the day his daughter died. Harry knew that murder spreads its ripples wide. Close friends as well as family would never find things the same again.

Since the era of Merseybeat, for example Ray Brill's reputation as a free-spending womaniser had overshadowed his musical achievements; it was impossible to think of one decent Ray Brill single since '64. At least Clive Doxey and Benny Frederick had prospered; presumably Benny in particular had been less close to the girl. How would the three men react if confronted with the notion that Carole had not died at Edwin Smith's hands? Would they pooh-pooh it as absurd - or resent an attempt by a stranger to rake up a past they might prefer to forget? Or was it possible that one or two skeletons might be ready to tumble out of cupboards?

First things first. He was building too much on a single conversation. He must look up the file and then speak to Miller again, with a view to pressing for more concrete information. The old man's conviction that the case deserved further investigation had been strangely compelling, but Harry knew himself well enough to beware his own eagerness to find a puzzle where once there had been none.

Fighting for breath in the teeth of the gusts, at last he came in sight of his destination. A hundred yards from the ferry terminal stood a small and inconspicuous hut with a steel door. Thick mesh grilles sealed the windows of the building and no sign or nameplate gave a clue to its purpose. He fished a large key from his pocket.

As he locked the door behind him, he found his teeth chattering. The place seemed even colder than the windswept waterfront outside. He peered through the gloom to the other end of the small landing on which he stood, where a flight of steep stone steps disappeared down into the black unknown.

Flicking a switch, he swore when the light failed to come on. The air was damp and the surface of the steps greasy. He gripped the iron handrail and started counting as he put one cautious foot in front of another and edged his way downstairs.

With each step he took, the place smelled mustier. No matter how many times he came here, he could never acclimatise himself to its atmosphere. It always put him in mind of decline and decay. He found himself yearning for a quick return to daylight.

'Twenty-four,' he said to himself at last, uttering a silent prayer of thanks as his feet touched solid land.

Groping for the basement light, he found to his relief that it was working. The fierce glare from the naked bulb made him blink as he tried to adjust to his surroundings. He had arrived in a large square chamber cut into the sandstone. An opening led off into a narrow passageway and he walked towards it.

He was about to enter the Land of the Dead.

Chapter Five

We always bury our darkest secrets

On the right-hand side of the passage were two double glass-paned doors, in front of which he paused. Above them in faded paintwork he could barely distinguish the legend PIERHEAD BALLROOM. Through the dusty panes he could make out the dim shapes of chairs, desks and cupboards heaped on top of each other as if in anticipation of Bonfire Night. Not since Hitler marched into Poland and changed the world forever had the smart couples of Liverpudlian society taken the floor in there.

The open space in which he stood had once been the lobby. A fenced-off shaft occupying the far side now lacked the lift that had whisked people up to street level. During the war, the cavernous ballroom had become an air-raid shelter. It had survived the might of the Luftwaffe, but peacetime austerity had seen it utilised for storage and the main entrance hall above the ground had been demolished to make room for a car park.

Next to the shaft, a complex mass of sewage pipes climbed one wall, in macabre parody of wisteria festooning a country cottage. Walking on, he heard the echoing of his footsteps. Even in the middle of the day this was a place which belonged, he felt, to lost souls. He could almost believe he heard from behind the double doors the faint strains of a band playing Jerome Kern numbers and the delicate tread of ghostly figures in evening dress, dancing cheek to cheek.

Suddenly, a saxophone began to play, a frantic sound. Harry froze, thinking for an instant that his fantasy had been realized and the old sybarites had returned to haunt him. He did not dare to breathe.

Then he recognised the mangled tune. 'A Hard Day's Night' had been written long after the Pierhead Ballroom closed to customers. And a professional musician would never have played so many false notes. He laughed and told himself not to be ridiculous. Passing through another doorway, he entered a long and wide corridor with white-washed walls disfigured by huge moist patches. Every few yards small metal trays had been placed on the ground. They contained poison, he knew. The intention was to kill the rats for whom this place was a natural home. Necessary, he supposed. Yet he always had a sense of nausea whenever he saw the trays.

The saxophone sounded louder here. Harry paused outside a door on his left, listened for a while, then threw it open. A slender fresh-faced young man wearing shirt, tie and pinstriped trousers was kneeling on a wooden crate and leaning backwards as he blew. His cheeks were puffed out like tennis balls.

Harry put his hands on his hips and grinned. 'I know the devil has all the best tunes, but I didn't expect to hear them subjected to torture in the Land of the Dead.'

The saxophone gave a maddened squeal as the lad lost his balance and toppled to the floor. He scrambled to his feet, flushing with embarrassment.

'Sorry. I'm Adrian, I'm articled with Kim Lawrence. Her firm rents storage room here. What did you say about - about the Land of the Dead?'

'It's the name I give to this place. Where all the solicitors' files are laid to rest. With all their secrets, all their memories. I'm Harry Devlin, by the way. Crusoe and Devlin, a two-man band from Fenwick Court.'

They shook hands and he added, 'We keep our old papers here as well. Don't tell Jock what I call his second home. He'd be mortally wounded - the cellar archives are his pride and joy.'

Adrian gave an eager nod. 'He was happy for me to play here before work starts at nine and during my lunch break, said I wouldn't be disturbing anybody. He's a really good bloke. He told me he's always loved music himself.'

'Wouldn't "Subterranean Homesick Blues" be more appropriate?'

'Jock prefers ballads. He says nothing beats a decent melody.'

Harry resisted the temptation to make the obvious joke and said goodbye. As he moved away, Adrian started to do his worst with 'The Long and Winding Road'.

Further down the passageway a heavy door was set into the wall. Next to it were two rows of numbered buttons. Harry entered a four-digit security code and pushed the door open.

Facing him was a large desk, on which stood a visual display unit and keyboard. Sitting behind them was a bald, neatly bearded man with half-moon spectacles perched on the end of his nose. The archivist who dwelt in the Land of the Dead, known to all who came here simply as Jock, was studying columns of figures with the avidity of a cricket buff devouring the first-class averages in *Wisden*.

'Morning, Harry,' he said in a Glaswegian accent which many years in Liverpool had done little to soften. 'What brings you here so soon after opening time?'

'Not the pleasure of listening to young Adrian down the corridor, that's for sure.'

'Ah, he's only a wee lad, Harry. Needs somewhere to practise. I thought, he's a decent kid, what's the harm? You don't object?'

''Course not. You're doing a public service, Jock, keeping him out of sight and underground. I never knew till now a saxophone was an instrument of cruelty. John Coltrane must be turning in his grave.'

'To say nothing of John Lennon. Ah well, we all had to start somewhere. Were you looking for anything special, or just having a mooch?'

'No offence, but I'd rather mooch around Smithdown Cemetery. As a matter of fact, I'm looking for an old file.'

'You could have phoned,' Jock pointed out. 'Or sent someone over. I reckon I can lay my hand on most things inside five minutes if I'm given the correct index number.' He gestured to the flickering screen in front of him. 'The system enables me to...'

'This isn't an ordinary dead file request,' said Harry, speaking quickly. The Scot was an amiable fellow, but once embarked on an exposition of the technical wonders at his command, he was not easily hushed.

'Something out of the ordinary? Grand, gives a little spice to the day,' said Jock, rubbing his hands. Not even the dank atmosphere of the Land of the Dead could quench his boyish enthusiasm.

'It's an old matter from the days of Tweats and Company.'

'Ah.' Jock tutted, cheerfully disapproving. 'You may be asking for something there, Harry. No method, that was the trouble with the Tweats archive. No method whatsoever.'

'I appreciate your problems. Knowing Cyril, I expect half the wills he drew finished up as sandwich wrappings. So I thought I'd best come down here myself and give you a hand.'

'Fine.' Jock pressed a couple of keys and brought up a new menu on his screen. 'So tell me the name we're looking for.'

'Would you believe Smith?'

'Like to set a challenge, don't you? Any more clues, or have you got all day?'

Harry leaned over his shoulder. 'The client's first name was Edwin. It was a criminal case.'

'Criminal, eh?' said Jock abstractedly as he watched the cursor scurry down the screen. 'What sort of thing?'

'Murder.'

'Really?' He turned to face Harry, not attempting to disguise his interest. 'You mean - this Edwin Smith killed somebody?'

'He was certainly convicted on that basis,' Harry said. 'Whether the verdict was fair may be a different story.'

What did he do?'

'Killed a young girl in Sefton Park, supposedly. Strangled her.'

'Good grief - oh, bugger it! I've wiped the screen clear in all the excitement.'

Jock was agog. Murder did this to people, Harry had discovered. It was the ultimate taboo: nothing could touch it for thrills.

'The file would finally have gone to storage in the mid to late sixties.'

Jock fiddled with his computer. 'Bear with me.'

Storing Crusoe and Devlin's records here had been Jim's idea. Until six months ago the firm's dead files had been kept beneath the office in the basement of New Commodities House. Harry had preferred it that way; if he needed to refer to old papers, he liked to think they were close at hand. As time passed, however, the sea of unstored documents had threatened to drown them and Jim had pointed out that, so disorganised were their records, there was barely a hope of tracing an individual file in any event. The imminent acquisition of Cyril Tweats' practice had forced them into a move to the Pierhead cellars, which boasted up-to-the-minute facilities: an easily accessed database, a full-time archive clerk with computer skills and security sufficient to satisfy the most pessimistic insurer.

But the publicity leaflets said nothing, Harry reflected, about there being enough warfarin here to wipe out every single member of the Liverpool legal profession. He leaned over Jock's shoulder. 'How are we doing?'

The clerk watched the list of names as it sped up the screen. 'Edwin Smith, you say? I think we're in business.' He noted the reference on the pad and said, 'If you're in a hurry to be off, I can send it over.'

'No problem, I'll take it myself. I may have to do a lot of waiting around the court today. The file will give me something to scan.'

'Follow me, then.'

They walked down an aisle lined by built-in cupboards. Jock led the way, a short, slightly built man whose working clothes were sweatshirt and jeans. The two-bar radiator by the side of the desk seldom burned and Harry marvelled that his guide had never succumbed to pneumonia. He was aware of his own gooseflesh as they turned into a large cellar containing rows of shelving which reached from floor to ceiling. Each of the shelves sagged under the weight of fat packets bearing numerical codes.

'If only they could talk, eh, Harry? Plenty of stories there. Shattered reputations, unsuccessful scams. Broken marriages, disputed wills.'

Shaking his head in wonder, Jock marched into a second large room. Long metal racks were piled high with books and buff folders and there was a collection of the bizarre oddments accumulated over the years by a dozen firms of solicitors. Rusty filing cabinets leaned like Pisa's tower under the weight of big black deed boxes bearing such inscriptions as BRIGHTWELL DECEASED and ESTATE OF THE LATE COLONEL TOLMIE. Cardboard crates were scattered over the floor, making the men's progress an obstacle race. Harry peered inside one of them and caught a glimpse of the detritus of Liverpool's glory days: old mariners' charts and pictures of ships in frames with cracked and dirty glass. Another held a trophy case entombing a morose stuffed trout: an unwanted legacy, perhaps. There were chairs with missing legs, a settee with its springs sticking out and even a lumpy mattress in a bilious floral design.

Jock pointed towards the mattress. 'I've heard it said that during the Blitz the senior partner of Maher and Malcolm entertained the wives of wealthy clients in his private office on that.'

'I'd feel more comfortable on the floor outside, taking my chance with the rodent population.'

As they came to the back of the cellar, Jock indicated a crater in the distempered wall, with exposed sandstone visible inside the cavity. 'If a rat dug that out, I wouldn't fancy bumping into the bugger.'

'If you'd met some of my clients, you'd take it in your stride. So, where do you keep Cyril's stuff? I realise he bequeathed a load of garbage, but we must be under the Mersey by now.'

'Not far off. I reckon that when we get a thirty-foot tide, I can hear the water washing up not a stone's throw away. As for the material from Tweats and Company, I'm still logging it on the system. It'd be easier to catalogue Dale Street litter.'

'You have my sympathy. Total quality management meant less to Cyril than Sanskrit.'

'Hey! I think we've struck gold!'

Jock bent down to a shelf just above the floor and picked out three files of papers held together by a rubber band. He flourished his find in front of Harry's nose.

'"SMITH, EDWIN, MURDER." All right?'

'Jock, you're a genius. Thanks.'

'So what is all this about?' asked the little man as they picked their way back through the detritus. 'A murder case thirty years ago - where do you come in?'

'I don't know yet that I do come in. But I've been asked to look into the old papers, see what I make of them.'

Jock raised his eyebrows. 'I've heard you have a name as a part-time private detective. Tramping the mean streets of Merseyside.'

'So someone's told you I'm a nosey sod? Well, I don't suppose I'll be sueing for slander. I can't deny I have an inquisitive streak. And yesterday I met a man who thinks there may have been a miscarriage of justice in the case of Edwin Smith.'

'Get away.' Jock flourished a dog-eared Ross Macdonald paperback which he had pulled from the back pocket of his jeans. 'Fact is, I like a good murder mystery myself. You'll have to let me know what you discover. Who knows? I might get a chance to play Watson to your Holmes.'

'Don't hold your breath. The man I spoke to may be way off beam.'

'But if he isn't?'

'Let's see what yesterday's papers tell me. Whether Smith was guilty as charged or just unlucky in his choice of defence lawyer.'

Puzzled, Jock stroked his jaw. 'But Cyril Tweats was a good brief, by all accounts. He may not have known about keeping proper records, but he was a champion of the ordinary man, not any kind of fool.'

Harry gave a sceptical grunt and nodded back towards the endless shelves of old documents.

'You know what they say - doctors bury their mistakes and architects build them. Solicitors simply file them.'

Chapter Six

and I feel no sense of guilt at all.

When Harry emerged into the open air, the Pierhead was as cold and grey as before. Yet in comparison to the Land of the Dead, it suddenly seemed as bright and warm as Malibu.

On his way to Derby Square, he wondered again whether there could be any doubt that Edwin Smith had strangled Carole Jeffries. A thin layer of dust lay over the papers in the folder tucked under his arm. Cyril Tweats hadn't agonised over the case, hadn't kept going back to it, striving to find a way to prove Smith's innocence. Once Smith's mother had paid his bill, he'd closed his file and consigned it to the vaults. Harry could picture him discussing the trial at his club, shaking his head and saying that it was a sorry business, but although he had done his best, the evidence had damned his client. Yet, Harry reminded himself, the conviction of Kevin Walter had once seemed equally sound.

On Kevin's twenty-fifth birthday, a jeweller's home in South West Lancashire had been burgled. He had been watching television when a masked man brandishing a gun burst in and bound and gagged him before stealing rings, watches and silver worth a small fortune. The jeweller was a mason, a member of the same lodge as several senior officers in the local force, and the investigating team was under pressure from the start to find the guilty man. Kevin Walter, a robber with a violent streak whose curriculum vitae read like a teach-yourself guide to the British penal system, headed the queue of the usual suspects.

Under questioning, Kevin claimed that on the evening of the break-in, he and Jeannie had quarrelled furiously because he had accused her of seeing another man. He had hit her and then stormed out to celebrate his birthday with a one-man pub crawl.

But he could not provide an alibi and after eighteen hours in the cells, his nerve snapped. He confessed and said his accomplice was a man he'd met in a pub whom he knew only as Terry. It had all been Terry's idea, of course, and Terry had conned him good and proper: he'd never seen any of the proceeds of the raid. Long before the trial came around, Kevin changed his story and was vehement in protesting his innocence. He'd been bullied into making a false confession and Terry was a figment of his own mind. But the jury didn't believe him and the judge sent him down for ten years.

He would still have been doing time had it not been for a stroke of luck. One fine morning another jeweller was offered several of the stolen rings and watches. He became suspicious and called in the police; for once their enquiry went like a dream. They traced the fence who had supplied the hot property and he identified his own supplier, a young villain from Toxteth called Gurr who had no known links with Kevin Walter. When Gurr was charged he exercised his right to silence. Meanwhile Kevin remained inside.

After they had spent so long apart, Jeannie remembered her husband's virtues more clearly than his vices and began to campaign actively for his release. She sacked his original solicitor and instructed Harry instead, whilst urging the media to help put right yet another miscarriage of justice. Harry discovered from transcripts of the interviews prior to Kevin's confession that he had been denied proper access to legal advice and that the interrogation had been oppressive. Revealing a flair for publicity which any kiss-and-tell bimbo would envy, Jeannie Walter soon began to attract support from journalists and pressure groups. Clive Doxey, no less, was one of those who had penned a column espousing her cause, Harry remembered. Gurr went to jail, still without opening his mouth, and Kevin remained inside. But a bandwagon had started to roll.

Jeannie dubbed the case Waltergate: the papers loved it and made the tag their own. She had once been a disco queen and when she organised a Jive for Justice at Empire Hall, it sold out and made national headlines. A tabloid paper bought exclusive rights to her story and portrayed her as a modern Joan of Arc. Even when a rival rag, disappointed to lose out in its bid for the biography of Jeannie for Justice, broke the news that she had picked up a couple of convictions for prostitution during Kevin's years inside, she revelled in the limelight. She was a victim of society, she said, just as her innocent husband was. It was easier to make a monkey blush than to embarrass Jeannie Walter.

Before long, the Home Secretary, who was heading for retirement and wished to be remembered as a man of conscience, referred the case back to the Court of Appeal. The three judges, perhaps appalled by the threat of a Strip in the Strand outside London's Law Courts if Kevin did not walk free, promptly ruled his conviction unsafe and unsatisfactory.

Since then the Walters' quest had been for compensation. The Home Office, keen to sweep the case under the carpet, had offered a handsome sum which Jeannie promptly denounced as derisory. Kevin wanted ten times as much after all he had been through, she proclaimed. And so they had opted to resist all settlement overtures and hazard everything on suing the police. The truth was, Harry guessed, that the Walters wanted blood: preferably that of the detectives who had stitched Kevin up.

By the time he arrived at the courthouse, it was filling with people and the ashtrays were already piled high with half-smoked stubs. Men and women with anxious faces and urgent voices were talking too much in a feverish effort to pass the time before their case was called. They had waited a long while for the day when they must take part in the legal lucky dip.

He caught sight of his court clerk, Ronald Sou, arms full of files and books, at the far end of the ground-floor lobby with Patrick Vaulkhard. Although he was on his home territory, the barrister too seemed tense and expectant and his fox-like features were twitching in anticipation of the battle ahead.

Harry walked over to say hello. Ronald Sou, habitually inscrutable, gave a scarcely perceptible nod, but said nothing. Harry and Jim Crusoe had once speculated on what it would take to prompt Ronald to express surprise. Doubling his salary might do it, they agreed, but so far they had not been able to afford the temptation to put their theory to the test.

Vaulkhard said, 'So, Harry. A crucial cross-examination for us this morning. Let's see if we can bait the trap.'

A Liverpudlian born and bred, he had kept close to his roots, and life at the Bar had never rubbed the Scouse edge off his accent. His reputation was that of a crafty and cynical individualist, someone who did not quite fit in. The old men in smoke-filled rooms who made such decisions had never allowed him to take silk and Harry guessed they never would.

'Here come our clients,' said Harry, glancing through the glass windows into Derby Square. He could see twenty or more journalists crowding Kevin and Jeannie Walter and throwing questions at them as if feeding fish to dolphins. It was plain that the real focus of their interest was Jeannie. Although her husband might be the plaintiff seeking huge damages, she was the character with reader-appeal. Love her or loathe her, Jeannie Walter had star quality and even the most hardbitten members of the pack were hanging on her every word.

Pushing through the swing doors, she detached herself from the group of journalists and, her husband lumbering two paces behind, headed towards the lawyers. She moved as if on a catwalk, slinky and self-confident. Harry guessed she had been up as early as he had that morning, contriving her platinum curls into that exotic cascade. He had a gloomy feeling that she nurtured ambitions of becoming a new icon for the fashion industry.

'How's my favourite pair of briefs?' She squealed with laughter, as she always did when she cracked that joke, then rushed on without waiting for an answer. 'Rarin' to go, Paddy? Great!'

'Ready to give them bastards hell, I hope.' Kevin Walter's years in prison had left him with a carefully preserved sense of martyrdom and a vocal whine that set Harry's teeth on edge. His skin was pallid, his shoulders hunched; he had suffered at the hands of the legal establishment and, like a cantankerous invalid, was bent upon making the most of his misfortune.

'The moment of truth.' said Jeannie, her eyes gleaming.

'It'll be a day to remember,' said Vaulkhard wryly, 'if we hear the truth in this court of law.'

As he sat in the courtroom, listening to Vaulkhard question the detective sergeant who had taken Kevin Walter's confession, Harry recalled a conversation from *Crime and Punishment*. He had read it as a schoolboy and the story of Raskolnikov's downfall had made a lasting impression. In later life, it had even given him a little understanding of the forces that moved his own clients to their pointless acts of self-betrayal. A few lines about cross-examination stuck in his mind: Porfiry's explanation of the method of starting an interrogation with trivial irrelevances as a means of putting the witness off his guard before stunning him with the most dangerous question of all. It seemed to him that Patrick Vaulkhard had taken the message to heart.

The early exchanges were low-key, little more than a series of pleasantries. Vaulkhard lingered over the sergeant's past record, and the commendations he'd received for shrewd detective work. The sergeant, a heavily built man in his forties, was on the alert for traps and for some time his responses were cautious and monosyllabic. But gradually he began to unbend and by the time Vaulkhard moved on to his part in the Walter case, he was in the mood to defend his actions with vigour.

'I suppose you will say that you were working long hours?'

'As a matter of fact, I was. We all were. It was an important investigation and we had plenty more on besides.'

'But you put considerable effort into detecting the man who committed this particular robbery?'

'You can say that again.'

'Yet no-one seems to have quizzed the real perpetrator, Denny Gurr, in any detail about the crime.'

The sergeant shrugged. 'I was only one of the team. I can't answer for everyone.'

'So,' said Vaulkhard. He paused for a moment before continuing and allowed himself the faintest of smiles. 'The fact that you bullied Kevin Walter into his so-called confession had nothing to do with the fact that Denny Gurr was, at the time, going out with your only daughter, Tracey?'

The silence seemed to last forever. Harry could see spots of sweat shining on the sergeant's forehead and watched as the man's hand moved to loosen his tie. It seemed as if his legs were starting to buckle beneath him and he stretched out an arm to steady himself.

Vaulkhard's face seemed more vulpine than ever. 'Yes or no will suffice, sergeant.'

The man turned to the judge. His naturally florid complexion seemed to have darkened. 'My Lord ...,' he began, but his voice was barely a whisper and it trailed away into nothingness.

'Are you feeling unwell, sergeant?' asked the judge.

For answer, the man clutched at his chest. He was gasping for breath. Then, as everyone looked on in frozen and fascinated horror, he slowly crumpled to the floor.

The silence was broken by a cry of alarm from someone in the public gallery. Harry was immobile. *So Dostoyevsky had it right*, he thought. And from the row behind him, he could hear the voice of

Jeannie Walter: 'It's fantastic, absolutely fantastic! Paddy's killed the bugger!'

'I've heard of deadly cross-examinations,' said a voice in Harry's ear, 'but this is ridiculous.'

He was standing outside the court cafeteria. The sergeant had been whisked away to intensive care: the paramedics reckoned he had suffered a coronary. Kevin and Jeannie Walter had departed to give their media minders their exclusive reaction to the morning's sensational development and the staircase and corridors of the courthouse were no longer buzzing with excitement. The rest of the cases on the list today were humdrum by comparison: the usual assortment of broken marriages and shattered lives. The judge had adjourned the case until the following Monday, although over a coffee Patrick Vaulkhard had expressed the view that that was due more to old Seagrave's fondness for a four-day week than to any serious expectation that the sergeant would soon rise Lazarus-like from his sick bed to explain why he had never drawn his daughter's brief fling with Denny Gurr to the attention of his superiors.

He looked round and saw a lean woman in white shirt and black jacket and skirt. A Greenpeace badge was pinned to her lapel and an Amnesty International magazine peeped out of the briefcase at her feet. Kim Lawrence, partner in another small city-centre practice and specialist in civil liberties law.

'So you've heard about our little sensation in court?'

'You know what this place is like for gossip, and any new twist in the Jeannie Walter saga is hot news.'

'She's become a legend in her own time, I agree. And after this case, what's the betting but that she'll make a career out of it?'

'Out of campaigning for justice?'

'No, out of being Jeannie Walter.'

Kim Lawrence's habitually watchful expression relaxed into a smile. Her blonde hair was brushed off her forehead and held in place by a slide; she shunned make-up and the only jewellery she wore was a pair of CND earrings. A career spent trying to bridge the gulf between truth and evidence had etched frown-lines into her forehead, and she wasn't someone he had ever socialised with. But looking at her now, his interest was awakened, and not simply because she currently chaired the Miscarriages of Justice Organisation.

'As it happens, I wanted to have a word with you. I'm interested in a case which is right up MOJO's street.'

Kim leaned forward. MOJO campaigned on behalf of those who claimed to have been wrongly convicted, whether through mistake or malice, yet whose cases were deemed by the authorities to be closed. It had supported the original fight for Kevin Walter's release although Jeannie's bandwagon had soon developed a momentum of its own.

'Another dodgy prosecution?'

'Too soon to say - even though the case in question dates back thirty years.'

'Thirty years? You're going back in time, aren't you? How come you're involved?'

Harry described his meeting with Ernest Miller and outlined what he knew about the Sefton Park Strangling. She listened with care and he enjoyed the feeling that she was concentrating her attention upon him, even if only to hear the story he had to tell. He knew that, as he spoke, she was weighing up the facts, assessing the strength of the case against the convicted man. As soon as he had finished, she slipped into the role of devil's advocate.

'So - if Smith was innocent, did he plead not guilty?'

He hesitated before replying. 'Apparently not. His confession stood and the jury took it at face value. Don't forget, those were the days when most people thought the British bobby could do no wrong and it was inconceivable that someone might untruthfully admit to having committed murder.'

'Okay, but what makes you think there's anything in Miller's story? The world is full of oddballs who like to spin strange yarns.'

'Don't I know it? Half of them seem to wind up on the other side of my desk. But sometimes those oddballs turn out to be telling the truth.'

She nodded and he knew that she understood. The people for whom she took up the cudgels were also apt to be social misfits and committing herself to their cause often meant a long and lonely struggle against judicial hostility and public indifference. Harry knew her prime concern was always to do her best for her clients, however unlovely they might be, rather than for Kim Lawrence.

'True enough. Most of MOJO's campaigns begin with one person who refuses to accept the received wisdom.'

'Miller might be such a man. He makes my flesh creep, but he's no fool. I'm sure he knows more about the Sefton case than he's let on so far, enough to convince him Smith may well have been innocent. But at the same time he's still gathering evidence. I simply wondered whether MOJO would be willing to become involved if I did find proof of an injustice.'

'Sorry, we have enough on our plate at present with contemporary disasters. But if it would help, I'd be glad to look at anything you turn up myself. If Smith didn't kill the girl, he deserves to have his name cleared.'

'Thanks. I'll let you know if I find anything of note in old Cyril's file.'

She gave him a sceptical look. 'If I know Cyril Tweats, you're most likely to find a trail of paper which exists solely to prove that he strove mightily but to no avail. Did you ever hear of that eighteenth-century breach of contract claim where the plaintiff turned out to be a highwayman? Not only did he lose the action, but he was hanged into the bargain. I often suspect he was represented by Tyburn's answer to Cyril Tweats.'

Harry laughed. 'Good old Cyril. Yet his clients loved him. When they phone up now and find he's retired, they're desolated by the thought they now have to depend on Crusoe and Devlin. Cyril made them feel good. It's a rare skill for a lawyer - and it earned him a few bob over the years.'

'Another miscarriage of justice.'

Jim Crusoe was in reception when Harry stepped over the threshold of New Commodities House. He was a big, bearded man whose mane of hair was turning grey prematurely - something he always attributed to the strain of being in partnership with Harry Devlin.

'I gather the police case collapsed this morning.'

'In more ways than one.'

'So Ronald Sou told me. He reckons the odds are that the police authority will make a much-improved offer.'

Harry groaned. 'From the gleam in your eye, you've already spent the fees.'

'I wasn't thinking only of the money. But of course, we ought to invest sensibly. New technology, that's what we need. A bar-code system for recording the time we spend, visual display units for every typist, an upgraded accounts package. There's a new debt-collection program on the market which...'

'Christ, the office will look like the Starship Enterprise by the time you've finished with it. Didn't we leave Maher and Malcolm to escape the tyranny of computers? Talk about looking over your shoulder. That place made Big Brother look like someone who was happy to keep himself to himself. I don't want Crusoe and Devlin to turn into a law factory.'

Jim's brow darkened. 'Look, old son. The law's no place for Luddites. We're in business, remember? We need to compete, to provide a decent service.'

'I haven't heard Kevin or Jeannie Walters complaining.'

'You've done a superb job, I'm the first to say so. But we must move with the times. We can't keep living in the Dark Ages.'

Harry shrugged and ambled back to his room. He knew his partner's arguments were unanswerable and that in time he would have to surrender. His reluctance to agree to change was not born of stubborn stupidity, but rather of an unwillingness to acknowledge that he was first and foremost a businessman, that simply seeing justice done would never in itself pay the mortgage. He resented, not his partner, but the failure of the world to match his more romantic notions of what was right and what was wrong.

A heap of messages awaited him, but the excitement in court had quenched any thirst he might have had for desk work. What he wanted was to take a look at the file he had retrieved from the Land of the Dead. He slipped off a couple of clips that held the old bundle of documents together and the papers spilled on to his desk. Statements of witnesses, correspondence, typed notes of evidence from the committal proceedings, instructions to counsel tied up with pink string, together with a couple of handwritten sheets in a young person's unformed hand.

He looked at those last two pages. They comprised a record of the trial at the old Liverpool Assizes. Cyril Tweats' clerk had faithfully taken down every word uttered when Edwin Smith was tried for the murder of Carole Jeffries. Yet not much had needed to be said, in view of Edwin's guilty plea.

Once more Harry asked himself the question that had been nagging away at the back of his mind ever since Miller had first accosted him. *Why* was the man so sure Edwin Smith was innocent?

He turned to the correspondence. Cyril had written the usual letters to his client and to the police. A reference in one letter made

Harry pause for thought. He turned to the separate set of notes on the meetings between Cyril Tweats and Edwin Smith. Soon he found what he was looking for.

One day in April, not long after his arrest, Edwin had asked to see his solicitor. When the two men were alone together, Edwin had insisted that he had not killed Carole Jeffries. His confession to the crime had been false.

Harry caught his breath as he read the neatly typed notes. At last - an indication that Miller might be on the right track and that Carole could have been murdered by someone else. Yet Edwin had not denied the crime in court. Following his change of heart, what had gone wrong?

The answer was: Cyril Tweats. He had simply not believed Edwin's retraction. It was clear from the papers that he felt sure that his client had simply panicked at the thought of what lay ahead. Stronger men than Edwin Smith had been terrified by the prospect of the rope. So Cyril had laid down a challenge to the young man: how do you explain your knowledge of facts of which only the murderer could be aware? No answer had been forthcoming. Harry could imagine the young man trembling as his solicitor pointed out that a not guilty plea in a case such as this would mean that he must give evidence on his own behalf and face up to rigorous interrogation from a prosecuting counsel who held all the cards.

Edwin's nerve soon broke; within twenty-four hours he withdrew his claim to innocence. By changing his tune again, he kept things simple for everyone: his defence team, the police, the courts and himself. He said he was willing to stand by his confession after all, plead guilty and allow the law to take its course.

Harry wondered if that was the moment when, overcome by the relentless inevitability of the legal process, Edwin Smith had decided that he could bear it no more and that, one day when the opportunity presented itself, he would put an end to his torment by taking his own life.

Chapter Seven

I doubt whether people would believe me even if I admitted everything.

Harry licked his forefinger and turned back through the file to find the copy of the statement in which Edwin Smith had confessed to murder. How plausible was the young man's claim to have strangled the girl? In this bundle of papers, surely, must lie the answer.

He read slowly and, to his surprise, with a sinking heart. For the terms of the statement were unequivocal and he realised he had from the outset been hoping that Miller's instincts were sound and that the Sefton Park case was a mystery unsolved.

Edwin explained how he knew Carole Jeffries as a neighbour. He had always regarded her as pretty but unattainable. She had given barely a sign that she was aware of his existence, but he sensed she knew of his two criminal convictions: one for exposing himself to a woman walking her dog in Otterspool and another for the theft of knickers from a nearby washing line. He guessed that, if she ever thought of him at all it was with disgust and he did not blame her for such a reaction: sometimes he disgusted himself.

On the last afternoon of Carole's life he had been on his way home when he saw her a few yards ahead of him and on the other side of the road, walking along the path which skirted the boundary of Sefton Park. She seemed to be wandering aimlessly and when he caught sight of her face as she passed beneath a street lamp, he saw that her expression was miserable, which made him sad, since he thought a girl who had everything ought surely to be happy all the time.

Something prompted him to change course and follow her into the park. Perhaps he would be able to cheer her up and thereby earn her favour. He described her as wearing a brown sheepskin jacket and green silk scarf, as well as black leather boots. After a couple of hundred yards or so he caught up with her and tried to strike up a conversation.

'Bitter weather, isn't it?'

Carole took no notice.

'You look a bit fed up,' he ventured.

She continued walking.

'My mum says, a trouble shared is a trouble halved.'

She didn't falter in her stride as she said, 'Why don't you just piss off?'

He kept pace with her in silence for another couple of minutes. It was a grim winter's evening, cold and dark enough to have deterred even the most resolute of dog walkers, and the park was deserted. Their path took them by the side of the lake for a while before branching off through a dip in the landscape bordered on either side by large spiky shrubs.

Edwin decided to dare everything. 'I wasn't going to tell you this. But the truth is, I really fancy you.'

At last he'd got through to her. She halted and faced him. 'You fancy me? So what am I supposed to do? Grovel with gratitude at the admiration of a subnormal little pervert like you? You're pathetic, Smithy. Now fuck off and go and play with yourself like you usually do in that garden shed of yours and leave me alone.'

The harsh response would always stay in his memory, word for word. Yet according to Edwin, it was the contemptuous sneer on her pretty face that made him snap. He wanted her and he had the chance to do something about it. Without another word, he seized hold of her and dragged her into the bushes. She struggled and screamed as he tried to undo her jacket. He was not a strong young man and, once she had recovered from the initial shock, she fought back fiercely enough to make him fear she was about to break free. He had no weapon to frighten her. All he could see ahead was misery and humiliation. He felt he must do something to avoid that. Anything.

So he pulled the silk scarf tight around her neck. She kicked out wildly, but he did not let go. As he increased the pressure on her throat, gradually her resistance weakened. Within moments - or so it seemed to him - she was limp in his arms. He had not meant to kill her. The sight of her blue face horrified him, repulsed him too. He shoved her body aside and ran blindly down the path, desperate to make his escape before the park keeper came to lock him in for the night with his victim's corpse for company.

Harry read every word of the confession before he put it down. Each page was initialled and at the very end was a terse paragraph.

This statement is true. I make it of my own knowledge and belief and I have been told that I may alter, add or delete anything in it with which I do not agree.

Underneath was a large, childishly scrawled signature, *Edwin Smith*, followed by the date.

It was as clear and convincing an admission to murder as any Harry had read. Its simplicity gave it the ring of truth and so did the crucial corroborative details. Edwin knew what the girl had been wearing when she met her death. Even more significantly, he knew how she had been killed, and with what ligature. Harry was certain that such information would not have been public knowledge at the time Edwin was taken in for questioning. The police were bound to have held it back. Even in the sixties attention-seekers with a taste for confessing to crimes were not unknown and a detective wishing to verify a witness statement would be looking for precisely the kind of specific and accurate information that Edwin Smith had been able to provide.

Harry sighed. So what was he to believe? Flicking again through the mass of paper, he concentrated with the ease of long experience on the key points to emerge from the documents, tracing every development in the case.

Carole had died on a Saturday. According to a statement taken from her father - still devastated by the killing and by his own admission scarcely able to take it in - she had gone shopping in the city centre during the morning, leaving home at around the same time as he set off to meet a group of his students. From the statements of Shirley Basnett, Benny Frederick and Ray Brill, it appeared that Carole had called in at Benny's shop for a chat, even though it was her day off. Ray had called in while she was there before he drove down to London for a gig. Carole and he had had a tiff - about nothing in particular, he claimed - and she had left, saying she was going to catch the bus back home.

Clive Doxey had visited the Jeffries' house shortly after lunch, hoping to catch Guy. The two of them were working on an idea for a book called *Liberty, Law and Labour* and Clive had come up with some fresh thought for the synopsis. Carole had been alone in the house at the time and she had seemed her usual self - warm and vivacious was how he described her. They had chatted for a while, but although Carole said she expected her father home soon, Clive could not stay.

Guy Jeffries missed his friend, Carole told him, by a few minutes only. He explained that he had been delayed by a colleague from the University and his daughter gave him a brief summary of her morning, implying that she regarded the squabble with Ray as something and nothing. After that Guy had retired to his study, to work on an article for *The New Statesman* for which he had a strict deadline. At about four o'clock, whilst he was bent over his typewriter, Carole had popped her head round the door and said she was going out for a stroll in the park, but would not be long. He had not, he told the police, even bothered to turn his head to catch a glimpse of his daughter for the very last time. The article had absorbed all his attention and only when Kathleen arrived back from Manchester shortly after six and Carole was still nowhere to be seen had he started to become anxious about her fate. He had looked round the part of the park nearest to the house but found no trace of her. Calls to her friends yielded no result. Eventually, at Kathleen's insistence, they had called the police.

Vera Smith, Edwin's mother, had confirmed that she was out of the house for most of the weekend in question, paying a visit to an old schoolfriend who lived on the other side of the Pennines. She could not give Edwin an alibi. All she could do to help was instruct Cyril Tweats to act on her son's behalf.

'Your first mistake,' muttered Harry under his breath.

The file contained a careful note of Cyril's interviews in prison with his client. At their first meeting, Edwin had been uncommunicative. Psychiatric reports indicated that he had a low IQ and poor self-image. He appeared to be dazed by all that had occurred since the police had picked him up. When they met again, however, the young man was more eager to talk. The gravity of his own position had finally dawned on him and he began by insisting that he was not a murderer. He claimed to have made up the confession, although he did not allege that the police had beaten it out of him. But when Cyril had pressed for more information, he had retreated into his shell, refusing to explain how he could have known how Carole was dressed and how she was killed. The following day, he summoned Cyril again and formally retracted his protestations of innocence.

Cyril had briefed Mr Hugo Kellerman of Brasenose Chambers to act as defence counsel. In his written instructions he had referred to the discussion in which Edwin had denied his guilt. Yet he had made little of it and no barrister would have experienced any difficulty in reading between the lines. Cyril thought his client knew too much and had confessed too readily for there to be any chance that he was innocent.

Kellerman had evidently taken the same view when Edwin had discussed the case with his legal advisers. According to Cyril's notes on the conference, the pros and cons of a guilty plea had been debated. There was no evidence of undue pressure on the part of the police and the prosecution had not only the confession but also Edwin's damning knowledge about the scarf. The chances of an acquittal were negligible and if Edwin pleaded guilty he would not have to cope with the intense strain of giving evidence in hostile surroundings, knowing that his life might depend on it.

How would I have reacted if I had been unjustly accused of murder? Harry asked himself. An easy one to answer: he would have striven to defend himself to the last drop of blood. Yet experience had taught him that many criminal clients saw the world differently. They were fatalists, not fighters, people who saw life as a lottery in which they were destined to lose.

As Cyril completed his preparations for the trial, the news came through that Edwin had been found in his cell by a warder, more dead than alive. He had used a shoelace to try to hang himself. The file did not explain how he had obtained the means for suicide, but Harry knew that prisons were places where blind eyes were often turned and anything was possible. Somehow, he felt, it was characteristic of Edwin that he had even bungled his first attempt to kill himself.

Eventually Edwin's injuries healed. *They wanted his neck to be perfect, with the skin unbroken and the wounds all healed - so that they could put it in a noose*, thought Harry, remembering what Miller had told him. He found it difficult to choke back revulsion at the picture in his mind of doctors checking the prisoner, to make sure no-one would be embarrassed by a beheading when the time came for him to mount the scaffold. Harry had in his own life met murderers who, he felt, deserved to die, but he hated the cold-bloodedness of capital punishment.

The trial took place at last in the classical surroundings of St George's Hall, scene over the years of cases more celebrated by far than that of the wretched murderer of Carole Jeffries. Its outcome had been swift and certain. The judge described Edwin as a savage and dangerous young man and, donning the black cap, sentenced him to death for his heinous crime.

The file contained a short note recording that straight after the trial Cyril had visited his client in the cells. Apparently Edwin had thanked him for his efforts. No question of any appeal arose and there was no indication as to whether anything passed between the two men other than anodyne, half-embarrassed remarks. The purpose of the note was to help justify Cyril's fees - and, no doubt, to cover his back: if his legal skills had ever matched his survival instinct, Cyril would have made it to the House of Lords.

A press cutting that Cyril had preserved in the file announced that, in the August before judgment was passed on Edwin, two men had been hanged for murder, Gwynne Evans at Strangeways in Manchester and Peter Allen at Walton Jail here in Liverpool itself. They had the dubious distinction of being the last men to go to the gallows in Britain. In October, a Labour government came to power and the end of the death penalty was in sight. Cyril conferred with Kellerman and they debated the possibility of a reprieve. And then they learned that their client had saved everyone a great deal of trouble. He had again attempted to commit suicide and this time, for once in his wretched life, he had achieved success. He had slashed his own throat and bled to death on the floor of his cell before anyone felt inclined to raise the alarm.

A messy end and yet one which, Harry guessed from the faintly relieved tone of the final letters on file, Cyril had regarded as bringing the case to a neat conclusion. Dead clients don't complain. Nor are they in a position to revive their claims of innocence. Until Ernest Miller had come along and started to ask questions, no-one had doubted that Carole Jeffries' killer had suffered poetic justice at his own hands after the legal system had flinched from inflicting the ultimate retribution.

Harry wondered what to do. It was easy to understand why Cyril had taken the line of least resistance. Edwin was one of those clients who don't help themselves. The likelihood was that he had sought to withdraw his confession only when the extent of his peril had begun to sink in. When he came to understand that there was little hope of escape, he'd given up.

Yet Harry had in his time known other inadequates prepared to accept punishment for crimes they had not committed. The old file did not disprove Miller's theory, although if Edwin was innocent, much was unclear. How had he learned about the scarf and what Carole had been wearing? What had prompted him to confess? And did he have any idea, however remote, of the identity of the true culprit?

The telephone rang. Suzanne, the switchboard girl, had a clutch of messages for him.

'I'm on my way out,' he said hastily. After the unexpected adjournment of the Kevin Walter case, he told himself, he could afford an hour or two off. It was past one o'clock and his breakfast at The Condemned Man was no more than a distant memory. He decided to escape in search of a sandwich and the opportunity to muse about Edwin Smith's fate free from the intrusion of clients and computer salesmen alike.

At the bottom of the steps which led from the building, he ran into Leo Devaney, who ran the second-hand record shop in the basement in partnership with a boyfriend called Simon. A thin man in his late forties who seemed to have worn the same scuffed leather jacket and jeans since his student days, Leo had the pallid skin of someone who regards fresh air as a health hazard and the pinched, abstracted look that comes from endless hours spent listening to music on ill-fitting headphones.

'Harry, I was meaning to call you. That old Dionne Warwick album you were asking after has come in.'

'I'm looking for another record at present. Do you have anything by the Brill Brothers?'

Leo shook his head. 'Sorry, madrigals by Meat Loaf are easier to find.'

'Don't tell me the records of such a minor duo have become collectors' items?'

'You'd be surprised how sought after many of those sixties albums are, especially those in good condition. Bear in mind that the records weren't manufactured in big numbers. They were always sure to prove scarcer than something like *Sergeant Pepper*, which sold by the million. But I'll keep an eye out for you, if you like. Record fairs are often the best bet and there's a good one at Empire Hall next week. Simon and I will have a stand there and you might like to look in.'

'Sure. In the meantime, what can you tell me about the Brill Brothers?'

Leo pondered for a second, then began to speak rapidly. 'Formed in late '61, a couple of good-looking lads who met at the Cavern and decided they could do as well as the acts on stage. They soon proved themselves right. Ray Brill sang like a gospeller, Ian McCalliog was a quiet boy who played the bass. Like most of their rivals they covered hits from the States. "Please Stay", an old Drifters track, was one, Chuck Jackson's "Any Day Now" another. Most of them were written in the Brill Building song factory in New York. Some people even thought Ray took his surname from the place, but in fact it appeared on his birth certificate. A pleasing coincidence.'

As Leo paused for breath, Harry said, 'Now I see why you were asked to contribute to *The Pop Encyclopaedia*.'

'If only I knew as much about balance sheets as I do about pop, I'd be rich enough to buy out Richard Branson.'

'What happened to the Brill Brothers?'

'Overshadowed by the Beatles, like everyone else. When the young girls stopped screaming for them, they lacked the originality and the staying power to survive. No shame in that, they did well enough for a couple of years. They were managed by Warren Hull and after their own Svengali died, they soon began to run out of steam.'

'Warren Hull? I've heard the name. Wasn't he a sort of poor man's Brian Epstein?'

'Got it in one. Warren was a pianist who accompanied several acts in the fifties without ever making the big time. When rock 'n' roll came along, he turned to pop star management with mixed results. So the story goes, he let Brian have the Beatles because he didn't like their looks. I can't believe it's true, because by all accounts he would have fallen head over heels for both Lennon and McCartney.'

'So Hull was gay? What happened to him? Did he kill himself, by any chance, like Epstein?'

'I think you're wrong about Brian. The best guess is that he took an accidental overdose. In any event, Warren Hull's death was very different. He was battered to death in his own bedroom. The police found his naked body there. Presumably he said the wrong thing at the wrong moment and his rough trade turned violent.'

'Who killed him?'

'God knows, some back-street rent boy, I suppose. As far as I'm aware, no-one was ever charged.' Leo grimaced. 'Let's face it, we're talking about the dark ages, long before the age of equal opportunities. Gay love was illegal and the police weren't going to bust a gut to avenge someone they'd have been happy to give a good kicking themselves.'

'This was when?'

'The Christmas of '63.'

'Did you know Ray Brill's girlfriend was strangled a couple of months later?'

'Murder's more your province than mine, Harry.' Leo gave him a searching glance. 'Am I right in guessing that's why you've taken a sudden interest in a couple of guys who were hardly in the class of the Everlys or the Righteous Brothers?'

'Turning detective yourself? Yes, you're spot on. I wonder - do you happen to know what Ray Brill is up to now?'

'He stayed in the business, of course, after the two of them split and Ian found himself a proper job as a number-cruncher for some shipping line. He formed a foursome which he called the Brilliants, but it didn't last long. Once the Beatles moved on and Merseybeat's golden age began to look a little tarnished, he found it as hard as everyone else. Nobody is forgotten as fast as yesterday's teen idols.'

'I'm almost glad I never was one.'

'Personally, I could have coped with the adulation. Anyway, Ray kept recording solo for as long as he could find people willing to invest in pressing his vinyl, but none of his songs meant a light after he went on his own. Now, can I take some money off you for that Dionne album?'

Harry followed Leo downstairs into the Aladdin's cave that was Devaney Records, but his mind was no longer on the record he had spent twelve months hunting for. What fascinated him at the moment was the Sefton Park case and the mixed fortunes of the people linked to it.

Two people close to Ray Brill, his manager and his sweetheart, had been brutally slain. One of the crimes had never been solved; the other had seemed at the time to be an open and shut case. It had all happened within the space of a couple of months. A fatal coincidence - and Harry wondered how much it had scarred Brill.

'Any idea where I could find Ray?'

'You're not just after his autograph, are you?'

'No, I'm interested in the girlfriend who was killed - but that makes me interested in Ray as well. Didn't he have a reputation as a ladies' man?'

Leo winked. 'It takes all sorts.'

'I suppose he married eventually, did he?'

'Three times, at the last count. Ray was alway unlucky in love, you might say. The first was an air hostess - she soon blew off with a pilot. Then came a barmaid and after that a black girl who was on the game. None of them stayed with him for long, but it was his own fault. He liked them young and willing and he liked plenty of them. And he was a betting man as well. Not just an odd flutter on the gee-gees, but anything at all. When I saw him doing a gig in one of Southport's seedier clubs a year ago, he had a couple of teenagers making eyes at him and he was giving odds as to which of them he'd manage to lay first. He was incorrigible. I think he was living up there at the time, though whether he's still in the neighbourhood, I haven't a clue.'

'You're sure he is still alive?'

Leo grinned. 'Certain of it. The price of his merchandise would have shot up if he'd gone to the Cavern in the sky. Have you ever wondered why so many pop stars die young? It's a great career move, that's why. No, Ray Brill isn't dead yet.' He paused and added, 'Though with his lifestyle, he bloody well ought to be.'

Chapter Eight

I shall put the facts down on paper

The telephone was ringing as Harry walked into his room after lunch. He had slipped in through the back entrance to New Commodities House, hoping to avoid Suzanne's eye. No chance: she was a mistress of all the receptionist's black arts and knew intuitively when he was within her reach.

He glared at the set steeling himself not to answer, but as usual Suzanne's persistence prevailed. Swearing under his breath, he picked up the receiver.

'Mr Ernest Miller for you.'

He felt a sudden foreboding as the careful voice came on the line, enunciating every syllable with sly precision.

'Mr Devlin, I heard the lunchtime news on Radio Merseyside about this morning's dramatic development in the Kevin Walter case. My congratulations. You must be very pleased.'

'Kind of you to ring.'

'Ah, do I detect a touch of irony? Well, I must confess that there was another purpose behind my call. I did wonder whether you might have had the opportunity to give any thought to my request for your assistance.'

'Didn't you say there was no hurry?'

'Indeed, indeed. But since we spoke yesterday evening I have talked to Edwin Smith's former lady love, Renata Grierson - or Yates, to use the maiden name by which he knew her. Most intriguing. As a result of our telephone conversation, I am now absolutely convinced of Smith's innocence. All the more reason, therefore, for me to press on with my enquiries.'

'And what exactly did she tell you?'

'If you do not mind, I would prefer not to discuss it on the telephone. But I am certainly willing to reveal something of my researches when we next meet, if you wish, and as a separate matter I have a little legal business with which you may be able to assist me.'

'Don't tell me you've been arrested?'

'No, no,' said Miller, chuckling. 'That would never arise, I can assure you. My need for help is much more prosaic - I think at my time of life I ought to make a will and I have no acquaintance with any other solicitors' firm. Not, of course, that I have a great deal to leave.'

Harry resisted the temptation to say that he had never known a client, however affluent, who actually claimed to have a great deal to leave. 'Fine, shall we get together sometime?'

'Perhaps we could meet as soon as you have ascertained whether you can trace the old Tweats file.'

'It's sitting in front of me as we speak.'

'Already? Marvellous! I realise that you are a busy man and I am most grateful that my request...'

'I wanted to satisfy my own curiosity,' interrupted Harry.

'And did you?'

'No, I'm left with more questions than answers.'

'Excellent! So at least you appreciate that it is by no means a straightforward case. May I ask if anything struck you in particular?'

'Edwin Smith withdrew his confession.'

'I see, I see. How interesting.'

Harry had the odd feeling that his news had hardly come as a bombshell to Miller. It was as if the man had already had an inkling of what the file would reveal and his satisfaction lay in having his supposition confirmed.

'Cyril Tweats wasn't impressed by the retraction and neither, by the look of things, was the barrister he instructed on Smith's behalf. In any event, Smith soon abandoned any attempt to claim innocence. By the time of the trial he seems to have been reconciled to pleading guilty.'

'But Mr Tweats' judgment was not always sound.'

'You speak as if you knew him.'

'Oh no.' Miller became cautious. 'I assure you I never met the fellow. I can only go by his reputation.'

Harry felt once again he was not being told the whole truth, but he let it pass. 'You're right, as it happens. Cyril took pains in his correspondence with Smith's mother to discourage her from any thought that her son had not committed the crime. He didn't probe deeply - in fact, he didn't probe at all. But whether probing would have yielded any results, we can only speculate.'

'And speculation is fascinating, is it not? Very well, can we arrange to meet? You may even be agreeable to my having a look at the documents in the file. Where would suit you?'

'Anywhere, provided it's not in the Wallace. I prefer not to have to fight for breath when I sup a pint.'

'In that case, let us try talking in the open air. I can suggest a perfect venue. Why don't we meet at Sefton Park itself?'

'You want us to become murder tourists?'

'There is surely some appeal in our visiting the scene of the crime together. I hope my suggestion does not seem too macabre. I prefer to think of myself as having a sense of place - and of history. Besides, it is a pleasant spot and not inconvenient for a busy man working in the city centre. Could we say one o'clock tomorrow at the seats by the side of the lake nearest to the Aigburth entrance? By then, who knows, I may have gleaned further information. I am hoping to speak to Carole's boyfriend, the pop singer, this afternoon. I shall be fascinated to hear what he has to say.'

Not for the first time, Harry felt repelled and fascinated by Ernest Miller in roughly equal measure. Of course, Miller was using him and had judged that the promise of further revelations would prove irresistible - but Harry did not deceive himself. The truth was that he had no wish to resist.

As the clock struck six, he walked into the Dock Brief to find Ken Cafferty standing at the bar, glass in hand, chatting to a barmaid whose cleavage was an incitement to riot.

'Here you are, love, this is the feller who's paying. He's had a good day in court, it ought to be drinks all round.' He grinned at Harry. 'I gather Paddy Vaulkhard excelled himself this morning. The word is that your people must be heading for a record award. They'll be set up for life.'

'It will be spent within the year.'

'Paying off your fees?'

'The taxpayer is funding this litigation, as you well know. Lately, a horde of financial advisers have been flitting round the Walters like flies over a corpse, but the investment strategy hasn't been devised that could constrain Jeannie's urge to spend, spend, spend. When we parted she was talking about buying a yacht and mooring it in the Mersey Marina.'

Ken put his hand in the inside pocket of the overcoat he had draped over an adjacent bar stool and withdrew a bulky brown envelope. Furtive as a double agent, he slid it across the counter.

'As promised. I hope you realise I've risked my job to honour our agreement. These are confidential documents. Not to be removed out of the office and all that crap. Summary dismissal even for first-time offenders.'

'I'll fight your case if they sack you.'

'I won't pretend I'm reassured. You're the kind of brief who ends up in the same cell as his client.'

Harry picked up the envelope and pulled out a thick wad of papers in an elastic band. 'This is your filing system?'

'Technology may have revolutionised the newspaper industry, but pockets of resistance still remain. The management keep threatening to put all these bits and pieces on microfilm, but at the moment we're still in the dark ages, thank God. Personally, I'd be happy to scrap all the technology and go back to two-finger typing on a rusty old Remington. You know what they say: to err is human, but to really bugger things up requires a computer.'

'You're a man after my own heart.'

'I know, that's what bothers me.'

The papers comprised old cuttings on which dates had been scrawled in ballpoint and a few flimsy sheets of typed stories in draft. Harry was immediately entranced. The first item in the pack, headed GIRL STRANGLED IN SEFTON PARK, set the shock-horror tone for everything that followed. During the first few hours of the investigation, the police had given very little away and Harry, digressing for a moment, marvelled that in those days the public respect for the bobby on the beat had apparently been so much stronger than today, when every force had its own slick public relations team. Perhaps there was a lesson in that.

Even at a distance of thirty years, he could almost hear the exultant shouts in the newsroom when the journalists learned that the victim was not only pretty but also had a famous father. It must have seemed like a stroke of luck, giving an added dimension to a tragic killing, making it certain that the story would run and run.

Guy Jeffries' photograph appeared in many of the cuttings that followed. Even in smudged black-and-white portraits that might have been taken by a boy scout using a box brownie for the very first time, Guy's appearance was compelling. With his thick shock of dark hair, even teeth and aquiline nose, he gave the impression that he expected admiration and flattery as his due, that he had no doubt he was a man of destiny. There was just one picture that told a different story; unlike the others, it had been taken on the day after the murder, when a persistent paparazzo had caught him leaving his home by the back door. His head was bowed and his shoulders hunched as if in acknowledgement of defeat. A quote on one of the cuttings seemed to capture his mood: *I should never have let her go.* Harry felt a flash of sympathy; he knew all too well the pain of losing a loved one to a sudden and senseless slaying.

In the reports, Jeffries was described variously as a celebrated academic, a best-selling political author and a noted left-wing thinker. His two principal books, *Our Sterile Society* and *The Identity of a Socialist*, received more mentions than a thousand press releases, launch parties and literary luncheons could guarantee. Profiles traced the upward graph of his career: from being the cleverest boy in the school, through outstanding achievement as a student, to a position of eminence in the intellectual, literary and political firmaments. Like his friend Clive Doxey, he had been a private adviser to Harold Wilson and there was even talk that he might stand for Parliament when the scandal-wracked Conservatives finally called a general election. The world was his for the taking.

Yet beneath the recitation of Jeffries' accomplishments and the florid accounts of his distress at the loss of his only child, Harry thought he detected a trace of journalistic *schadenfreude*.

He said as much to Ken, who scratched his nose. 'From what I can gather, he was never flavour of the month at our paper. He and Doxey both used to write soapbox columns for the other lot and the editor we had in those days equated a socialist government with barbarians at the gates of Rome. Besides, Jeffries had it all, didn't he? Good looks and a great career. Nothing delights a lesser mortal more than to see a paragon finding out the hard way that life can be unkind to everyone.'

Harry gave him a sharp look but said nothing. He flicked through the pieces of paper, pausing whenever he came to a new twist in the tale or a photograph of one of the cast of characters. Now and then he allowed himself to be sidetracked by snippets from other stories on the reverse of the clippings. They gave him a flavour of the times. The Great Train Robbers were on trial; in South Africa, a lawyer named Mandela had been jailed for life. Mary Quant said that Paris fashion was out of date and Mods and Rockers fought on Clacton Beach. The Beatles took New York by storm and back at home Cilla Black topped the hit parade with 'Anyone Who Had A Heart'. Ah, the sixties, an almost mythical age when the world seemed full of infinite possibilities. Harry found himself feeling nostalgic for a time he could not ever remember.

So far as the Sefton Park Strangling was concerned, the police had made their breakthrough quickly. The arrest had been a lead story and the details soon emerged. First Smith's age was given, then his job - he worked as a storeman for a firm of builder's merchants - then the fact he lived in the same road as the victim. As soon as his name was released, his picture was printed.

Harry stared at the man who was supposed to have killed Carole Jeffries. Smith had freckles and prominent eyes, no chin but a giraffe's neck to compensate; he seemed like someone born to be suspected of anything and everything.

His victim, on the other hand, was worth looking at. Day after day photographs of Carole Jeffries appeared. Her face would have sold papers even without its connection with sudden and violent death. Despite the poor quality reproduction of old snapshots, Harry could recognise the beauty in her cast of features as well as the artful way she lowered her eyelashes for the camera.

'I see she is described as "fun-loving",' he said.

'Damning, eh? I was never a believer in the *de mortuis* school of thought. I think we can make an educated guess that she was a bit of a slag.'

Harry didn't hide his resentment at the casual slander. 'She was only sixteen, for Christ's sake.'

Ken shrugged. 'Even in those days, some kids grew up fast. She'd left school, don't forget, and taken a job. Found herself a boyfriend who was adding a few decibels to the Mersey Sound.'

'Look, even Edwin Smith's own confession didn't suggest she led him on. Quite the opposite. The red mist descended because she didn't show any interest in him.'

'So you've tracked the old file down? Does it cast any light?'

'He retracted his original statement at one point, but Cyril Tweats managed to persuade him he was really guilty, after all.'

Ken laughed. 'Good old Cyril. How he kept his practising certificate, I'll never know. Perhaps the truth is, he did keep practising throughout his career. He just never got it right.'

'There's something else. My informant now believes he has confirmation that Smith was no murderer.'

'Does he, by God?'

'Which raises the question - if Smith didn't kill Carole, who did?'

'Don't tell me you seriously expect to find out?'

Harry spread his arms. 'You never know till you try.'

'You can't tell me that even if by some chance Smith was innocent, you could trace whatever passing maniac happened to strangle the girl and then elude detection for thirty years.'

'Suppose,' said Harry, articulating an idea which had been germinating in his mind since his meeting with Miller, 'suppose it wasn't a random attack. Suppose instead someone Carole knew had a motive for murdering her - or maybe just did it in a fit of rage?'

'And by a stroke of luck found that Smith was ready, willing and able to take the blame?'

Harry leaned forward. 'It's not impossible. Suddenly the case becomes interesting, don't you think? Maybe what happened in Sefton Park all those years ago was the perfect murder - committed by mistake.'

On arriving back in his flat late that evening, Harry picked up the television remote control and zapped his way from programme to programme whilst he tried to summon the strength to make some black coffee. His session with Ken had lasted longer than either of them had intended and the cold blast of the night air on the walk home had not been strong enough to focus his thoughts.

He moved quickly on from a Swedish film with subtitles, scarcely pausing to take in the highlights of a welterweight boxing match or an alternative comedian who talked a lot about farting and impotence. Harry yawned. Wasn't *Chinatown* due on tonight? He had seen it half a dozen times and on each new viewing he gleaned something fresh from it.

The regional newscast carried the story of the sergeant's collapse in court. His present condition was described as 'serious but stable', which in Harry's experience of hospitalspeak probably meant that he was already being measured for a shroud. A mouthpiece for the police authority, interviewed briefly, described the sergeant as 'a dedicated officer'. He looked as glum as if he was expecting the compensation for Kevin Walter to be deducted from his personal salary.

But there would be no payday for Edwin Smith, even if Miller was right to believe in his innocence. Perhaps, thought Harry, that was all the more reason to care about clearing his name, if justice demanded it.

Outside, a gale began to howl. He could hear it even through the double glazing. The heating was on, but he felt a slight chill. He knew it came from the lack of someone warm to share the night with. Since Liz had walked out on him, he had had affairs, but few relationships that had meant anything. He found himself thinking about Kim Lawrence, then reminded himself that the word in the law library was that she was involved with a social worker. A bloody waste, he told himself, though he was honest enough to admit that even if she was here beside him and in the mood for love, he would probably want to keep her up for hours, talking about the Sefton Park case.

Eventually he began to doze and when he awoke with a start, he realised he had missed much of the film. Yet he could still take pleasure in the way Polanski captured the suffocating atmosphere of thirties LA during a drought and in Jack Nicholson's private eye discovering a conscience. J.J. Gittes' quest to expose the corruption of a wealthy businessman brought, not salvation, but death to a woman he had begun to love. The last thing he remembered before he drifted off to sleep again was the sense of menace he felt when he heard Nicholson's nasal tones.

'You may think you know what you're dealing with, but believe me, you don't.'

Chapter Nine

so that when my own life is at an end,

He arrived at Fenwick Court the next morning to find the office in a state of uproar. A police car was parked outside and one of the large windows which looked out on to the courtyard had been smashed. In the reception area, a couple of chairs and a table had been upturned and all the staff were standing together in a small group, talking in hushed yet urgent voices.

'You're late!' complained Suzanne as he approached.

He couldn't deny it. Already the clock showed ten past nine. He had overslept after a night interrupted by two or three wakings from grim dreams in which the sight of Ernest Miller's corpse was a recurrent and inescapable image.

'Never mind that. What's going on?'

'We've been burgled!' said the girl, opening her eyes wide and making a dramatic gesture with her arms.

His immediate reaction was amazement rather than shock and as if reading his mind, Jim Crusoe walked through the door, accompanied by a young woman constable to whom he was saying, 'Who would want to rob us? After all, most of the petty thieves in Liverpool city centre are our own clients.'

'If this is the work of anyone I act for, you shouldn't be short of clues,' Harry told the policewoman. 'Fingerprints, fibres, driving licences, you name it, my clients usually scatter them at the scene of the crime. They aren't exactly master criminals. I sometimes think Charlie Pearce must be spinning round in his grave.'

A faint smile spread across the woman's face. 'Burglars just don't take a pride in their work these days.'

'This is Detective Constable Lynn DeFreitas,' said Jim. 'Lynn, meet my partner, Harry Devlin.'

'Pleased to meet you,' she said, extending a hand. She was slim and pretty and had an air of quiet authority. 'Well, at least you seem to have got off quite lightly.'

'Much taken?' asked Harry.

Jim shook his head. 'Not as far as I can see. The door into the book-keeper's room hasn't been forced and the typewriters and office equipment seem to be all present and correct.'

Harry could have sworn there was a note of regret in his partner's voice. No excuse to buy a new computer system on the contents insurance, then.

'Looks like the work of one of two kids,' said Lynn DeFreitas. 'I gather you don't keep much money on the premises.'

'Barely enough to pay for an hour of your overtime,' said Harry. 'It makes more sense to rob a church poor box than a solicitor's office. Mind you, there are blank cheques, of course...'

'Not touched,' confirmed Jim.

'Did the alarm go off?'

'It was disabled. The buggers knew what they were doing.'

Amazing, Harry thought gloomily. The salesman had sworn it was a state of the art system and it had certainly caught him out on his nocturnal office visit last December. So much for security technology. 'Is that my window they came in through?'

'Yes. They seem to have started there and begun working their way back through the building before leaving in a hurry. Maybe they were disturbed.'

They had reached Harry's door. 'Anything of mine gone?'

Jim gestured toward the paper-strewn room and shrugged his shoulders. 'Frankly, old son, who can tell?'

Harry winced as he stepped inside. The files he kept stacked on every available surface had collapsed on to the floor, spilling their contents everywhere. 'You don't understand my methods, that's all. Normally, I can always lay my hand on a file any time I want it.

But now it looks like a bomb has hit the place. Christ, I don't know where to start.'

'Personally,' said Jim to Lynn DeFreitas as they followed him in, 'I think this room looks just the same as usual. Tidier, if anything.'

'Could they have been looking for anything in particular amongst your working papers?' she asked.

'In Harry's room?' scoffed Jim. 'Talk about needles in haystacks. They'd have had to stay all night.'

'But might there be sensitive information in one of your files?' she persisted. 'Something that someone would like to be kept quiet?'

Harry ran through his current caseload in his mind before shaking his head. 'I can't think of anything out of the ordinary.'

Lynn DeFreitas tiptoed through the mess towards the door. 'Perhaps it was spite? A client who feels you've let him down?'

'There are no such people,' said Jim hastily. 'This feller somehow manages to have the villains eating out of his hand.'

'Chummy with the criminal classes, are you?'

'Don't worry, we know when to keep our distance.'

'The last solicitor who said that to me is in Strangeways at present, serving eighteen months for assisting a client to escape from police custody.' She smiled again to soften her words and Harry noticed the frank interest with which Jim returned her gaze. Pleasantly, she said, 'Looks like common or garden vandalism, then.'

'I guess. And thank God, it could have been so much worse.'

Harry followed them out and back down the corridor, but he said nothing. It had occurred to him that in his briefcase was one set of papers which would have meant nothing to any of his clients yet which might have been the object of the burglar's search. He must look again at Cyril Tweats' file on the strangling of Carole Jeffries.

He left Jim and the policewoman deep in conversation and his secretary Lucy to the thankless task of bringing a semblance of order to the chaos of his room. He had a date in court with Tina Turner.

Unfortunately, Bettina Mirabelle Turner, a twenty-seven-year-old white Caucasian female from a tower block in Dingle, was less glamorous than her celebrated namesake, although equally vivacious. This Tina was up for the umpteenth time on a soliciting charge and when the magistrates imposed a fine that she could pay off with a couple of afternoons' work in one of the big city centre hotels, she blew them a kiss in relief and almost found herself locked up for contempt of court.

'How's business?' asked Harry outside. He knew perfectly well that if the prospect of AIDS or a beating did not deter his client from her chosen profession, judicial sanctions were hardly likely to do so.

'Never better, chuck,' said Tina, showing countless teeth in a vast smile. 'If I had another pair of legs, I'd open up in Manchester. Mind, some of me clients have fallen on hard times, like. Last week I asked this feller if he'd like a blow job and all he wanted to know was whether it would affect his dole money.'

Harry laughed and said goodbye, but rather than heading back for the office, he ensconced himself in the passenger seat of his MG and began to reread the Edwin Smith file.

Not one word, not one unguarded sentence gave him an inkling as to why any burglar might be desperate to steal the file from him. The only suggestion that Smith was innocent of the killing of Carole Jeffries came in the note of his prison cell retraction, which in turn had been so speedily retracted. Harry reflected that Lynn DeFreitas' assumption that the break-in had been the work of a juvenile vandal, like so many simple solutions to seemingly baffling puzzles, was probably correct. He sighed and set off for his meeting in Sefton Park.

Everywhere was quiet as he parked his car opposite the lake. The trees were bare and the wind was sweeping through the wide open spaces. The place was deserted apart from the usual dauntless dog-walkers, a couple of truanting schoolboys and Ernest Miller, who was sitting on a bench overlooking the water, deep in thought. An empty plastic sandwich box, a thermos flask and the document case which seemed to act as his comfort blanket were at his side. Not until Harry was within a dozen yards did the old man look up.

'You have made good time, Mr Devlin. Thank you for coming.' The muscles around his mouth twitched in a smile as he waved a hand towards a neatly tended shrubbery. 'So this is where it happened, all those years ago. Carole's body was found over there, look. She was attacked on the path you see to your right and her killer then pulled her as far as a clump of bushes which used to grow where I am pointing.'

Harry contemplated the scene. It seemed so quiet and empty that a man with less imagination would have found it impossible to picture the crime. But the words from Edwin Smith's confession statement echoed in Harry's head. *I wasn't going to tell you this, but I really fancy you.* Could this conversation with Carole on that fateful day have been fiction? Or was Miller mistaken and everyone else right all along?

He sat beside the old man and placed his folder of papers on his lap. 'Here is the file. I can't let you take it away. But feel free to look through it.'

'I do appreciate your assistance,' said Miller, yet although he stretched out a hand for the folder, he did not fall upon it with the greedy relish that Harry had anticipated. Instead he leafed through the documents as casually as a guest glancing at a dull host's holiday snaps.

'Look at Edwin's confession. You'll see why the police thought it had the ring of truth.'

Miller turned to the statement and raised his eyebrows after reading it. 'I take your point, but where is the retraction?'

Harry turned to the pages which recorded Cyril's meeting with his client. 'His solicitor didn't pay it much heed.'

After studying the notes, Miller gave a brief nod. 'Thank you.'

'Intriguing, isn't it?'

'The notes and correspondence are immaculately typed, don't you agree?' said Miller, evading the question with an enigmatic smile. 'And remember, this was in the days when people took a pride in secretarial work, long before word processors robbed us of yet another skill.'

'I thought you would be more concerned with Edwin Smith's attempt to claim innocence.'

'Yes, yes, it bears out what I have been arguing, does it not? And I think his denial is entirely plausible, even though your predecessor poured cold water on it.'

'Cyril Tweats was hardly infallible.'

'And yet a man's life rested on his advice.' Miller shook his head. 'The power that lawyers exert ... it is remarkable.'

'I never noticed it myself.'

'Come now. When careers end, reputations are ruined, marriages crumble or death comes, you and your professional colleagues are consulted. People dare not move a muscle without your say-so. Oh yes, if I had my time again, I would be a lawyer. As it is, I would be grateful if you could assist me with my little bit of legal business. If you remember, I have decided that I really ought at last to make a will.'

'You need to speak to my partner, Jim Crusoe. I know as much about the law of inheritance as I do about the second law of thermodynamics.'

'I doubt whether an appointment will be necessary. My wishes are straightforward and I have written them down.' He opened the document case but as he did so, a couple of red files slipped out together and fell to the ground, with several sheets fluttering out of them. Miller bent down to pick them up, wheezing and cursing himself for his own clumsiness as he stuffed them back into place.

'I am not a fit man, Mr Devlin, as you can tell. It is right that I should put my affairs in order.'

He replaced one file in the case. It was marked CAROLE JEFFRIES and Harry recognised it as the one he had seen in the Wallace. From the other, marked PERSONAL, Miller drew out a sheet of lined paper bearing a list of figures and instructions scripted in immaculate calligraphy which he handed to Harry. 'I trust you and your partner will not object to acting as my executors?'

Probates were where the money lay. Harry nodded his agreement, his interest rising as he took in the details of assets and savings, personal effects and shareholdings.

'You were too modest on the telephone. I see that your estate is quite sizeable.'

Miller shrugged. 'I had a reasonably well-paid job for many years and neither my late wife nor I were extravagant with money, quite the reverse. Even so, I recognise the truth of the old saying. I can't take it with me.'

He had set out, in clear if pedantic prose, the intended destination of his wordly goods and Harry opened his eyes wide as he read the instructions.

'You propose to leave everything to the Miscarriages of Justice Organisation?'

'They are a worthy charity, are they not? And short of funds, too, I should guess, like so many other deserving causes.'

'Of course,' said Harry. If anything could make Kim Lawrence whoop with delight, he suspected it would be the news of Miller's gift. He had not imagined the old man as an altruistic benefactor. 'But...'

'You are plainly startled by my largesse. Let me try to explain. I said to you when we first met that I find the question of justice

83

fascinating. People sometimes say that justice delayed is justice denied, do they not? I suspect the reality is that justice is invariably delayed and often denied altogether. Well, if the relatively modest sum I have to give will be of value, that is enough for me.'

'Don't you have any family at all?' Harry did not feel he was being disloyal to Kim Lawrence in putting the question. The last thing she would want would be for some long-lost relative to turn up out of the blue and contest the will. Now was the time to discover if there were any likely claimants.

'I am a widower, as you will have gathered. My wife died ten years ago and we had no children, nor any other family ties. I left Germany as a young man after the death of my parents and I had no brothers, sisters or cousins. If you and Mr Crusoe do agree to act as my executors, I think you will find the task straightforward.' Miller gave him a stern look. 'No excuse for over-charging.'

Harry grinned. 'I'd say "trust me", but I don't expect you're the kind of chap who trusts anyone and I can't blame you for that.'

'Mr Devlin, you strike me as tolerably honest, if that is not damning you with too much faint praise.' Miller passed him the file. 'Here you will find a few odds and ends that your partner might need in preparing the document. No doubt you will return them to me when the will is ready for signature.'

'It won't take long. I'll ask him to let you have it as soon as possible.' He glanced inside the folder and picked out a small booklet and a clip of yellowing papers. 'I see you have a pension and some insurance. What did you do when you were working?'

'I was personnel manager with a small firm of printers in the city. I spent years doing battle with the trade unions, but in the end it was computerisation which hit us hardest. I made half the workforce redundant and then found myself out of a job as well.'

Harry nodded. So much for Jim's belief that technology was the answer to everything, he thought. Along with its benefits, it brought cuts in employment: not all the changes it made to people's lives were for the better.

'I've seen it happen before.'

'Perhaps it was for the best,' said Miller. 'I had always suffered badly from asthma and I found the pressures of business life were becoming intolerable. Besides, I realised in the end that I was not ideally suited to the work I was doing and in particular my role as welfare officer.' He smiled his discomfiting smile. 'People have always intrigued me, you see. Yet eventually I discovered I *like* very few of them.'

'Misanthropy isn't the ideal qualification if you're planning to reincarnate as a solicitor.'

'But you do not have primarily a welfare role. You delve for facts, organise them, then present your case. It does not matter if you loathe your client. You certainly need not love him.'

'Maybe it's as well,' said Harry, thinking of the thieves, rapists and murderers for whom he had acted over the years.

'As for Mr Tweats, my impression is that his main concern was to wash his hands of young Smith. He never seems for a second to have doubted his guilt.'

'But you must agree that the evidence was damning. How could Smith have known about the scarf, for instance, unless he actually committed the murder?'

'Could it be that he saw Carole Jeffries wearing the scarf that day and, knowing she had been strangled, made a fortunate guess at the murderer's means?'

'But why?'

'I am no psychiatrist, Mr Devlin. I cannot explain the workings of an inadequate mind. But that is my best guess, following my telephone conversation with Renata Grierson.'

'What did she tell you?'

'At first she was most reluctant to say anything, but when I pressed her, eventually she said that she was positive that it was impossible for Edwin Smith to have killed Carole Jeffries. When I asked why, all she would say was that she had not learned of that impossibility until after Smith's own death. Hence her silence until now. Evidently I am the first person in whom she has confided the truth.' Miller gave a satisfied smile. 'So far she has been reluctant to divulge all she knows about the case but I am hopeful that soon she will be more forthcoming. I plan to meet her in the near future, but in the meantime I think you will agree that her remarks are as fascinating as they are significant.'

'It all sounds vague to me. Are you sure she wasn't simply telling you what she guessed you wanted to hear?'

'Of course that thought has crossed my mind, but I am happy to trust my instinct. I do not doubt her sincerity.'

'What of Ray Brill, then? Did he shed any light?'

Miller fiddled with the buttons of his coat. Harry could sniff evasion in the air. 'He was unable to add anything of substance so far as the murder of Carole was concerned. Although he had seen her on the morning of the twenty-ninth of February, he then set off to London in the company of his singing partner, Ian Brill. There was no way that he could have been the culprit.'

Miller was choosing his words with even more care than usual. Taking a leaf out of Patrick Vaulkhard's book, Harry decided that gentle flattery was the method most likely to draw him out. 'You have obviously been busy. How many other people involved with the case are you hoping to see?'

'Frankly, Mr Devlin, I am far from sure. Benny Frederick and Clive Doxey, of course, are in the public eye and easy enough to find, should I wish to do so. Renata proved by far the most elusive of those connected with the case: in the end, I had to resort to advertising in the local press. All I knew was her maiden name, but happily she saw my advert and called me up. It was much easier to trace the whereabouts of Kathleen Jeffries; Shirley, the girl with whom Carole worked; and Deysbrook, the policeman who headed the murder team. Fortunately, all of them still live in Merseyside.'

'Did Kathleen ever remarry?'

Miller shook his head. 'By all accounts, she has been something of a recluse since her husband died.'

'And Shirley, what has happened to her?'

'Thirty years ago, her surname was Basnett. She has changed it several times since then. I gather her third husband, a man named Titchard, died recently, leaving her a wealthy widow.'

'So you might speak to each of them?'

'As I say, I may decide to change my original plans. After all, I have established to my own satisfaction that Smith was not guilty of the crime. On reflection it would, perhaps, be hoping for too much if I were to press on with my investigation in the vain belief that I might be able to identify her killer.'

'That's not the way you were talking when we first met.'

'Perhaps I became carried away with myself on that occasion. But I feel I shall probably rest content once I have met and talked in greater detail to Renata Grierson and ascertained precisely why she is so confident that Edwin Smith was no murderer.' Miller smiled his infuriating smile and handed back the old Tweats file. 'Thank you, Mr Devlin. I do appreciate your help.'

Harry found himself becoming irritated. At the precise moment when Miller had aroused his curiosity in the Sefton Park case, the old man was giving the impression that his own enthusiasm was beginning to wane. Or was he simply seeking to discourage further inquiries now that he had seen Cyril Tweats' papers? Harry decided it was time to tease him.

He tucked the file under his arm and said casually, 'Better look after this. I have the idea you aren't the only person interested in it.'

He felt a childish sense of gratification to see Miller's eyebrows shoot up. 'Oh really?'

'My office was burgled during the night. Nothing seems to have been stolen and it crossed my mind that the intruder might have been looking for this.'

Miller stared at him. Harry had the impression that the old man's mind was working rapidly, but when he spoke again, his manner was elaborately patronising. 'A far-fetched notion, surely? You and I are the only people who knew of my interest in the file.'

'Unless,' said Harry gently, 'you happened to mention it to Renata Grierson, say - or Ray Brill.'

'Oh ... I am sure I did not. No, Mr Devlin, you are mistaken. Depend upon it.'

But looking at Ernest Miller's pensive expression, Harry suspected that he had made no mistake.

Chapter Ten

people can judge my confession

'Is he dying?' demanded Jim Crusoe an hour later.

'Not as far as I'm aware,' said Harry. Miller is one of those characters who always seems to be ailing but the old bugger will probably outlive the lot of us.'

'His will is straightforward. I can let you have the engrossment before the end of the day if you want.'

'Thanks. I may want an excuse for another word with Mr Ernest Miller before too long. So if you can prepare it quickly, so much the better.'

'No problem. Mind you, if we had the latest software, we could turn out any document based on the standard precedents in a matter of minutes at the press of a button. Do you know what we're missing by not having the latest packages?'

'No, but from the evangelical light in your eyes, I'm afraid you're going to tell me.'

His partner sighed. 'I suppose it's no use asking if you'd be interested in seeing a rep offering a fifty per cent discount on promotional videos for solicitors' firms?'

Harry pulled a face. 'Only if my part will be taken by Richard Gere.'

'Peter Falk might be better casting.'

'And I suppose you'd want to be played by a young Sean Connery?' A thought occurred to him. 'Wait a minute. Who made this approach to you about the video?'

'I received a mailshot a couple of days ago. The follow-up phone call came today. The company is Frederick's, the people who made the management video-tape you vandalised.'

'I told you, it was the only spare cassette I could find the other night. I wanted to record *The Postman Always Rings Twice* - the Lana Turner version, that is, from the days when the postman didn't spend most of his time delivering computer-generated junk mail to impoverished businessmen. But I might just be willing to make amends. Pass me the literature and I'll give it the once-over.'

Jim's bushy eyebrows lifted. 'I don't believe I'm hearing this. Harry Devlin showing an interest in PR?'

'I might even be interested in a meeting to see if they could do anything for us. On one condition.'

Jim gave him a suspicious look. 'Go on.'

'That we meet the organ grinder, rather than the monkey. I don't want to waste time with a junior salesman. I'd like a presentation from Benny Frederick himself.'

Benny Frederick was away at a conference in London, the monkey told them, and although he would be willing to see any prospective new customer, he would not be available until after the weekend. Harry had to accept that as good enough, but he could not help chafing with impatience. His conversation with Miller had puzzled him and he could not push the Sefton Park case out of his mind.

He was at a loose end the following day and in the morning he wandered into town, telling himself that he needed to pick up a few odds and ends for the flat as well as food for the week ahead. Yet he did not really fool himself, and before long he found his way to the Bluecoat Gallery, where posters on the railings outside announced an exhibition of *Snaps of the Sixties*, photographs from the Beatles era taken by Benny Frederick. He paid his money and strolled inside.

A girl at the door handed him a leaflet which told him a little about Benny's career. He had inherited his father's studio as a young man in 1961 and had proved to be in the right business in the right place at the right time. His candid camera had caught pop singers, poets and comedians and made him as much of a star as most of them: what Patrick Lichfield was to high society and David Bailey to the world of fashion, Benny Frederick had been to the age of the Mersey Sound. As the city's golden decade had drawn to a close, he had recognised the need to move with the times and his nose for commerce had prompted him to diversify into video, but it was for his photography that most people knew him best. With justice, Harry thought: despite the self-deprecation of the exhibition's title, he could see that the photographs were the work of a talented artist. Benny could capture a personality in a single shot, whether it was Ringo Starr cavorting on Blackpool Beach, Ken Dodd clowning at the Empire or Bessie Braddock haranguing a heckler at an election meeting. Brian Epstein was pictured standing offstage at the Cavern, watching with rapt attention as a young John Lennon sang 'Baby, It's You', but Harry was more intrigued by a photograph of a nightclub pianist. His hair was plastered with lotion and his lips curled as if he held his piano in contempt. The caption said simply WARREN HULL AT THE PEPPERMINT LOUNGE - 1961. So this was the Brill Brothers' guru, yet another man who would later die violently and long before his time. But of Ray and Ian Brill themselves there was no sign.

For a minute or two, Harry flirted aimlessly with the girl on the door, but then her boyfriend arrived and it was time to move on. He had decided to watch the soccer at Anfield in the afternoon, but even after a liquid lunch at the Dock Brief, he still had time to drift into the second-hand bookshop in Williamson Lane. Normally he haunted the fiction room, thumbing through shabby copies of long-forgotten mysteries by the likes of Anthony Berkeley and John Dickson Carr. He relished the sorcery of the old books, with their bodies discovered in rooms that had every door and window locked and barred and their murders in Turkish baths committed by daggers made of ice. The Golden Age of crime fiction seemed to him to be a time of innocence and charm: between the wars, artifice was everything and only authors, not policemen, indulged themselves in creating elaborate fictions.

For once, though, he concentrated on the true crime shelves, keen to see if anyone had ever written up the strangling in Sefton Park. There were endless accounts of the cases of Charles Bravo and Constance Kent, while Florence Maybrick and James Wallace had a whole row to themselves - but he could find nothing on the killing of Carole. Her death had caused a sensation in its day, but it held no interest for the murder buff: there was no suspense in a case that everyone regarded as open and shut.

What if Miller could establish with Renata Grierson's evidence - whatever it might be - that Carole Jeffries had not died at the hands of Edwin Smith? Would the public interest be stirred and would the men who had known her, the likes not only of Ray Brill, but also Benny Frederick and Clive Doxey, at last come under the microscope? Might long-forgotten motives suddenly emerge?

The thought fascinated him as he made his way upstairs. Perhaps he should do a little background reading. The first floor of the shop was dusty and quiet and he suspected most of the stock stayed on the shelves from one year to the next. Never before had he bothered to search out books about politics or the social sciences - they were subjects he would ordinarily travel a distance to avoid - and it took him a while to find his way around. But in the end he came up with a fat hardback and a dog-eared Penguin that made his visit worthwhile. *Our Sterile Society* by Guy Jeffries and *Radicalism And The Law*, a collection of articles by Sir Clive Doxey. A little light reading for after the match.

At home that evening, Harry listened to Dionne Warwick asking the way to San José while he studied his purchases. Guy Jeffries' face appeared on the back of his book's dustwrapper. He was giving the camera a youthful grin: the photograph must surely have been taken in the early fifties, years before first publication. Harry had little experience of the literary world, but he had noticed before that in real life authors always seemed far older than their publicity pictures made them appear. The biographical notes were more up-to-date, recording the glittering prizes Guy Jeffries had earned so rapidly during his academic career and including an encomium from a future Prime Minister.

There is no more fluent exponent of the integral link between politics and philosophy in Britain today than Guy Jeffries, Harold Wilson had proclaimed, and although it was hardly an epitaph that would have encouraged Harry to glance inside the book in normal circumstances, now he opened it at once.

Even before he reached chapter one, he was struck by the dedication which came immediately after the title page. *To Carole, whom I adore.* Both Harry's parents had been killed in a road accident when he was a boy but somehow he had never doubted that his own old man, taciturn and undemonstrative though he had been, would have done anything to spare his son from pain. Again he tried to guess at the grief Jeffries had felt at the death of his daughter. To lose one's mother and father when young was a cruel blow, but to lose an only child must be a hundred times worse.

Guy's writing was fluent and - even in a chapter on the unpromising subject of British industrial policy - passionate. There was no denying the strength of his convictions or the verve with which he propounded them. The strangler, Harry reflected, had not only robbed Carole of life but also her father of the will to continue his march down the path to fame and fortune.

Late in the evening, Harry turned to Clive Doxey's book. It had been written during his socialist phase and the biographical note at the front did not reflect the author's subsequent political metamorphoses although the elegant style of the main text was familiar to Harry from Doxey's more recent journalism. A forceful essay on *Punishment* made it clear that he belonged to the school of penal reform that believes in fining householders careless enough to allow themselves to be burgled and concentrating the resources thereby acquired on the rehabilitation of those driven by deprivation to commit the burglaries. What, Harry wondered, of the person who had committed the murder in Sefton Park? If neither Smith nor some other inadequate was guilty, he came back to the possibility that the culprit was someone who had known Carole well. Someone who had been able to cast his crime aside and carry on living in civilised society without apparent strain or shame.

Unless, thought Harry as his eyelids began to droop, that someone was Ray Brill and the decline of his career was due to something more significant than his failure to come to terms with the changing world of pop.

When he woke the next morning, he was still haunted by the same idea. Now he could pinpoint Miller's change of attitude towards the Cyril Tweats file. Even after speaking to Renata Grierson, he had been curious about its contents at the time of his telephone call on Thursday. But that same afternoon he had been anxious to choke off any interest Harry might have in the case. Could it be that Ray, taken off balance by Miller's news that Smith seemed to be in the clear, might have said something that amounted to an admission of his own guilt?

Yet the more Harry debated with himself, the more fanciful his guesswork seemed. Hadn't Sherlock once said that it was a capital mistake to theorise without data? What he needed was hard facts and Miller's determination to play his cards close to his chest simply had the effect of making him more eager than ever to find things out for himself. Yet where should he start?

Best to begin close to home, he concluded. At least he knew the man who had been at the heart of things thirty years ago. The time had come to pay a call on Cyril Tweats.

It was not a decision he took lightly. He had always found Cyril an infuriating companion and had reacted with horror to Jim's suggestion, when the practice of Tweats and Company came on the market, that they should put in a bid.

'Are you serious?' he had demanded. 'We'll be the laughing stock of Liverpool.'

'Laughing all the way to the bank, if the figures I've seen stack up,' his partner had replied. 'Cyril's comfortably off and he's not seeking much money for the goodwill.'

'Goodwill? Most of his files are marked with the black spot.'

'You exaggerate, as usual. Say what you like about Cyril - and you usually do - he has plenty of profitable work-in-progress in his cabinets. Besides, his overheads are minimal.'

'Of course they are. He pays his staff peanuts and never moves a muscle on any of his files unless someone forces his hand. What about the risk of negligence claims?'

'Warranties and insurance,' said Jim with a wave of the hand. 'Believe me, we can afford a bank loan to pay him what he's looking for and wait for the money to roll in.'

'If it's such a good deal, why aren't our competitors biting his hand off?'

'Same reason you're so nervous. Cyril has a wonderful reputation with his clients, quite the opposite with other solicitors. Besides, most firms are trying to move upmarket. They're aiming for the corporate business, that's where the money is supposed to be. I tell you, though, Harry, I've examined Cyril's accounts as sceptically as if they had been prepared by Robert Maxwell and as far as I can see, we simply can't lose.'

So the deal had gone through and although Harry still had the occasional nightmare that one day a knock on their door would herald the arrival of joint envoys from the Fraud Squad and the Law Society, he had to admit that thus far their investment had paid off. But he still thought it a fluke: rather like the entire career of Cyril Tweats.

As soon as he had studied the last football league tables in *The Sunday Times* and consigned the business and personal finance sections to the wastepaper bin unread, he set off for Aigburth. Cyril had retired to a palatial villa in a quiet road with views over the cricket field. *Only a stone's throw away from Battlecrease House where Florence and James Maybrick lived,* thought Harry, but then he bit his lip and told himself to watch out: crime was rapidly becoming not only his bread and butter but also the obsession of his every waking hour. As he turned into the drive, he saw a man bending over a drain underneath one of the downspouts on the side of the building. Harry thought it was a tramp but when the man straightened, he realised his mistake. Cyril himself had been clearing out a handful of soggy brown leaves. In his donkey jacket and elderly trilby, he hardly looked like a distinguished professional man, but Harry reflected that was fair enough, since he had not been one.

Cyril's whole career might have been planned to prove that it is better to be born lucky than rich. His rise to fame and fortune had become the stuff of Liverpool legend and these days it was hard to separate truth from the layers of accumulated myth. He seemed always to provoke exasperated amusement, and every solicitor in the city had a Cyril story to tell.

He stood up at the sound of the car and waved as Harry walked towards him, a vague gleam in his watery eyes.

'My dear fellow, how are you? Good to see you.'

'Hello, Cyril. How's retirement?'

'Splendid, absolutely splendid. I seem to be so busy about the garden that I can't recall now how I managed to fit any legal business into my working day. Come in and have a cup of tea and a jaffa cake.' He led the way to the house, calling out, 'Dolly! We have a visitor.' Turning at the door, he confided, 'She looks after me damned well, you know. Not that I'm much trouble.'

'I'm sure.' Privately, Harry entertained the greatest respect for Cyril's widowed sister. Amiable as the old man was, prolonged exposure to him would test anyone's patience. But Dolly Harris would have made Job seem like a chain-smoking neurotic.

As they entered the lounge, Cyril pointed to the huge aquarium that was his pride and joy. Perhaps the open mouths of his exotic fish reminded him of clients past. He tapped the side of the tank and said, 'Exceptionally thick glass, you know. It would stop a bullet.'

'Very handy, if someone wants to assassinate your fish.'

Cyril shook his head sadly and settled himself into an armchair. 'Oh Harry, Harry. You're so sharp that one day you'll cut yourself. Well, young man, what brings you here? I suppose you've come to pick my brains?'

God forbid, thought Harry, but aloud he said, 'Sort of, Cyril.'

Cyril gave a comfortable nod. He always liked to say that he had had a marvellous education in the university of life and he saw nothing risible in the idea that a professional colleague might seek to benefit from his accumulated wisdom.

People said he had only scraped through his exams because the Law Society could not face marking any more of his resit papers. The principal who had signed his certificate of fitness to practise once he had completed his articles had been either drunk or simply desperate to get rid of the lad. After gaining a little more experience at the expense of a series of luckless clients, Cyril had put up his own nameplate outside an alcove in the Cunard Building, less from a desire to become a sole practitioner than from a growing awareness that no-one else would have him. He made a vow early on not to narrow his horizons through specialisation and as a resul he applied his inverse Midas touch to an infinite variety of les problems. His conveyancing clients ran the risk of finding a main road running through their back yard within months of completion and people who came to him for advice on a divorce could count themselves fortunate if they were not reduced to penury by the financial settlement. Yet for all that, his unflappable, if insensitive, good nature coupled with a native Liverpudlian's ability to talk himself out of trouble helped him to make ends meet. And then one day, Cyril Tweats struck gold.

It began in a small way, as *causes célèbres* often do, when he was consulted by a Toxteth resident aggrieved by the noise and smell from a local glue factory. Impressed by Cyril's talk of taking the attack to the multi-national which owned the offending premises, the client encouraged a dozen of his neighbours to make similar complaints. Cyril duly wrote a ferocious letter to the company and when its failure to disclose any realistic cause of action prompted the managing director to consign it to the waste bin, he issued a writ and promptly forgot about the matter.

As the proceedings lumbered along, head office in Illinois was informed and hotshot in-house lawyers came on to the scene. When their powerful defence failed to persuade the litigants to throw in the towel, they sent a letter making a token offer of settlement with a view to saving time and expense. Cyril, as was his custom, ignored the offer and in due course the Americans increased it in the hope of ridding themselves of the case once and for all. Further correspondence and telephone calls provoked no reply and as time passed a degree of panic set in. The company was engaged in a fierce takeover battle and needed to be squeaky clean. As the day of the hearing drew near, the commercial cost of ~he dispute mounted and before long the need to resolve it became ~nerstone of boardroom policy. Cyril had scarcely turned his details like the need to brief counsel when nerves finally ·he other side of the Atlantic. The lawyers put forward a ~d to make every plaintiff rich. When Cyril laughed at it, they took him to be hell-bent on making legal history rather than simply unable to credit the sum being mentioned and so they hurriedly doubled it. The name of Tweats and Company became the toast of Toxteth; Cyril's reputation was made. Thereafter he was often described as a pioneer of English environmental law.

Yet he was not a man to brag. 'Ah yes, the case of the glue factory,' he would say. 'Damned sticky business.' And he would smile in his charming manner.

'So what can I do for you?' he asked when Dolly had served tea in china cups and a plateful of biscuits.

'Cast your mind back thirty years. Do you remember a client by the name of Edwin Smith?'

'Remember him? As if it was yesterday, my dear boy, how could I ever forget? The press were buzzing round like wasps over a rotten apple. The city hadn't seen a bigger murder trial since the Cameo Cinema case.'

'I happened to look at the old file the other day. I have it here.' Harry slid the folder across the table. 'I hadn't known that he actually retracted his confession.'

Cyril frowned. 'Well, yes, I recall that he did. Of course, they often do.'

'Who?'

'Criminals, of course. For all manner of reasons, but mainly because they hope to get off. And quite frankly, given the state of justice in this country nowadays, they are usually in with a good chance of that.'

'So it never crossed your mind that the retraction might be genuine and his confession to the police false?'

'Good heavens, no.'

'But with the benefit of hindsight, might you think differently?'

'Whatever for? The chap was as guilty as a monk's thoughts in a nunnery.'

Harry bit his tongue. 'Tell me about him. What sort of man was he?'

Cyril dipped a biscuit into his drink and took a bite out of it as he collected his thoughts. 'Unprepossessing lad. Freckles, no chin, too much neck. In a word, shifty. No backbone. Far too much of a mummy's boy.'

'I see from the papers that mummy paid your fees.'

'Quite correct. Young Edwin could never keep a job down, never made two pennies of his own to rub together. All the same, there was money in the family. The father had died years before, a stroke, I think, but he was in cotton in the days when there was still something to be made from textiles and he left his widow a few pennies, as well as an enormous house on Sefton Park. She was a forceful character too, but the boy was a sore disappointment. Her own fault, I suppose, all that mollycoddling. Unhealthy. Of course, a heavy price was paid. Poor young Carole Jeffries wasn't the first person he'd molested.'

'He was hardly a major criminal. I gather from the file that he had a history of exposing himself and stealing knickers from a washing line.'

Cyril clicked his tongue. 'You know as well as I do that with such a pathetic specimen, one thing invariably leads to another. As it did with young Smith. One day, he simply went too far.'

'He had had a girlfriend of his own, though.'

'Yes, I believe there was someone, but that only made things worse. He admitted she'd finished with him around the time he strangled the girl, if memory serves. Obviously, the rejection tipped him over the edge.'

'Name of Renata Yates, according to his statement. Did you ever see her?'

'Lord, no. She'd made herself scarce and besides, I could tell she was going to be bad news. I mean, from the little he said about her she was no better than a street-walker.'

'So you never heard any suggestions that her evidence might have exonerated Edwin?'

'Good gracious me, certainly not. Wherever did you get such an idea?'

'From the same person who tells me that Edwin was an attention-seeker, the sort who might admit guilt simply to claim his fifteen minutes of fame.'

'Look, Harry,' said Cyril in his most fatherly manner, 'don't you believe all that you hear in those saloon bars of yours.'

'Okay, okay, so tell me about the victim, Carole. What was she like?'

'Pretty girl. Headstrong, by all accounts, possibly rather spoiled. Her mum was a bit of a tartar, I remember, but Carole was the apple of her father's eye, he thought she could do no wrong. Her death finished him, you know. He'd been a powerful figure in the Labour movement, but after his daughter's death, he was never the same man again. Of course, you might say that's the inevitable fate of people who devote themselves to the Labour movement. Even so, I often thought that he was Edwin Smith's second victim.'

'Although he survived Edwin by - what? - nearly fifteen years?'

'Yes, killed himself on the day Margaret Thatcher came to power, would you believe? Ludicrous, absolutely ludicrous. You don't need me to tell you she was the finest Prime Minister this country ever had. And how did her own party reward her?'

Keener even than usual to avoid a discussion about the Iron Lady, Harry said hastily, 'Smith cut his throat in prison. It was careless of the authorities to let him have the opportunity. Wasn't he marked down as a suicide risk?'

'You know how these things occur,' said Cyril in his man-to-man tone. 'I'm afraid my client was an unpopular fellow. I suspect a warder turned a blind eye to the possibility of *felo de se*. It happens, as you know.'

Looking at the amiable, contented face, Harry marvelled. Cyril was a man who had always been at ease with himself, no matter what disasters befell those for whom he had acted.

'What about the people close to the Jeffries family? Clive Doxey was one of them, wasn't he?'

'Ah yes,' said Cyril with a chuckle, 'he experienced quite a crisis of conscience, as I recall. He'd been an outspoken advocate of abolishing capital punishment, but when his best friend's daughter was murdered, he seemed to have second thoughts for a while. I remember it well.'

'I suppose there was never any suggestion that the police should have cast their net more widely in searching for suspects?'

'Lord, no. Everyone regarded it as an open-and-shut case.'

'Carole's boyfriend, the pop musician - was he ever a suspect?'

Cyril smiled a superior smile. 'Ah, Harry, you never change, do you? Constantly seeking a complex explanation where a perfectly simple one exists all the time. I'm surprised you have time for all this nonsense, with such a busy practice to attend to. When I was your age...'

'The musician,' prompted Harry.

'Oh yes, I remember the chap you're referring to, though I forget his name, but I'm quite certain he had an alibi for the killing. As you will appreciate, it was one of the first things the police had to check.'

'And the strength of the alibi?'

A dismissive shrug. 'I don't believe there was ever the slightest indication that he might have committed the crime.'

Succumbing to frustration, Harry said, 'All right, Carole worked for Benny Frederick, didn't she? Did anyone consider whether he might have had a motive for killing her?'

'My dear fellow, I don't think I'm talking out of turn when I say that Frederick was well known for being rather more interested in young men than young girls.'

Harry decided to fly a kite. 'Homosexuality was illegal in 1964. She might have been blackmailing him.'

Distaste spread across Cyril's placid features like a stain. 'A lurid suggestion, Harry, and frankly a slanderous one. I do urge you to think carefully before you make some of your more outrageous statements. Yes, I really do advise that you look before you leap.'

Harry felt it was a sound principle to do the opposite of whatever Cyril advised, but he simply nodded and said, 'Would you like to look at your old file? It may trigger one or two memories.'

Cyril picked up the folder and started to glance through it. Every now and then he gave a small grunt of pleasurable reminiscence, rather like a minor celebrity leafing through an old album of press cuttings.

'A well-organised file, though I say so myself. Quite immaculately presented. Say what you like about her, Mrs Miller was certainly a good secretary.'

The name struck Harry like a slap across the cheek.

'Mrs Miller?'

'Yes, yes. Marlene was her first name, although we were never on such familiar terms. Let me see, she must have worked for me for the best part of twenty years. An immaculate typist, precise and well organised, the best I ever had.'

'She wasn't by any chance married to a man called Ernest?'

Cyril tutted. 'My dear fellow, I can hardly be expected to recall the Christian name of the spouse of an employee who worked for me donkey's years ago. And yet, as it happens, you may just be right. The two of them were Germans, of course, though I did not hold that against them. Now I come to think of it, I believe he changed his name from Mueller.' Cyril beamed at his feat of memory. 'Yes, I'm sure that was his name. Ernst Mueller, who became Ernest Miller. Is that the chap you're asking about?'

Chapter Eleven

to the ultimate crime.

Harry stared at Cyril Tweats. 'So Marlene Miller was your confidential secretary and did all the typing on the Smith file? Tell me, how long did she work for you afterwards?'

Cyril was genial in his condescension. 'You are flitting about today. One minute you're immersed in a case that closed thirty years ago, the next you're getting excited about my typing arrangements. Really, Harry, is it possible you may be suffering from over-tiredness?'

'Please, Cyril, I'm interested.'

Cyril beamed again to show that he was willing to humour him. 'I should say she stayed with me until about twelve years ago. Then another firm offered more money. I sensed she was reluctant to go, kept hoping I would increase my offer. But I have my principles.'

Glancing at the sumptuous furnishings all around, Harry had to admit that Cyril's principles had kept him in a style to which many would be glad to become accustomed.

'Did you know Marlene had died?'

Cyril rubbed his chin. 'I believe I did hear that. I think her husband let one of the girls in the office know.'

'You never met him?'

'I always made it a rule never to fraternise with my staff or their families,' said Cyril sternly. 'I regard it as a basic tenet of good management. One must keep one's distance. Otherwise standards start to slip. Another jaffa cake?'

'Did she ever speak of him?'

'Possibly. I never knew a woman yet who didn't indulge her taste in gossip - and usually at the most inconvenient time. But it will have washed over me, I'm afraid. I used to find that the occasional

"Oh really?" sufficed as a courtesy whenever one of my girls was chattering about her loved ones. But do tell me - why the sudden interest in the woman who worked on this file?'

'I've met Mrs Miller's widowed husband. He's the person who persuaded me to take an interest in the Sefton Park case. And thanks to you, I now know why he was so convinced Edwin Smith was innocent. His wife must have told him about the retraction.'

Cyril brushed the retraction away as if swatting a fly. 'My dear Harry, I do feel you are paying far too much attention to a brief episode in a lengthy case. After all, Smith did plead guilty at trial.'

'On Hugo Kellerman's advice?'

'Of course. It was plainly the right thing to do. Kellerman - he died of a coronary a few years ago, God rest his soul, too many dinners at Lincoln's Inn, I suppose - had no doubt. When Smith asked about the chances of an acquittal, he said, "You're pissing in the wind, Smithy, simply pissing in the wind"'. Cyril smiled in reminiscence. 'He didn't mince words, Hugo didn't. The Bar is the poorer for his passing.'

Harry could imagine that Cyril would have instructed a barrister who was a kindred spirit. Already he could picture Kellerman: a ruddy-faced blusterer with a technique of persuasion as subtle as that of a timeshare salesman.

'So Edwin surrendered?'

'He saw reason,' corrected Cyril with a sweet smile. The old rascal had charm, Harry reflected. With a hide so thick, he should have gone into politics. He had a flair for presenting the acceptable face of incompetence and expecting it to be kissed.

'And after sentence was passed, he committed suicide.'

'He'd made one previous attempt, as I imagine you are aware, before the parliamentary vote to abolish the death penalty.'

'A vote that did no good for Edwin.'

'It did no good for all those people over the past thirty years whose killers might have been deterred by the prospect of the rope,' said Cyril, suddenly stern. 'But you're right. Edwin Smith was no psychopath. He was bad, but not mad: a pitiful individual, wholly lacking in backbone. Yet I believe he was genuinely overcome by remorse for what he had done. When the state was ready to spare his life, he took what he thought was the honourable course. And I could respect him for that.'

Harry thought that in days gone by Cyril would have been the first to pass a pearl-handled revolver to a disgraced colleague and suggest that he pop next door to the library and do the decent thing. With an effort, he subdued his rising temper and said, 'So you still believe he was guilty?'

Cyril smiled again. 'Oh yes. As sure as I am sitting here, sipping tea and eating more biscuits than are good for me. Take it from me, Harry, for his terrible crime, young Edwin Smith certainly deserved to die.'

After saying goodbye, Harry sat in his car for a few minutes, mulling over what Cyril Tweats had told him. He found it was easy to discount the views of Cyril and Hugo Kellerman about their client's guilt and at last he understood why Ernest Miller had been equally convinced that Smith's confession was likely to have been false. One mystery, at least, had been solved. No doubt Marlene had discussed the case avidly with her husband and now, in his retirement, he had decided to poke around.

But in poking around, would he find that the embers of the Carole Jeffries case were far from dead? Harry felt a surge of anxiety on Miller's behalf. The old man was playing with fire. He resolved to talk to Miller again and find out for certain exactly what he had learned.

The will provided at least a thin excuse for making a weekend call. Jim had kept his promise and had the document typed up before close of business on Friday evening. Harry drove through the quiet city centre streets back to his office and collected it, together with Miller's red document folder, before setting off for Everton.

The journey took Harry to a maze of back-to-back houses. Every other Saturday from August to May the streets in this part of the city were thronged with supporters making their way to the match. It was a place of fierce loyalties, home to many of its inhabitants from cradle to grave, and yet Harry felt surprised that a man like Miller had stayed here so long. He was not a native of Liverpool and during his working life must have earned good money, with a useful second income whilst his wife was alive. According to the information he had given Harry, he was comfortably off, so why had he not moved upmarket? Had he simply grown accustomed to this place, too set in his ways to contemplate a change - or had the close ties that still kept this community together bound in even such an awkward cuss as Ernest Miller?

Miller's house stood at the end of Mole Street and commanded a view of an iron foundry and a gasworks. The lace curtains at the windows were in need of a wash and the door had probably not been painted since the Brill Brothers were in the charts. In contrast, the step outside the house next door shone smugly, as if it enjoyed a through scrub once each day. As he parked, Harry noticed a twitching of the neighbour's curtains. He guessed Ernest Miller seldom had visitors and the arrival of an MG was cause for curiosity.

He pressed the bell and heard its muffled ringing inside. No answer. He tried again with equal lack of response and was about to turn back to his car when the door of the adjoining house opened. A woman of about sixty with impossibly bright auburn hair peered at him like an ornithologist studying a rare species.

'After Ernie, are you?'

'I seem to be out of luck. Any idea when he'll be back?'

'I can't understand it. He's not taken his milk in today, or his *News Of The World*.'

Puzzled, Harry glanced at Miller's empty doorstep and letter box. The woman explained, 'A couple of kids pinched the bottles and the newspaper this morning. They were out of sight before I could get to my front door, the little monkeys. Only seven or eight, they were. If I was their mum, I'd give 'em a good hiding. It'll be cars they're stealing next and then who knows what will happen?'

'Is it unusual for Ernest not to be about on a Sunday?'

'Put it this way, I've lived next to him for years and I've never known it before.'

'You think he's gone away?'

'Not without leaving word with me. I always keep an eye on the place for him when he's gone on holiday and such-like.' She had the simple confidence of the indispensable. 'Besides, he was there yesterday. I heard him.'

'Could he have been taken ill?'

Her expression blended concern, curiosity and excitement at the prospect of drama. 'That's what I'm wondering.'

Harry lifted the lid of the letter box. The hall inside was dark and yielded no sign of life. 'Mr Miller,' he called, 'it's Harry Devlin here.'

'You're a friend of Ernie's, then?' asked the woman.

'I'm a solicitor,' he said firmly, relying on her membership of a generation which retained a residual respect for the mystique of the law.

'Ah, legal business,' she breathed.

'I don't suppose you have a spare key so that we can go in and check to see that he hasn't had an accident?'

She shook her head in regret. 'Oh, Ernie would never let me have a key. He's always been very close, always kept himself to himself.'

Without much hope, Harry gripped the door handle and gave it a twist. Unexpectedly, the door swung open.

The woman's eyes opened very wide. 'Yet he hasn't been out for the last twenty-four hours. I would have known.'

Harry did not doubt it. Living next door to GCHQ would have carried less risk of surveillance. 'I think we ought to go inside, don't you?'

Thrilled, she said, 'And you don't reckon we should call the police, Mr...?'

'Devlin. Harry Devlin.'

She stretched out a hand gnarled with arthritis. 'Gloria Hegg. Pleased to meet you.'

Harry stepped over the threshold. The hall carpet was patterned with hideous red and yellow flowers; it seemed not to have been swept for weeks. The paper on the walls was peeling at the edges and spiders had traced cobweb patterns down from the picture rail. There were two doors on the right, a third under the staircase and a fourth, in glass, at the end of the corridor. As he took a pace forward, a musty odour made him wrinkle his nose.

Behind him, Gloria Hegg said in a whisper, 'Something's not right, Mr Devlin. I can feel it.'

Harry could feel it too. The stillness of the hallway troubled him, but more than that, he felt a chill down his back which he had experienced before. Gritting his teeth as he strove to summon up the courage to go on, he gestured towards the first two doors.

'Sitting room and dining room?'

She had turned pale. 'And that one leads down to the cellar. The one at the end takes you into the kitchen and scullery.'

Harry felt her hand grip his shoulder as he opened the sitting-room door. Even before he looked inside, he knew what he would find. When his companion screamed and pitched forward at the sight of the shrivelled body stretched across the floor, he was ready to break her fall.

Chapter Twelve

In the aftermath of death,

A fter he had helped Gloria Hegg into the dining room, found a bottle of brandy in a wall unit and poured her a generous measure, he dialled 999 and summoned the police. His immediate duty done, he felt the numbing shock he had experienced at the discovery of Miller's corpse begin to give way to a dull ache of despair. Although he had not cared for Miller, the ending of a human life always left him with a feeling of emptiness. Whoever it was who died, how could anyone not mourn the extinction of a fellow human being? And more than that, in the presence of death, how could anyone fail to be reminded of their own mortality?

He decided to pour another brandy for himself. The sight of those sallow features, twisted in an agonised parody of the habitual crooked smile, had filled him with nausea. And yet, for all his anguish, his mind had not seized up. Miller's death was more than a mere source of misery. It presented him with a new puzzle to solve.

How had the old man died? There was a gash on his head and there were stains of blood on the corner of the stone hearth in the sitting room as well as the carpet. The position of the body seemed consistent with Miller's having fallen, possibly as a result of a dizzy spell, cracked his head open and died from the combined effects of shock and the injury. He had been in poor health and there were no signs of a break-in or of a struggle.

'I can't believe it,' said Gloria Hegg indistinctly. Her head was in her hands and she was sobbing softly. 'I simply can't take it in that we've found him dead.'

Harry knelt beside her chair and put an arm around her. 'Have a good cry,' he said softly, 'you'll feel better for it.'

He did not find it quite so difficult to believe that Miller was dead. Even before his arrival in Everton he had become apprehensive for the safety of the old man who was now lying next door, waiting for the officials of the state to take him on his final journey. His manner in Sefton Park had suggested that he had learned something new from his meeting with Ray Brill. Perhaps he had enjoyed the hoarding of information too much for his own good. Harry could not help wondering if Miller had at last come into possession of dangerous knowledge and if it was possible that the old man might have been given a helping hand into the next world.

Two and a half hours later, he was sitting in Gloria Hegg's own front room, drinking her tea and dispensing more sympathy.

'It's a dreadful, dreadful thing,' Gloria said, for perhaps the twentieth time. She cradled her chin in her right palm and stared at the flying ducks on the opposite wall, as if hoping they might offer a solution to the mysteries of life and death.

'Were you close to him?' he asked gently.

She looked up and gave him a sharp glance. 'As close as anyone, I suppose, though that's not saying much. Like I said, he kept himself to himself, did Ernie. He was a very private man.'

But there was no privacy in death. The police officers and medics had been brisk and efficient, neither callous nor pretending false concern. To them, the discovery of an old man's body was all part of a day's work. Even a constable who did not look old enough to shave was experienced enough already to have learned detachment; without it, his job would have been unbearable. Gloria and Harry had given brief statements explaining how they had come to find the corpse. The constable's questioning had not been rigorous; from the outset, he gave no hint of suspecting foul play. Gloria mentioned early on that Miller was often severely affected by asthma attacks and all the preliminary indications were that he had fallen and cut his head while overcome by such an attack. The time of death was unclear and the precise cause of death would need to be ascertained at the post mortem, but at present everything seemed straightforward.

Harry had said nothing about the Carole Jeffries case; he had shown the constable the will and the young man had been naive enough not to express surprise that a solicitor should call on a Sunday to discuss a routine matter. He had treated Gloria with barely concealed condescension and she had responded to each patronising question with monosyllables. Yet Harry sensed that something was on her mind. Once or twice she had started to speak, but each time the constable interrupted with another question and the moment passed.

With little fuss and even less ceremony, the body had been taken off to the mortuary. Naturally, the police wanted to know about Ernest Miller's family, but Gloria was adamant that he had none. His wife had died a decade ago, so she understood, and he had spoken of being alone in the world. When popping in over the Christmas period, she had never noticed any cards that might have come from relatives. When Harry confirmed that was also his understanding, the young constable frowned and remarked that the house needed to be made safe. Gloria had been quick to take her cue and offer to look after the key, which she knew Miller kept in a pewter mug above the fireplace.

'How long had you known him?' Harry asked when they were alone again.

'Nigh on eight years. I bought this place after my husband left me. We'd lived in Walton, but I wanted to get away and start again.'

'And his wife?'

'She died a year or two before I came here. He never spoke about her much, but I think he must have missed her.' She pushed a hand through the bizarre auburn curls. 'Certainly he never seemed interested in any other woman.'

'Did you see much of him?'

'I like to be a good neighbour,' she said, a trace of colour rising in her cheeks, 'and after he retired, obviously I saw more of him about the place. These houses only have small yards at the back, but he used to potter around. I'd often invite him in for a cup of tea, but mostly he said no.'

'He didn't know what he was missing,' said Harry, pouring for each of them from a fat chocolate-coloured pot.

'Thank you, Harry - may I call you that? - you're a gentleman. I make a good cup of tea, though I say it myself. But I can tell you, poor Ernie wasn't much interested in a drink and a natter. I don't like to speak ill of the dead, but he did have a sarky way with him at times. He could be sharp and that used to upset me. I never meant to be a nosey parker, I was only trying to be friendly.'

Harry could hear the hurt in her voice and he wondered if Gloria had ever set her cap at Miller and been rebuffed. He found it easy to imagine both her curiosity about her odd neighbour and, equally, Miller's irritable reaction. It seemed unlikely that she could cast any light on the Sefton Park case, but there was no harm in asking.

'Tell me, Gloria, as a matter of interest, did you know Ernie was an amateur criminologist?'

She shook her head, puzzled.

'So he never mentioned to you his researches into a murder case from years back, the killing of a young girl named Carole Jeffries?'

'No, though I'm not surprised he would get mixed up in that sort of thing. He was morbid, was Ernie. Do you know he used to read nothing but books about famous murders! As if there isn't enough misery in the world without people adding to it in books! It doesn't do for me, I'm afraid. I'm in the local library and I reckon to read three Mills and Boons every week.'

'Did he have many friends?'

'None, as far as I could tell. He wasn't popular in this street, you've probably gathered that.'

Harry had. After the arrival of police and ambulance, a knot of local people had gathered in the street. Women in curlers had whispered behind their hands and scruffy young children had pointed and jigged about with excitement. Everyone had been fascinated by the activity, but even though word soon got around that Miller had died, no-one gave any appearance of sorrow. For the people of Mole Street, it seemed that their neighbour's demise was a source of entertainment to match anything on the telly rather than a cause of dismay.

Yet that was not true of Gloria Hegg. Whether or not she had ever fancied Ernest Miller, at least she mourned his passing. Her eyes were still brimming with tears and the puffiness of her skin made her look even older than her years.

'Did he have any regular visitors?'

'No, I hardly ever heard his doorbell ring. People collecting for charities only called once on Ernie, I'm afraid. He always sent them off with a flea in their ear.'

'Yet he instructed me that he meant to leave his money to charity.'

She dabbed at her cheeks with a small handkerchief. 'Just goes to show, doesn't it? He wasn't the mean old sod that people said.'

'And no-one called yesterday, for instance, or earlier today?'

She hesitated before replying. Again he had the feeling that she was about to unburden herself.

'Yes, Gloria?'

'It's probably nothing,' she said slowly.

'Tell me anyway.'

She gave him a grateful glance. 'At least you don't speak to me as though I'm a stupid old woman, like that young whippersnapper from the police. Whatever you may think inside.'

'Of course I don't think you're stupid. Come on, Gloria, you've had a grim experience and I can see that something's preying on your mind. Why don't you share it?'

'All right. As a matter of fact, someone did bang on Ernie's door last night. I remember, because it was so unusual.'

'A sales rep or someone rattling a collector's tin?' Harry was sure that Gloria would have had her face pressed to the window at the sound of activity next door. An inquisitive man himself, he recognised Gloria as a woman capable of turning nosiness into an art form.

'I've no idea,' she said with evident regret. 'I heard the knocking, but as it happens, I was on the phone to my sister in St Helens and I could hardly ring off. But no-one called on me, so when I thought it over afterwards, I felt sure it hadn't been anyone selling or collecting.' She gave him a fierce look and added defensively, 'I like to know what's going on in my street. When you're a woman living alone, you never feel safe.'

'Do you know if Ernie invited his visitor inside?'

'I suppose so. I didn't hear anyone leave later, but there's no reason why I should have done. I was talking to Myrtle for over an hour. She lives alone and she likes a good natter once in a while.' She hesitated and said, 'It doesn't matter, does it, that I didn't mention it to the policeman?'

'Don't worry about it, Gloria, don't fret yourself any more.'

Yet as he finished his tea, he mulled over the implications of what she had told him. Suppose Miller's visitor had been someone connected with the Sefton Park case. Ray Brill, for instance. What if the old man had some reason for suggesting that Brill's alibi for the killing of Carole Jeffries would not stand up to scrutiny? Might his visitor have struck him down and then, realising the old man was dead, have panicked and fled, leaving the door to the house open? Guesswork, guesswork, guesswork. He needed to know what

Miller had learned and the answer, he felt sure, lay in the old man's file on the case.

'I think,' he said carefully, 'I ought to have a quick look round the house before I go.'

'Yes, yes of course. As his solicitor, you need to make sure everything is secure.'

He gave her a smile on his way out, thanking his lucky stars that she did not know that his own office had been burgled less than forty-eight hours earlier. Letting himself back into Miller's house, he thought the place had the atmosphere of a graveyard. The dust irritated his sinuses and the musty smell was as strong as before. He knew he was trespassing in the secretive old man's castle and he felt uneasy, as if from somewhere Miller was watching his every move.

He padded up the stairs and took a look around. As well as a bathroom there were two bedrooms of reasonable size together with a third scarcely big enough to accommodate a pygmy. He glanced into each room. Miller slept at the front of the house in the double bed he had presumably once shared with his late wife. The second room he evidently used as his study and the third was filled with junk accumulated over the years: an old mattress, bundles of old suits and a radiogram from the days of 78 rpm records and the BBC Light, Third and Home programmes. No prizes for guessing that he had never listened to the Brill Brothers here.

Harry concentrated his attention on the study. It was the only neat room he had seen in the entire house. This, he felt sure, was the place Ernest Miller loved to be. On a large mahogany desk stood an anglepoise lamp and a plastic tidy full of paper clips and drawing pins. A bookcase was full of cheap true crime paperbacks: turgidly written accounts of murder from Whitechapel to Wisconsin, books stuffed with theories about the Ripper's identity and gory details of how each of his victims had died. There were grisly studies of sadism and murder, chock-full of pictures of sociopaths who mostly looked like the man on the Clapham omnibus and psychobabble which pandered to readers who like to cloak their voyeurism with a pseudo-academic fig leaf.

A two-drawer filing cabinet stood next to the desk. Its key was in the lock. Harry opened it and rummaged through the suspensions, each of which held a red file of the kind Miller favoured. Every file and suspension was neatly marked: bank statements, building society correspondence, savings certificates, long-term investment, bills and all the rest. Nothing of interest there, he thought. The real question was: where was the one marked CAROLE JEFFRIES?

He checked through the cabinet a second time and looked to see if anything might have slipped to the bottom, but again he drew a blank. There was, however, at the back of the lower drawer, one suspension that bore no name tag and contained no file. He scratched his head. It was impossible to believe that a well-organised man like Ernest Miller would have used one more suspension than was absolutely necessary.

And all too easy to believe that last night's intruder had searched here for the file on the Sefton Park Strangling and stolen it to conceal facts which revealed that he, rather than Edwin Smith, had murdered Carole Jeffries.

Chapter Thirteen

I relished the sense of having settled old scores.

'Bloody bad news,' said Jim Crusoe the next morning when Harry told him about Miller's death. He gazed at the heavens as if in reproach. 'If only you'd managed to get him to sign his bloody will, we'd be quids in. Normally we have to wait years to convert a loss leader on the fee for a will into profit on a probate.'

'I don't think Ernest Miller meant to be inconsiderate. I'm sure he would have preferred to hang on for a while himself.'

'And now the bloody government will get the lot.' Jim shook his head and then a thought occurred to him. 'No suspicious circumstances, are there?'

'Why do you ask?'

'I've learned from experience that you and sudden death seem to go hand in hand. Being your partner has probably doubled the cost of my life insurance.'

'As a matter of fact, the whole business bothers me.' No exaggeration, this: thinking about Miller's death, and that of Carole Jeffries, had kept him awake for half the previous night. 'You see, it goes back thirty years...'

'For God's sake,' Jim interrupted, 'you haven't got time now to give me a history lesson. Tell me later on today. Have you forgotten you're due back in court in half an hour? What's the latest on the sergeant, by the way?'

'Still in intensive care, last I heard. One thing's for certain, he won't be finishing his evidence this morning.'

'And the chances of a settlement offer even the Walters can't refuse?'

'Improving with every hour. The police authority must be desperate to put an end to it all.'

Jim clapped him on the back. 'Go for it, then. And this time make sure that Kevin doesn't keel over until the money's safely in the bank.'

Patrick Vaulkhard and the Walters were waiting for him when he arrived at the court building. Jeannie was at her most glamorous: he guessed she had been up since the early hours applying the make-up in readiness for a triumphant press conference later in the day.

'So, what's the latest?' he asked. 'Are they ready to cough up?'

'Let's wait and see,' said Vaulkhard. 'I don't intend to make the first move this morning. The police are under pressure: we're ready to proceed. Let them make the running.'

'We're going to make 'em sweat,' confirmed Kevin. In his wife's presence, he seemed to need to assert his identity, to make it clear that he was relishing the occasion.

Jeannie nudged Harry in the ribs. 'Uh-oh. The Gnome's coming over here.'

She had thus christened the barrister representing the police authority and Harry had to admit the truth in her gibe. Gordon Summerbee was a tubby man with a red moustache and beard who looked as though he was born to hold a fishing line and squint out over a herbaceous border.

'Patrick,' he said, 'I wonder if we might have a word?'

As the two barristers moved off into a corner, Kevin gave Harry a wink. 'What d'you reckon?'

'Fingers crossed.'

'Whatever they offer,' said Jeannie, 'it can never be enough. Not after what my Kevin's been through.'

She gave her husband a smile, intended to be fond, which put Harry in mind of a miser beaming at his gold.

Kevin nodded vigorously and said, 'Y'know, I could never have made it without Jeannie.'

His wife preened, but did not forget to utter the sentiment she always expressed in her interviews. 'I've only done what any woman would do in the same terrible circumstances.'

She shrugged her overcoat off her shoulders and passed it to Harry, who in her presence often felt like a courtier. Today she was dressed for the photographers, wearing a tight black jersey and a microscopic skirt which revealed seemingly endless legs. Her impressive bosom bore in extravagant orange stitching the legend - WALTERGATE - MY KEV WAS INNOCENT.

Her Kev said excitedly, 'Bugger me, that was quick. He's coming back already.'

Harry could tell it was good news. Vaulkhard was walking towards them with a sportsman's swagger.

'Well?' demanded Jeannie. 'What have they said?'

'The authority is now willing to make a much improved offer.'

'So I should bloody well hope,' said Kevin.

'How much?' asked his wife.

'You need to consider their proposal with care.'

The way he's dragging it out, thought Harry, *it must be well into six figures.*

'Yes, yes,' said Jeannie impatiently.

Vaulkhard named the sum on offer. It was far more than Harry had expected, more even than he had hoped for in his most optimistic moments.

Kevin whistled. 'That's more like it!'

'Shut up,' Jeannie snapped. She addressed Vaulkhard. 'We want another thirty thousand.'

The foxy features twitched. 'I really would advise...'

'Another thirty,' she repeated, 'or we go back into court.'

Vaulkhard looked at her and then at her husband. 'If they withdraw the offer...'

'They won't withdraw it,' said Jeannie. 'Go back and tell them we fight on unless they decide to be more realistic.'

A spasm of uncertainty creased Kevin's face. He turned to Harry. 'What d'you think?'

'It's a gamble, Kevin, but if you're willing to...'

'Listen,' cut in Jeannie. 'We've bloody gambled all the way along the line. Now we've got them in a corner and I'm betting they'll cave in.'

'It's your decision,' said Vaulkhard sombrely.

'Too bloody right,' she said.

Chewing his lower lip, Kevin said, 'Look, love...'

'What are you waiting for?' she demanded of the barrister. 'Go on. Put it to them.'

'Very well.'

As Vaulkhard walked back to where Summerbee and his cohorts were standing, Kevin swore softly.

'Jeannie, if you fuck this up...'

'Listen. You'd still be sewing sodding mailbags if it wasn't for me. Now all you need do is keep your trap shut and wait for the busies to cave in.'

As they bickered, Harry's thoughts strayed. What would the late Edwin Smith not have given for a last taste of freedom, he wondered, let alone the prospect of financial recompense?

A new note of urgency in Jeannie's voice brought him back to the here and now. 'Look, Paddy's on his way back!'

Harry needed merely to glance at the barrister to know that the miracle had occurred. Vaulkhard had on his face an uncharacteristic expression of wonder, like that of a child at Christmas time.

'Well, what did they say?' called Jeannie. 'Don't keep us in suspense!'

'I must congratulate you, Jeannie, on your eye for a bargaining position.'

'You mean,' demanded Kevin, who always wanted things spelled out, 'the busies have actually agreed to the extra thirty?'

'Every penny.'

The couple stared at each other, then each let out a whoop of joy that had the tabloid hacks a few yards away scrambling for their pencils and notebooks. But Jeannie, the true professional, composed herself within seconds.

'It's a lot of money,' she said in a grave tone, 'but cash can never compensate for what we have suffered.'

She was right, reflected Harry. Cash could not redress every wrong. What of Edwin Smith, he thought again, what if there was indeed a chance to clear his name? In this case money genuinely did not matter. Only if the real murderer of Carole Jeffries was identified could justice finally be seen to be done.

The Walters' jubilant press conference over and done with, Harry walked back to the office with Ronald Sou. As usual, the clerk did not encourage conversation: he could make the average Trappist seem like a chatterbox. Harry found himself wondering what Ronald really made of their clients. The only clue he had was the quirk of Ronald's lips when Jeannie told the man from *The Sun* that the court case had not been about money, but a matter of principle.

He had to admit that it was a perfect outcome for Crusoe and Devlin as well. Even on legal aid rates, the fees would smooth the wrinkled brow of their accountant for a long time to come. The only snag was that Jim would want to invest the proceeds in more information technology, while Harry would have been content with a quill pen and a few scraps of vellum. At present the only information he was anxious for was whatever Ernest Miller had kept in the missing red file.

When they reached New Commodities House, he headed straight for his office. Lying where he had left it on his desk was Cyril Tweats' file for Edwin Smith. He picked it up and tucked it under his arm. He had finally convinced himself that the burglary here and the disappearance of Miller's papers were no coincidence.

The file was best kept in a safe place. The sooner he returned it to the Land of the Dead, the better.

Jim poked his head around the door. 'The conquering hero!'

'You've heard?'

'Ronald has just given me the glad tidings. He was beside himself with excitement, by which I mean he gave me a half-smile. How about a celebration drink at lunchtime?'

'Love to.' He gestured to the file under his arm. 'And I'll tell you the story of Cyril Tweats' unluckiest client.'

With that he set off for the Pierhead. Crossing the Strand, he saw Kim Lawrence fifty yards ahead of him and put on a spurt to catch her up.

'Not in court this morning?'

She seemed genuinely pleased to see him. 'I've done my duty. A number of my clients were charged with breach of the peace. They're anti-nuclear campaigners, and they threw eggs at a junior industry minister who won't be content until even our tap water is radioactive.'

'Is every case a crusade with you?'

She gave him a long look. 'I hope so. And besides, you don't do so badly yourself. The place was buzzing with news of the Waltergate settlement. Well done.'

She was not a woman who gave out compliments like calling cards and he felt himself blushing. Quickly, he said, 'Patrick Vaulkhard handled the negotiations. I took a back seat.'

'He's the best man for a case like that, but I know you were living with it night and day long before he was briefed.'

They reached the hut on the Pierhead and he unlocked the door which led to Jock's underground domain. 'What brings you here? Not on your way to the Land of the Dead, by any chance?'

'I want to collect some files from archive,' she said, following him down the flight of stairs. 'I could have waited for the messenger to come round this afternoon or sent my articled clerk Adrian out

- it's become a second home to him anyway, since Jock let him practise the saxophone here - but I need the exercise.'

He appraised her lean figure and thought about saying that she didn't look in need of exercise, but he had the feeling that she was not a woman who would respond to such a clumsy line of chat. Instead, as they walked past the old deserted ballroom, he said, 'I'm glad you're here. I'm beginning to feel it's not safe for me to wander around on my own. Since we last spoke, my office has been burgled and I've stumbled across the body of a client of mine.'

'I thought that was par for the course with Harry Devlin. The talk round the courts is that you've been mixed up with as many mysterious deaths as Inspector Morse. You're not by any chance a fan of opera?'

'Hate it. I don't mind some of the tunes but I simply can't follow the lyrics. As for my own reputation, such as it is, blame my curiosity. It usually gets the better of me - although that isn't so hard to do. You remember I mentioned the Sefton Park Strangling to you? Ernest Miller, the man who interested me in the case, is dead. I'm more than ever convinced that Edwin Smith, who was found guilty, did not kill the girl. And whoever broke into my office went through all my papers but took nothing.'

A faint smile slid across her face. 'But apart from all that, nothing much has been happening? Who were your burglars, undercover investigators from the Legal Aid Board?'

'Can't have been, they didn't leave any forms behind for me to fill it. No, my bet is, the intruder was searching for Cyril Tweats' old file on the case.' He patted the folder under his arm. 'I've decided to bring it back here, where it's out of harm's way.'

'So you're sure Miller was on to something?'

'He was eccentric, perhaps, but no fool. Incidentally, the good news is that his heart turned out to be in the right place. He didn't have any family, so he instructed me to draw up a will leaving everything he had to MOJO.'

'You're kidding!'

'The bad news is, he died before he got round to signing it.'

Kim Lawrence stared at him for a moment, then shook her head and swore. 'So who gets the money?'

'The Crown, presumably. And before you say anything, I know the national finances are in a poor way, but I don't think the Chancellor of the Exchequer is implicated in Miller's death.'

They turned into the archivist's room and Harry said, 'Hello, Jock. I have something for you.'

The little Scot beamed with delight as he was handed the file. 'You're not returning the old file you took away the other day, by any chance? Splendid, absolutely splendid! So often I have to chase people up. They forget to send things back here, where they belong.'

'This is the best place for the file of Mr Edwin Smith. Look after it, though. Someone out there would dearly love to get his hands on it.'

'Harry's involved in another of his mysteries,' explained Kim.

'So I gather,' said Jock. 'Come on, for Heaven's sake, you must tell us the whole story.'

'It will take a while,' warned Harry.

'So much the better,' said Kim. 'Anything to put off the evil hour when I have to return my phone calls.'

'You're a woman after my own heart. Okay, here goes.'

He recounted at length how Miller had first interested him in the Sefton Park case, his discovery of the body and his growing suspicion that the burglary of his office was no coincidence. When he had finished, Jock scratched his bald head in bewilderment.

'What on earth makes you think all these incidents are connected?'

'Come on,' said Kim. 'Harry's a noted amateur sleuth. You ought to trust his detective instinct.'

Jock gestured to an old paperback of *The Big Sleep* nestling up to his visual display unit. 'See that? One of my favourite shamuses. I always fancied being a private investigator myself. Tell you what, why don't you tell us your own ideas and we'll let you have our theories?'

'Sounds like foul play to me,' said Kim. 'Miller tried his hand at blackmail and was murdered for his pains.'

'I'm not so sure,' said Harry. 'There were no signs of a disturbance in his house and the police didn't seem to think he'd been killed by a person or persons unknown.'

'I rest my case.'

He grinned. When their paths had crossed in court, Kim Lawrence had been earnest and determined, never revealing a sense of humour or irony. The more she relaxed, the more he liked her. 'And your prime suspect?'

'How about this man Ray Brill? I don't read many detective stories - real-life crime is enough for me - but as I understand it the man with the cast-iron alibi is invariably the one who dunnit.'

'Dead right, although I can't believe that the police didn't check Ray out thoroughly, even though Edwin was soon in their sights. After all, the finger would usually point at the boyfriend in a case like that.'

'I agree,' said Jock. 'Besides, surely Miller couldn't *prove* anything after thirty years? It doesn't make sense to me. Presumably there was no evidence of any kind to suggest that Edwin Smith wasn't guilty. So - even if someone else was accused, presumably he could laugh it off.'

Harry nodded. 'Exactly. And yet I can't help feeling that someone has taken Miller's enquiries all too seriously. True, the death and the break-in might have nothing to do with Miller's investigations. His visitor may have been the local pools collector and I may have been burgled by a teenage delinquent with time on his grubby hands. But I find it hard to believe.'

'Perhaps the answer is in Cyril's file, after all,' said Kim.

'If so, it's escaped me.'

'Shall I tell you my guess?' asked Jock. His dark brown eyes were shining: involvement in a real mystery, even at second-hand, clearly enthralled him. 'I reckon Miller was rattled by his visitor. A man who had killed Carole Jeffries might be ready to kill again. Perhaps he feared for his own safety and thought the best course was to say that the crucial information was in your hands, not his. Then with all the excitement he had an asthma attack and died. A genuine accident. The man stole Miller's own file but Cyril's was a red herring - yet he swallowed Miller's story and couldn't resist searching through your office for it even though he knew he would never be proved guilty of murdering either Carole or Miller.'

'Plausible,' said Harry, 'except for one thing. The burglary occurred before the unknown visitor knocked on Miller's door. Back to the drawing board, Marlowe.'

Jock sighed. 'I agree it's a fascinating case. Imagine all the skeletons that have safely been locked in their cupboards for the past thirty years.' He gestured at the file-laden shelves all around. 'And look at all this stuff. There must be so many secrets locked away down here, stories from long ago of crime and romance and greed. Yet I never get to know about any of them. It's a tantalising thought. So do keep me posted with your investigations. I'd love to have the chance to pit my wits.'

'I think I'm getting bitten by the detective bug as well,' said Kim. 'What's your next move?'

'First things first,' said Harry. 'I still have no proof of Edwin Smith's innocence. I need to trace Renata Grierson and find out exactly why she told Miller that her boyfriend was no murderer.'

Chapter Fourteen

she was always so provocative.

An hour later he was sitting at a corner table in the Ensenada opposite Jim Crusoe, who was raising a glass of Moët and wishing that every week brought a new Waltergate.

'Here's to justice,' said Jim. 'Long may it miscarry.'

'As long as the fees are good?' asked Harry mischievously.

'A man's got to eat,' said his partner, eyeing his steak with enthusiasm. 'Besides, I know our social conscience is safe in your care. I suppose this Sefton Park case is going to be another of your *pro bono publico* enquiries, is it?'

On the way to the restaurant, Harry had regaled him with an account of his conversations with Miller and what he knew of the Carole Jeffries case. 'I'm thinking as much of Edwin Smith's mum as of my own curiosity. She paid Cyril handsomely for poor reward. If her son now turns out to have been innocent all along, he deserves to have his name cleared.'

'Are you thinking of a posthumous pardon?'

Harry spread his arms, and almost sent a passing waiter flying. 'Why not? The poor idiot has spent thirty years being considered guilty of a crime he may not have committed - assuming that this Renata woman wasn't pulling the wool over Miller's eyes when she assured him Edwin couldn't have been guilty. I wish I knew how to get in touch with her. Perhaps the best idea is to follow Miller's example and advertise.'

'That won't be necessary.'

'Do you have a better suggestion?'

'As a matter of fact, I do.' Jim reached down for the briefcase he had brought along from the office. 'If only you'd let me get a word in edgeways earlier, I might have put you out of your misery. Look at this.'

He took out the red file Miller had handed Harry about his personal affairs and drew from it a single sheet of paper. 'I take it you didn't study the documents our client passed to you?'

'I glanced at the summary, but I didn't trouble with the rest of the paperwork. It's more your line of country than mine.'

'Not necessarily.' Jim passed him the sheet. 'When I was working on the will, I couldn't make head nor tail of this stuff. None of it had any bearing on Miller's instructions about his estate. But I think you may find it useful.'

'Too right,' breathed Harry as he stared at the sheet. It was headed CONTACTS and contained a list of names, telephone numbers and addresses in Miller's immaculate script. They were names that had begun to mean a good deal to him: Vera Smith, Kathleen Jeffries, Ray Brill, Clive Doxey, Benny Frederick, Shirley Titchard, Vincent Deysbrook - and Renata Grierson.

'I don't know how it got mixed up with the financial papers,' said Jim between mouthfuls of steak, 'unless Miller meant to pass it to you surreptitiously.'

'Nothing so melodramatic. I remember now he dropped his files when we met in Sefton Park and several sheets spilled out. He must have put this one back in the wrong file.' He grinned and took another sip of champagne. 'Wonderful! Maybe I'm now a step ahead of the character who nicked the rest of Miller's papers on the case.'

'Watch your step. If you're right in thinking he killed Carole Jeffries - and maybe Miller for good measure - he won't take kindly to your sticking your nose in.'

'No need for you to worry. Don't forget our cross-insurance.'

Jim wiped his mouth on the back of his napkin. 'I live in fear that the small print may exclude death in the course of detective work.'

'Anyway, I'm far from certain that he did murder Miller. I need to find out what the post mortem revealed.'

'I'll ask for you if you like. I'm ringing that policewoman who came round to the burglary - whatshername, Lynn - to find out if they have any leads, so I can progress our claim. I could ask her if she can find out.'

'Thanks, but there's no need. I'll speak to the constable I met at Everton. He ought to be willing to talk to me. I was the late Ernest Miller's legal representative, remember.'

***

As soon as he got back to the office he called the number Miller had listed for Renata Grierson. The phone was answered on the second ring. 'Is that Mrs Grierson?'

'Who wants her?' asked a woman's voice at the other end of the telephone line. The accent was broad Scouse, the tone provocative.

'This is Harry Devlin.'

'I don't care if it's *hare krishna*, love. What are you after?'

'I'd like to talk to you, Mrs Grierson. It's quite urgent.'

'You're getting me all excited, love, but what's it all about?'

No point in beating about the bush. 'Thirty years ago, you knew a young man called Edwin Smith who was convicted of murder.'

At once the woman became cautious. 'And what if I did? Not that I'm admitting anything, mind.'

'I'm not a policeman, I'm not asking you to admit a thing. I'd just like a word, that's all. Today, if it's convenient. If not, maybe tomorrow.'

'What's the hurry after thirty years? And why all the sudden interest after such a long time?'

'You've already talked to a man called Miller about Edwin, haven't you? He told me you had responded to his advertisement, claiming Edwin could not have strangled Carole Jeffries.'

'Are you a friend of this Miller?'

'I'm his solicitor. Or should I say, I was.'

'Sacked you, has he?'

'He's dead.'

After a shocked pause, Renata Grierson said, 'Dead? He can't be. I only rang him on Thursday. He said he wanted to fix up a meeting with me.'

'Don't hold your breath waiting for his call. I almost fell over his body when I called at his house. He'd collapsed in his own front room and now he's dead, I feel I owe it to him to find out more about the Sefton Park case.'

She snorted down the line. 'What's your real interest, Mr Devlin?'

'Miller persuaded me that Edwin Smith was done a grave injustice. If that's true, it ought to be put right.'

'Edwin died a long time ago, Mr Devlin.'

'Justice doesn't have a sell-by date,' said Harry, thinking as he spoke that it was worryingly easy to become the self-important lawyer of a thousand tired caricatures. If he didn't watch out, he'd start spewing out soundbites like a poor man's Clive Doxey. Less grandly, he added, 'Will you spare me half an hour?'

She took a deep breath. 'I was just getting ready to go out to work this evening, as it happens. I work in an Egyptian restaurant in the city centre, a place called Farouk's. You can see me afterwards, if you like.'

'What time do you finish?'

'No fixed time, but usually late. Come over and have a meal first, if you like. The food's one of Liverpool's best-kept secrets, you'll thank me for tipping you the wink.'

His next task was to chase up the result of Miller's post mortem. He always found contacting the police by phone a tedious business and was frequently tempted to make every message a 999 call, but eventually he collected the information he wanted.

The pathologist was sure that Miller had died following and as a consequence of a severe asthma attack. Time of death was never easy to fix, but early evening of Saturday was probably favourite. Although he had cut his head when he had fallen, the gash had not been serious. There was no clear indication as to the trigger for the attack; it could have had any one of a score of causes. It was a straightforward matter, Harry was assured. No suspicious circumstances at all.

'Then let me mention one or two. Mrs Hegg, my client's neighbour, heard someone call next door on Saturday evening ... No, she doesn't know who it was, she heard knocking whilst she was on the phone and thinks she heard the visitor being let in. And some important papers appear to be missing from my client's study ... No, nothing else, no money has gone. But the papers relate to a crime my client was interested in ... thirty years ago, although...'

The best he could do was extract a promise that a statement would be taken from Gloria Hegg. He had no illusions: there was enough crime in present-day Merseyside to occupy the forces of law and order, and the assumed loss of one file of documents about a case dating back to 1964 was hardly likely to call for all police leave to be stopped and the drafting-in of reinforcements specially trained in investigating miscarriages of justice.

As he put the receiver down, he reflected that Jock's guess as to what had occurred at Miller's house on Saturday was probably not far from the truth. Miller had not been murdered and the burglary of the office could be unconnected. Unless Ray Brill was the one who had feared that Cyril Tweats' file might reveal a secret he was desperate to hide.

Back in the flat that evening, Harry switched on the television whilst he changed in readiness for his trip to Farouk's, hoping to catch the regional news. It was being read by a plump redhead whose Mancunian vowels rolled as if she were auditioning for a part in *Hobson's Choice*.

'...who had been the head of the South West Lancashire Major Enquiries Squad for the past nine years resigned today after a record compensation payment for wrongful arrest was agreed in the case of Liverpool man Kevin Walter.'

As she summarised the main points of the case, the picture showed Kevin and Jeannie outside the Law Courts, grinning at a forest of microphones. At their side was Patrick Vaulkhard, permitting himself a sly smile of self-congratulation. Harry, no expert in media relations, had managed to find a place just out of camera shot.

'No money can ever make up for what my Kevin has suffered,' Jeannie announced to the camera, 'but all we want to do now is to get away for a quiet holiday and start to pick up the pieces of our shattered lives.'

It was a quote, Harry supposed, from the serialisation of her life story which would begin in one of the tabloids the next day. He did not expect to be buying a copy.

'Is this a good day for English justice?' a reporter asked Vaulkhard.

'Justice?' demanded the barrister. A caption across the bottom of the screen identified him for the viewers' benefit. 'A man loses his liberty and the people responsible have to be taken to court before they offer compensation even remotely sufficient to recognise the wrong they have done? Where is the justice in that?'

'You can't put a price on freedom,' said Jeannie.

The redhead reappeared and said, 'Tonight Sir Clive Doxey, the President of MOJO, the Miscarriages Of Justice Organisation, added his weight to calls for tighter regulation of police interrogation methods.'

A silver-haired man sitting in front of a bookcase full of imposing leather-bound volumes started speaking about unscrupulous police methods and how the case illustrated the need to preserve a suspect's right of silence.

'...national disgrace ... insist upon an urgent review ... courage of Mrs Walter...'

Harry paid scant attention. He was reflecting that it was a small world. What would Sir Clive say if it were suggested to him that Edwin Smith might have been a victim of a miscarriage of justice even graver than the one that had befallen Kevin Walter? Would he use his muscle to press for some form of enquiry into the old case? Or was this one time when he might be content to let bygones be bygones?

Farouk's was tucked away down an alley that led off Victoria Street. The fascia of the building was as inconspicuous as its location; there were no menus in its curtained window and only the tiniest of signs outside to proclaim its existence. Harry stepped inside and, climbing the steep and narrow staircase to the first floor, reflected that the owners seemed to have done their utmost to discourage passing trade. They must have the confidence to rely on word of mouth. Whether Renata worked as a waitress or in the kitchens, he was impressed that she had recommended the cuisine at the place where she worked. In his experience, people on the inside of most kitchens preferred to eat elsewhere: ignorance was bliss. When he opened the door at the top and peered inside, however, he saw that the place was almost full. The light was low and the air thick with smoke; in the background a swarthy man with a drooping moustache was playing a bouzouki.

'The name's Devlin. I rang earlier and booked a table for one,' he told the waiter who came to greet him.

As he was led to his seat, he saw that in the opposite corner of the room a large woman was dancing to the music. Her exotically tasselled green brassière, chiffon hip scarves and see-through harem skirt revealed far more of her ample form than it concealed. A fringe of coins dangled over her forehead; she wore tiny cymbals on her fingers and a pair of gold anklets. As Harry watched, she shimmied towards a couple of men in business suits who were sitting in a small alcove. Their eyes gleamed in anticipation as, with a wicked smile and flutter of improbably long black eyelashes, she thrust her pelvis forward and dipped her breasts towards them before shimmying out of reach and on to the next table.

Menu in hand, Harry was wavering between kibeh and tabouleh - and telling himself that it was a long time since that lavish lunch at the Ensenada - when a tinkle of finger cymbals told him that the dancer was approaching. He turned to look at her again. At close quarters he suspected she was closer to fifty than to forty. Her make-up could not quite disguise the laughter lines around her mouth and eyes; her stomach was flabby, her buttocks huge. Each wiggle was determined rather than sinuous and her vast breasts seemed in imminent danger of escaping their skimpy moorings.

A brisk swivel brought her body within touching distance. Her perfume was a heavy musk; it even blotted out the smell of the cigars. She smiled at him, putting her tongue between her lips and bent down so as to give him a better view.

'Mr Devlin?' she asked in tones more redolent of Anfield than of the mysterious east. 'Pleased to meet you. My name's Renata Grierson.'

Chapter Fifteen

She had only herself to blame:

The voice was unmistakeable: the wobbling breasts right under his nose belonged to Edwin Smith's one-time girlfriend. He was conscious that all eyes in the restaurant were upon him. Leaning back in his chair, he returned her smile.

'Thanks for letting me see you, Mrs Grierson.'

A pair of nipple tassels rotated mesmerically. 'Renata, please. I'm not one for formal introductions.'

'I've guessed as much.'

The lines on her face hardened. 'So you're poking around in a case best left dead and buried?'

'Like Edwin? I'd like to know the truth about the murder of Carole Jeffries. I think he may have suffered an injustice.'

'Maybe you're right. Though at one time I reckoned he deserved what he got.'

'When can we talk?'

'The waiters are lovely lads, but speed of service isn't their strong point. By the time you've had your meal, I'll be through.'

She smiled again before tilting her body away from him and started to glide to the next alcove. As he watched her go, Harry reflected that, had things worked out differently, Edwin Smith might now be a henpecked fifty-year-old married to a belly dancer instead of pushing up daisies in a prisoner's grave. Some people might not be sure which was worse.

At the end of the evening, Renata timed her return to perfection. While he stood at the till signing the credit card slip, she appeared beside him. Gone were the anklets and the finger cymbals. Even her perfume seemed less oppressive. In her tartan jacket and black leggings she looked like any other middle-aged woman who likes to dress young.

'Thanks for being willing to talk,' he said as he followed her down the stairs.

'That's all right. I've kept quiet long enough.'

'But you contacted Ernest Miller.'

Her tone became grim. 'I didn't much like the sound of him on the phone. He had a slimy voice. But I found myself starting to answer his questions. He said he had this idea Edwin was innocent. His late wife had worked for Edwin's brief and she'd told him that Edwin withdrew his confession before the trial - but the solicitor didn't believe him and bloody Edwin didn't have the bottle to slug it out in a courtroom.'

'So you said he was right, but didn't explain why?'

'I wanted to do it face to face. You see, Mr Devlin, the whole thing's been bothering me since 1964. I'd like to get it off my chest.' She forced a smile. 'Anyway, where are you taking me?'

He spread his arms. 'What did you have in mind?'

'Don't tempt me, young man. How about a drink in the Demi-Monde? Don't worry, I won't show you up. Now I've changed out of my dancing clothes, anyone would think I was respectable.'

A couple of minutes later they were sitting at the nightclub's bar and Harry had learned that Renata's tipple was a daiquiri and coke.

'Thanks, love. I need this. All that shimmying is thirsty work.'

He had to raise his voice to be heard above the thudding nineties musak. 'How long have you been doing it?'

She moved a little closer to him. 'On and off, for ten years. I love Egyptian dancing, it's perfect for me. For one thing, it's a positive advantage to have a big bum. Besides, it takes me out of myself. And at my age, how else could I get a whiff of the steamy passions of the caliph's harem?' She gave him a direct look and, even in the darkness of the disco, he felt himself blushing. 'Now, love. I've no-one to go home to at the moment. My feller drives an

HGV and he's down south tonight, so my time's my own. So what can I tell you about that poor sod Edwin?'

'How did you get to know him?'

'On a bus ride into the city centre. He started chatting me up. I was between boyfriends, so even though he was nothing to look at, I didn't give him the cold shoulder. Besides, it was obvious his family had a penny or two. he might have been a wimp, but his old feller had been a successful businessman and they had a posh house opposite Sefton Park to prove it.'

'So the two of you got together?'

She gave him a crooked smile. 'Oh, I played hard to get for a while. At least a week, as I recall. At first, he wouldn't introduce me to his mum. I gather she was a bit of a dragon, but all the same, I took it as a bad sign. Then one day he invited me round to the house. I was desperate to have a look at the place, so I could see if the Smiths were as well off as I guessed.'

'You were interested in a long-term relationship, even though he was a wimp?'

'Oh, I don't pretend it was a burning passion. I'm no angel, Mr Devlin, never have been. In 1964 I was a one-woman permissive society. School did nothing for me - the teachers said I was bright enough, they just couldn't control me. At the time I met Edwin I had a job in a tongue factory. I can remember the stench of the mess sloshing around on the works floor to this very day. I wanted to escape. If that meant getting hooked up with a creep like Edwin, I was game.'

'And so you went home with him?'

He could feel her warm breath on his cheek, see every line that time had dug around her made-up eyes. 'Maybe I was more innocent than I thought. I actually believed he was going to introduce me to his mum that afternoon. He pretended to be surprised when she wasn't there and it wasn't long before we finished up in his bedroom.' She paused. 'I'll never forget it. The date was the twenty-ninth of February 1964. Leap Year Day, but no way was I going to propose to him. Not after that fiasco.'

'Tell me.'

'Edwin admitted his mum was visiting someone in Yorkshire and wouldn't be back till the following day. He'd planned it to perfection so the two of us could have a wild time in bed without any fear of being disturbed. There was only one slight problem.'

'Which was?'

She wriggled a little on her bar stool. 'He couldn't make love to me, could he? His thing was as soft as a piece of plasticine. No matter what I did, it made no difference. I tried kindness and kinkiness, but none of it was any good. He admitted he'd never had a girl before. Not properly.' She shook her head and sighed. 'After a while he climbed off the bed. He was in tears. I remember that he parted the curtains and looked out. That was what suited him in life - looking, not doing.'

Harry sensed she was about to tell him something important. 'And do you know what he saw?'

'I got up and joined him.' Renata's voice was abstracted and he could tell she was reliving that Leap Year Day. 'He was watching a young girl walking into the Park through the gates opposite his bedroom window.'

He guessed what was coming next. The explanation to the conundrum that had been troubling him. 'A blonde girl, wearing a brown sheepskin jacket, black boots and a green scarf?'

'Got it in one. Carole Jeffries. At that time, I'd never heard the name, of course. Edwin told me she was a neighbour. I asked if he fancied her and he admitted he did, but said she had no time for him. I pulled him back on the bed, spread my legs wide and told him to make believe that I was her.' She shook her head. 'God, the things I've done for men in my time. But it was no good. His imagination - or something - simply wasn't up to it.'

'How long did you stay there?'

'For another couple of hours. In the end, my patience snapped. I felt I'd been short-changed. I didn't laugh at him, Mr Devlin, I'm not one of those women who mock a man who can't perform. Christ, if I was, I'd have been murdered myself a dozen times over. But I'd had enough.'

'What did Edwin do?'

'Begged me to stay, didn't he? I often wonder, you know, if things would have turned out differently if I had. But I've learned it's no use fretting over what might have been.'

It was a lesson of life Harry was still struggling to absorb. He signalled for more drinks and asked, 'What time did you leave?'

'I was dressed again and out of the house by ten past six. I went out through the back gate, so as not to attract any attention. For once in my life, I wanted to be on my own. I felt bitter and frustrated, you have to remember that. The gate gave on to a path which took me to the main road and I caught a bus home. My mum was there, pissed out of her mind as per usual. I never had a father.'

'And after you got home?'

'Packed a bag and caught the last train to London, didn't I? I thought maybe I'd make a fresh start. I didn't leave a note, mum would only have used it to light the fire.'

'How long did you stay down there?'

'Until the winter. By then I'd realised the streets weren't paved with gold. And after I get back here with my tail between my legs, what do I find? Only that Edwin Smith has just topped himself and everyone thinks it's good riddance to a self-confessed strangler.'

'Did the police ever approach you?'

She took a sip from her replenished glass. 'No, why should they? As far as I can make out, Edwin never put me forward as an alibi. Too ashamed of his lack of performance, I suppose. And I didn't even hear about the murder in Sefton Park while I was down in London.'

'Seriously?'

'I didn't have a telly in those days and I never bothered with the London papers. It was only when I got back that I read a few snippets in the *Echo* about the case. I worked out that this Carole was his neighbour, the girl he'd watched from the window. At first I thought that after I left he must have gone out himself, caught up with her and done her in. But then I realised it simply wasn't possible.'

'Why?'

She banged her glass down on the bar and concentrated her attention on him. In a fierce voice she said, 'Listen. I arrived at the house at half two. Looking forward to afternoon tea in the lap of luxury, bloody young idiot that I was. The earliest Edwin could have strangled the girl was a quarter past six.' She drained her glass, as if in need of strength. 'Yet the *Echo* said Carole Jeffries was murdered sometime between four o'clock and five at the latest. I couldn't make sense of it, so I rang the reporter, telling him some cock-and-bull story. But he was definite: there was no mistake. They could fix the time because Carole only left her parents' house at four and by five a courting couple had started canoodling on a bench only yards away from the bushes where her body was found. As the man said to me, the pair of them may have been engrossed with each other, but no murderer in his right mind was going to take the risk of dragging a corpse right under their noses whilst they were snogging.'

'Did you discuss this with anyone?'

'Who? Edwin had confessed, hadn't he? If he'd wanted to take the blame, who was I to stand in his way? Besides, he was beyond my help by then. It wasn't as though he was about to be hung - or even spend the rest of his days inside.'

'And what about his mother? She had to live with the belief that her son was a murderer.'

141

'I was seventeen,' said Renata helplessly. 'I'd never met her and besides, I didn't want to be any more involved with the police than I had to. While I was down in London, you see, I'd picked up a conviction. Soliciting. So much for the bloody glamour and the bright lights.' She finished the rest of her drink. 'Any chance of another?'

When it came, she tossed it all down in two or three gulps. 'Look, when I saw Miller's advert, I knew I had to give him a call. I've been married twice and had more men that you've had hot dinners, but until last week I'd kept my secret in silence. It's been preying on my mind for so long. When I spoke to Miller, it was like a dam bursting.' She shook her head. 'All this time, I've been wanting someone to realise that, for all his faults, that pathetic little creep Edwin never murdered anybody in his life.'

And as Harry watched, she cradled her head in her hands and, oblivious of the barmaid's baffled stare, began to weep for the young man she had walked out on thirty years before.

Chapter Sixteen

the fatal outcome was inevitable

Next morning Harry was back in the bargain basement of the legal system, down at the magistrates' court appearing on behalf of a couple of careless drivers and a positively negligent car thief who had managed to leave a letter to him from the social security office tucked under the dashboard. When the last case had been heard, he paused on his way out to look at the news-stand adjacent to the courtroom entrance. The face of Jeannie Walter beamed out at him from under a banner headline saying JUSTICE IS DONE - BUT WHY DID IT TAKE SO LONG?

Edwin Smith and his mother might ask much the same question, he reflected. In the small hours, he had finally poured a sobbing Renata into the taxi he'd called to take her back home. By then she had become maudlin and was blaming herself for Edwin's suicide. 'If only I'd stayed with him,' she kept saying, 'he would still be alive today.'

'You can't rewrite the past,' he'd told her, although he had himself often wanted to do exactly that.

At least, he thought, in death both Edwin Smith and Ernest Miller had been vindicated. Edwin was no killer and the strange old man's hunch about the case had been proved right. Harry could imagine Miller, following his retirement, recalling what his wife had once told him about Edwin's short-lived attempt to withdraw his confession; perhaps she'd had more sense than Cyril Tweats and had realised that it rang true. But only once one understood how Edwin knew what Carole had been wearing did it become clear that the corroborative evidence so crucial to the assumption of his guilt really had no substance at all. When, following the humiliation with Renata, he had confessed to the crime, he must have guessed at the ligature used by the real killer, knowing already that Carole had been strangled and was wearing a scarf when she took her last stroll through the park. Harry thought the conversation with Carole was too vivid to have been a total fabrication. He guessed Edwin had tried to chat her up on a previous occasion and received the crushing rebuff he had described to the police. As for Miller, what had he learned from Ray Brill about the case - and who had called at the scruffy house in Everton on the evening of the fatal asthma attack?

'Wondering how many copies to buy of Jeannie Walter's exclusive interview?' asked Kim Lawrence in his ear.

He turned to face her. 'I don't think I'll bother.'

'Why not? You're bound to be mentioned.'

'I don't think my ego would stand the strain. Besides, I've already come to earth with a bump after yesterday's excitements. Petty crime, fines and probation. No travesties of justice this time. How about you?'

'A shoplifting single mother. She turned up with a bruise under her eye - her boyfriend's been beating her black and blue.' Kim sighed. 'Any news about your Sefton Park case?'

'Only that Edwin Smith could not have strangled Carole Jeffries.'

He was rewarded by the widening of her eyes. 'Tell me more.'

As he did so, he found himself aware of how much he had begun to enjoy her company. She had a reputation in the city as an abrasive litigator famously quick to interrupt her opponents, but he was realising for the first time that she could also listen and he could not deny that he felt flattered by her interest in the case that so absorbed him. He could sense her mind working, testing Renata's story for flaws and contradictions, worrying away at possibilities for lethal cross-examination.

When he had finished, she opted for direct attack. 'And what makes you believe that after thirty years of silence this superannuated belly dancer is telling the truth at last? Maybe she's just spinning you a yarn for the sake of a little notoriety.'

'If you'd seen her dancing, you'd realise she's no need to tell tall stories to do that. But leaving that aside, I did believe her. Although she did nothing to save Edwin while he was alive, she didn't have any inkling that he needed to be saved. She had problems enough of her own to contend with at the time, but I'm sure the whole business has nagged at her ever since. That's why she was willing to spill the beans when she read Ernest Miller's advertisement.'

She gave a satisfied nod. 'Okay, I'll buy that. So - what next? Presumably it's time for you to speak to the people closest to Carole. But do you think they will co-operate?'

'Have you ever met a Liverpudlian who was unwilling to talk? Anyway, I've made a start. I called Shirley Titchard first thing and she agreed to see me this afternoon. But before that, I want to see if someone can give me an objective picture of them. So right now I'm going to call on the man who headed the murder enquiry.'

'And I thought your conscience would make you head back to your desk as soon as court was over.'

They exchanged grins, two advocates who regarded desks as designed for conveyancers and corporate lawyers. 'It can do without me for a while. Let's face it, I might still have been sitting behind Patrick Vaulkhard, watching him kebab the police authority's witnesses.'

'As a matter of fact,' she said after a slight pause, 'there is a meeting of MOJO tomorrow evening in one of the conference rooms at Empire Hall. Our speaker has cancelled at the last minute, so I've asked Patrick if he would be willing to talk about the Waltergate case. I wondered if you'd like to join us. That is, if you don't have anything else planned.'

He looked at her and said, 'No, I don't have anything else planned. I'd be delighted to come.' An idea occurred to him. 'And will your president, Sir Clive, be there?'

She smiled. 'I thought you might ask that and the answer is yes. But I hope you won't look on the evening solely as an opportunity to pump him for more information about the Sefton Park Strangling.'

'Oh no,' he said. 'I won't.'

***

Half an hour later, a pleasant middle-aged woman at the reception desk in Jasmine House nodded when Harry said he wanted to see Vincent Deysbrook.

'That's lovely. Vincent will be glad to see you. He doesn't have too many visitors. His son lives in Norfolk and his daughter moved to Sydney and married an Australian. One or two of his old colleagues from the police drop by now and then, but that's about all. Who shall I say it is?'

'My name's Harry Devlin, but that won't mean anything to Mr Deysbrook. He and I have never met. Even so, I'd be glad of a word if he's up to it.'

'I'll be right back.'

While he waited, Harry glanced around. The long low building stood in an acre of undulating grounds and from here it was hard to believe that a dual carriageway ran past the other side of the spiky trees. The atmosphere was so tranquil that the city might have been a hundred miles away. From one of the shelves opposite the entrance, half a dozen teddy bears grinned at him. Above them were hand-carved wooden trains and fluffy cushions, each individually priced and marked MADE BY THE RESIDENTS. On a noticeboard, posters in pastel colours spoke about bereavement counselling and gave contact names and telephone numbers. They were the only clues to the purpose of this place. Jasmine House, so different from the dank atmosphere of the subterranean world he lightheartedly described as the Land of the Dead, actually was the last home of the dying.

The woman returned, smiling. 'He's in better form this morning. Even though he doesn't know who you are, he said he'd be happy to see you. Remember, though, he tires very easily. And if he asks you for a cigarette, really we'd rather you said no. We don't have smoking here and it's done him harm enough already.'

'He's suffering from lung cancer?'

She nodded. 'He's been with us for three weeks. At first it was simply respite care, but he's not well enough to go back to his flat. Day by day, we can see him losing strength, but he's not short of willpower. He's fighting it, Mr Devlin, he's fighting it every inch of the way. Would you like to follow me and I'll show you to the lounge?'

She led him to an L-shaped room overlooking the rear of the building. Outside there was a patio, where a couple of old women were sitting on a bench, feeding the ducks in a small pond. A gaunt man in a dressing gown was in front of the television, flicking through the sports pages of the *Daily Mail*. When he heard the approaching footsteps, he rose to his feet, wincing with the pain of movement. Even after so many years and the ravages of disease, his features were still recognisable from the grainy photographs in Ken Cafferty's cuttings captioned *Chief Inspector Vincent Deysbrook: 'Arrest Expected Soon'.*

Harry grasped the withered hand. 'Thanks for seeing me. I won't take up much of your morning.'

'Take as much as you want. I've not much else to do with it.' Deysbrook gave a short laugh which turned into a prolonged cough. He waved Harry into one of the armchairs. 'Stupid, isn't it? My time's running out and yet I find myself feeling bloody bored.'

'I've never been inside a hospice before. I didn't know what to expect, but certainly not something so...'

'Peaceful?' Deysbrook nodded. 'It's a good place and the staff do a grand job. I just wish I wasn't a bloody resident, that's all. You wouldn't happen to have a cigarette, by any chance?'

'I gave them up a couple of years ago.'

'Wish I'd never started. Maybe if I'd broken the habit sooner, I wouldn't be here. Ah well, no use fretting over what might have been. Besides, I've always liked my cigarettes. All right, then, Mr Harry Devlin, what can I do for you?'

'I'm a solicitor in town and lately I've been looking into the murder of Carole Jeffries in Sefton Park.'

The old man gave him a sharp look. 'What in God's name for? It was over and done with thirty years back.'

'You remember the case?'

'I'll never forget it,' said Deysbrook huskily. 'Never. That poor young girl with everything ahead of her. Her life snuffed out by a pathetic worm.'

'I believe Edwin Smith was innocent.'

'Rubbish.' Anger brought spots of colour to Deysbrook's chalky cheeks and his mouth hardened. He had to fight for breath before he continued. 'Look, it was an open and shut case. You don't know what you're talking about.'

'Last night I spoke to someone who gave Smith an alibi.'

'They were having you on. The man confessed and pleaded guilty into the bargain.'

'It isn't unknown for innocent fools to confess to crimes.'

'We didn't kick that confession out of Smith, if that's what you're thinking.'

'It certainly isn't. I can understand why you didn't look any further.'

Deysbrook gave him a suspicious glare. He was a tall man, around the six-foot mark at least, but although his body frame was large, his clothes hung loosely over his wasted trunk and limbs.

Harry guessed that the illness had shrunk him by as much as eighty pounds.

'I never cared much for defence lawyers, Mr Devlin, I'll tell you straight. In my experience, they'll twist the truth any way they can to get their clients off the hook.'

'Whatever I find out can't help Smith. I'm not here to defend him, simply to learn a little more about the case.'

'A do-gooder, eh?' Deysbrook made a derisive noise. 'The world's full of them. People who like to say that black is white. Even if a bent brief can't help a criminal to walk out of court with a smirk on his face, you always find some social worker or probation officer willing to blame society for his rapes and muggings.'

'I'm no bleeding heart, Mr Deysbrook, and I'm not here to throw mud at the police investigation or at you personally. My only interest is to find out what really happened, not to make a fast buck.'

'I thought you said you were a lawyer?'

Harry grinned. 'Ouch. I'd like to explain how I come to be involved.'

'You'd better,' said Deysbrook without a smile.

The story did not take long to tell. Deysbrook listened carefully. In coming here, Harry had expected hostility. The retired detective was a sick man and no-one welcomes the news that they have been badly mistaken in a matter of life and death. Yet he sensed that Deysbrook's instinct was to give him a fair hearing.

'And what makes you think the woman isn't telling a pack of lies?'

'Did you never rely on your own nose for the truth?'

Deysbrook grunted. 'Often enough. But all the lawyers I ever knew liked hard evidence. Something they could see in black and white.'

'Everything Renata told me fitted the facts. She explained how Edwin could have had the knowledge that incriminated him, about the clothes Carole wore on the day she died. And she gave me a clearer idea of the sort of man he was, a passive inadequate humiliated by his own impotence. I can believe that he would have confessed to the murder to make himself important. When he got in too deep, he tried to save himself, but it was too late. His lawyers hardly listened; they were going through the motions. For Edwin Smith to be guilty was convenient for everyone. Including the real murderer.'

'And who might that have been?'

'Interesting to speculate, isn't it?' Harry felt he had hooked his man at last. One thing his job had taught him was how to persuade reluctant people to open up. 'I wanted to ask you about the police view. Was anyone other than Smith a suspect?'

Deysbrook rubbed his jaw as he cast his mind back. While he waited, Harry glanced through a glass panel in the door and saw a nurse walk past, her arm around the shoulder of a weeping woman who he supposed must be a patient's relative. 'The boyfriend, of course,' the old man said at last. 'With every murder, I always looked first at the nearest and dearest. Young Carole was going out with a pop singer, can't recall his name. Flash character, thought he was God's gift to the girls. I didn't take to him.'

Harry could imagine. 'Could he have killed her?'

A shake of the head. 'No way. He had an alibi.'

'Alibis can be organised. You know that as well as I do.'

'Bet you won't admit that in court, though, Mr Devlin, will you? You'd soon have no clients left.'

'Look, I've been wondering - he was a member of a duo, they were called the Brill Brothers. Is there any chance that his partner might have covered for him?'

Deysbrook made a scornful noise through his teeth. 'No-one could have broken his alibi. Not even he could have corrupted five hundred people. That evening the whatsit Brothers appeared in a concert at a big club in London. As far as I can remember, they'd arrived by mid-afternoon.'

Harry felt a tremor of disappointment. 'So you are absolutely sure that it was physically impossible for him to have been in Sefton Park when Carole took her last stroll?'

'Absolutely bloody positive.' Deysbrook burst into a fit of coughing and Harry waited until the old man had composed himself.

'Carole worked for a well-known photographer by the name of Benny Frederick. Was he in the clear?'

Deysbrook scratched his head. Harry could guess at the effort the man was making to step back thirty years, to a time when he was fit and strong and had a murder on his hands that he was desperate to solve. Finally, he said, 'Yes, we did speak to him. I soon guessed he was a queer, though he would never have admitted it. In those days, it was a crime. People like that were ashamed of themselves - and afraid. Now they expect a bloody medal and a government grant.'

'Any reason to think he might have had a grudge against Carole?'

Deysbrook shrugged. From the way he flinched it seemed that even this simple gesture caused him pain. 'He reckoned to be cut up about the girl's death, but who knows?'

'Any alibi?'

'Can't recall. It was a long time ago, Mr Devlin.'

'What about Clive Doxey - Sir Clive, as he now is?'

'Oh yeah, I remember him all right. Pal of the girl's father and a right pain in the arse. Important chap, even then, a bigwig and he made sure you knew it. I liked him even less than the other feller - and I could never stand queers.'

'You questioned him about his movements?'

'He wasn't at all co-operative. As far as he was concerned, we were wasting valuable time questioning him which we could have spent finding the killer.'

'I take it he had the opportunity to have committed the murder?'

'Maybe, though again I can't remember after all this time. To us, he was just another do-gooder - always making a fuss about police brutality, yet he was the first to complain when we didn't make an arrest within half an hour.'

'But now? Are you prepared to accept that Carole might have been killed by someone other than Edwin Smith?'

'I'd need to speak to this Renata woman of yours before I said yea or nay to that.' He sighed and added grudgingly, 'But supposing she's told you the truth - well, maybe we did make a mistake.'

Harry was unable to resist saying, 'Good job the death penalty's been abolished, eh?'

Vincent Deysbrook started to cough again, a hoarse retching sound, and Harry realised with a stab of dismay how sick the old detective was and how much it had cost him to talk for so long, let alone have the guts to admit the possibility that his own prejudices might have sent an innocent man to the gallows.

'That's where you're wrong, Mr Devlin,' he said when he was able to speak again. His tone was subdued, as if he knew that before long his own fight would reach its end, and Harry sensed that in his mind's eye he was seeing again the dark shadow of the X-ray of his lung. 'The death penalty hasn't been abolished, I can vouch for that. I only wish it had.'

Chapter Seventeen

and I had to gamble everything

Shirley Titchard had agreed to meet him in one of the shops she owned. After he had explained his interest in the Sefton Park case, her manner on the telephone had been crisp and businesslike.

'I can't imagine why you think I can tell you anything, but I don't mind giving you half an hour. I suppose it will make a change from keeping an eye on the girls. The manageress at Caesar Street is on holiday for the week, so I'm having to run the branch myself, but you can have half an hour, all right?'

The shop was tucked between a tobacconist's and a derelict snooker hall; the street was a dead end and noisy ten-year-olds were playing soccer alongside the burnt-out wreck of a stolen car. Jasmine House was no more than five miles away, but it might have been in a different country. Harry pushed open the door and stepped inside. At once the hubbub of voices died down and he was conscious of the scrutiny of a dozen scowling faces. The light was dim and the extractor fan did not seem to work: the smoke made his eyes smart and he couldn't help thinking to himself that a few of Shirley Titchard's customers would one day end their lives in the same despair as Vincent Deysbrook.

His only acquaintance with horse racing was through the novels of Dick Francis and they had not prepared him for the scruffy reality of this place. The walls were covered with cuttings from the sporting press and the racing pages of the national newspapers. Opposite the entrance, a washable white board was covered with offers of odds scrawled in every colour imaginable. In the middle of the room, a television stood on a pillar: a man in the kind of trilby Harry had never seen worn except in old movies was talking rapidly about runners and riders. Through thick mesh grilles he could glimpse two women cashiers, their attention caught by a loudspeaker voice announcing that a horse had withdrawn from the three o'clock at Sandown and that the latest prices would be coming through shortly. The punters were perched on stools or sitting round small tables. Most had cans of beer in their hands, but they had paused in their drinking and study of the form to examine Harry, but even as he looked around and absorbed the scene, one by one they turned back to the papers or the TV. Some started to scribble out bets on slips of paper. Gambling was a serious business and not even the sight of a stranger in a suit could distract them for long.

Someone tapped him on the shoulder. 'Mr Devlin?'

He turned to face a stocky woman with tightly permed blonde hair. Her short-sleeved blouse revealed muscular forearms and the cut of her jaw made it clear that she stood for no messing. She was weighing him up as though she'd been asked to give odds on how long he would survive in a fight with one of her regulars.

'That's me. And you are Shirley Titchard?'

A brisk nod. 'Come through.'

As she led him towards the security door which led from the public area, her path was blocked by a man with beery breath who had seized a teenage lad in denim by the throat. Without hesitating, she gripped the man's wrist and forced him to face her.

'Not here. If you've got a score to settle, do it somewhere else.'

The man gave her a baleful glance but did not argue. Instead he shook his fist at the youth and said, 'Next time, pal, next time...'

As she unlocked the door to the back part of the shop, she said to Harry, 'You need to show people who's in charge. Otherwise they take liberties.'

'You have much trouble?'

'Nothing I can't handle. An hour ago, a kid collapsed in the toilet. He'd been sniffing glue in there, the little bastard. His mates were doped up to the eyeballs and pissing themselves with laughter. I had to get things sorted sharpish. He could easily have died.'

'Jesus.'

She gave him a look of Thatcheresque severity. 'It would have been no loss, but I can't afford an interruption to business. My late husband built this chain up. I reckon I owe it to him to keep it going.'

They were standing behind a counter girl who was arguing with a punter who had not filled out his slip in the approved manner. Shirley Titchard shook her head and said, 'Let's talk in the kitchen. It's the only spot in here where we'll be able to make ourselves heard once the next race starts.'

She took him into a cubbyhole which, although equipped with a grimy sink and the wherewithal for making tea and coffee, was flattered by the name of kitchen. When she shut the door, the noise from outside was muffled but still audible. He wedged himself between the draining board and the fire exit at the rear while she stood with her back to the way in.

'Well now, Mr Devlin. What is it you want to know about my old friend Carole Jeffries?'

There was a derisive note in her voice that he found difficult to interpret. He said, 'As I said on the phone, a question has come up about whether the man who was jailed for killing her really did it.'

'Sounds a long shot to me. He confessed, didn't he?'

'Not everyone who confesses is guilty. Anyway, thanks for talking to me. I realise it's hard to look back so far in time.'

The blonde perm shook decisively. 'It's as if it was yesterday. I tell you, Mr Devlin, I remember Carole better than the first feller I married.'

He grinned. 'You were very close with her?'

'She fascinated me,' said Shirley Titchard simply. 'All the people I'd ever known before were ordinary, not glamorous like Carole's folk. My dad had a newsagent's just off Aigburth Road, my mum helped behind the counter and we lived over the shop. Carole's father was a celebrity, his name kept appearing in the press and on TV. Her mother was a formidable lady, just as clever as Guy, and strong-minded with it. I met them a couple of times when they came to the shop to see how she was settling in. They lived in a mansion opposite the Park.'

'Did you feel they looked down on you?'

'No, they weren't snobs, quite the opposite. Guy was crazy about Carole but he would never have sent her to a private school. She went to the same place as me and give her credit, she was always one of us, as often in trouble as anyone else. More often, if the truth be told.'

'You both left school at the same time?'

'That's right. For me, it was the obvious thing to do. I wanted to make my own way in the world and besides, I never passed an exam in my life. Carole was different, she was much brighter than me, even if she often didn't show it. The teachers said she was lazy and I suppose they were right. When I found a job at Benny Frederick's, Carole decided she would do the same. I remember our headmistress trying to talk her out of it, saying how disappointed her parents would be. Carole put her right on that score. "All my dad wants is for me to be happy," she said - and she was right. Even though her mother was livid, he didn't make a fuss at all. She could twist him round her little finger.'

'You enjoyed the work?'

'Took to it like a duck to water. I'd been brought up in a shop, and although I didn't want to stay at the beck and call of my mum and dad, I thought Benny's was great. Carole did too. She was crazy about the atmosphere and loved spotting the big names who used to come and go. Liverpool in the sixties was the place to be, Mr Devlin. So much kept happening.'

'Benny was a good boss?'

'Lovely feller, one of the few really sweet men I've ever met and I've met a lot of men in my time. He was always decent to me.'

'You knew he was gay?'

'I had eyes,' she said drily. 'He was always so pally with the young lads who used to hang around his shop. Though he had to be careful. Gay sex was a crime in those days, you know. And anyway, he wasn't above taking a fancy to us girls, as well.'

'Is that so?'

'He used to flirt with me all the time, though we never took it any further. But every now and then he'd introduce us to a woman visitor and say she was his girlfriend. He's always had an eye for a pretty face and a neat bum, has Benny, boy or girl, it's never seemed to matter to him. And he certainly took a shine to Carole once she arrived.'

'And how did she take to him?'

'Oh, she played up to him. She loved being in that shop, having the chance to meet the local celebrities.'

'Was that how she met Ray Brill?'

Her face darkened. 'Yes, as a matter of fact it was. But what you won't know is that I met him first. I'd already come across Ian, the quiet one, he was an old pal of Benny's and often called at the shop. A nice enough lad, but not really my type. The minute I saw Ray, I fell for him. I thought he made James Dean seem like the boy next door. He was good-looking, successful, and he seemed to fancy me.'

As Harry tried to regroup his thoughts, a ragged cheer came up from the shop. 'The favourite's won,' she said with a grim smile.

'Look, I didn't know this. You say you started going out with Ray Brill yourself?'

Shirley Titchard folded her arms, as if challenging him to disbelieve her. 'I knew he had other girls, but that didn't bother me. Ray had appeared on *Top of The Pops* and *Ready, Steady, Go!* He was a star and I was happy just to be with him.'

157

'Until you found out that he was seeing Carole?'

Pursing her lips at the recollection, she said, 'Yes, it hurt me badly, though I should have realised what would happen. I was so much in love with him that of course I wanted him to meet my best friend. I introduced them one night at the Cavern. I was so sodding naïve in those days. Carole was the prettiest girl in the place and she knew it. Ray took a shine to her from the first and I was glad, because I wanted the two of them to like each other. And they did, worse luck, they did. Ray started coming to the shop and I was flattered. I didn't twig that he was keener to see Carole than me.'

'How did you find out?'

'One of the other girls who worked at Benny's told me she'd seen the two of them kissing and cuddling down in Mathew Street the previous evening. She was a spiteful cow and I didn't want to believe her, but she was so jubilant I knew she was sure of her facts - and in my heart of hearts, I realised it made sense. I'd been off sick the previous day with a stomach bug. Ray and Carole had had the chance to get together and knowing them both as I did, I couldn't imagine either of them resisting temptation. They were well suited, that pair - they took their pleasures whenever they could.'

'What did you do about it?'

'I confronted her. I couldn't face Ray, he was too special to me. And besides, I knew he would deny it. He was like that, he would swear black was white rather than admit being in the wrong. Carole was secretive, always had been, but she was no fool. I knew that if I forced the issue, she'd tell me the truth.'

'And did she?'

'Yes, I can still picture the scene now. I spoke to her after work and she said straight away that she realised she'd done something very wrong, but she'd not been able to help herself. Apparently, Ray had called in the previous day, when I'd been down with the bug. He and Ian had a gig at the Cavern and he'd asked her to go with him. She said she'd done it simply to keep him company, but even I wasn't stupid enough to believe that. One thing had led to another and they'd finished up in bed together.'

'And how did you take that?'

Her strong features yielded a glimmer of an ironic smile. 'Oh, I wanted to scream and scratch her eyes out, but I never did any such thing. Carole could always charm the birds off the trees. She said she thought she was in love with him, but she swore she would give him up if I said she must. I didn't say a word, just went home and wept all night. Ray didn't call me and I stayed in all weekend. When I went back to work on the Monday, I knew Ray wouldn't phone me again. There was no point in fighting fate. I let her have him. We didn't talk about it: she could always read my mind, she knew I'd lost all hope. So she got her own way - as usual.'

'You must have hated her,' said Harry softly.

She shrugged. 'Perhaps I did, deep down. The pair of them had betrayed me - but there was nothing I could do, so I accepted it. Carole wasn't a fool, she didn't rub it in. She was kind to me in many ways. I sulked for a while but before long I began telling myself there were plenty more fish in the sea.'

'And did Carole talk about her relationship with Ray?'

'She did her best to make me think life with him was no bed of roses. He was sex mad, though she wasn't exactly prim and proper herself. But soon she was saying he certainly wasn't the love of her life. I wondered if she was trying to make me feel better about it all, but I guess the great romance was cooling off. If she hadn't been murdered, I doubt they would have stayed together much longer.'

'What about the day she died? She came to see you in the shop, didn't she?'

She closed her eyes. 'Yes, it was the last time I saw her. Ray came in and the two of them had a blazing row, then he headed off to London with Ian. She'd worked herself up into a state but then she had a private chat with Benny and that seemed to calm her down.'

'What did they talk about?'

'No idea. You'd have to ask Benny, he was always good with Carole. As I say, he liked her a lot.'

'And how did you feel when you heard the news about her death?'

She bowed her head. 'Strange. I felt strange, that's the honest answer. Yes, I was shocked, of course, but I couldn't help feeling other things.'

He waited, willing to take his time while she dug deep into her memory and tried to recapture her inner thoughts of thirty years before. Finally she lifted her chin and looked him in the eye.

'It sounds terrible to say, but it was the most exciting time I'd ever had. I became the centre of attention. I made out that I was heartbroken and everyone offered comfort and support.' She paused and added, 'The truth is, I felt she'd got her just deserts. She'd always lived dangerously and now Ray Brill had lost forever the girl he left me for.'

Harry said nothing and after another momentary pause she bit her lip and told him, 'I've never said that before to another living soul, but it's true. She fascinated me when she was alive and after all this time she still fascinates me. She hurt me badly, but I've never been able to get her out of my mind. So what do you make of my true confession, Mr Harry Devlin? I suppose you think I was depraved to feel that revenge was sweet when my friend had been so brutally strangled?'

'I don't think you'd be human if you'd experienced nothing but grief.'

She grunted and gave him a hard glance. 'You talk as if you know about these things.'

'My own wife was killed,' he heard himself saying. 'She'd left me two years earlier but I still loved her, I mourn her to this day. All the same, I can't pretend I've forgotten the way she behaved.'

With a nod of understanding, she said quietly, 'I suppose I'd kept telling myself that it wouldn't last, the relationship Carole had with Ray.'

'Did you think Carole would finish with him?'

'Maybe I did.' Her dark eyes glinted. 'After all, she was seeing another man, you know.'

Startled, he said, 'No, I didn't have any idea of that.'

'Oh, it had been going on for a while. Though she kept very quiet about him - like I said before, she was secretive. I had the impression he was an older man. Married, I assumed, though she never said as much.'

'Could you guess who it was?'

'Ah, she was too cagey to give the game away, although she liked hinting that she'd been taught as much as she'd ever need to know by this other fellow.'

'Could it have been Benny?'

'What makes you think that?'

'You said he liked girls as well as boys - and he was fond of Carole.'

She spread her arms. 'If it was him, they both deserve Oscars for their acting day after day in the shop.'

'Any other candidates?'

'Your guess is as good as mine.'

'What about Clive Doxey?'

'Sir Clive? What about him?'

'He was a friend of Guy Jeffries, handsome and sophisticated. Any young girl might have found him attractive. And he was an up-and-coming man with a reputation to protect.'

'God alone knows. In those days, I wasn't much interested in politics or writers. Can't say I've changed even now. Guy Jeffries I liked. He thought the sun shone out of Carole's arse and he was always giving her treats. Mrs Jeffries didn't approve at all, but she didn't get much chance to lay down the law. But although I can remember meeting Doxey once at the Jeffries' house, he never meant much to me. I could see he was smooth and successful, but he was over thirty. To me, he might as well have been eligible for a bus pass. I only had eyes for younger men. Like Ray.'

'Do you ever see Ray Brill these days?'

'God, no. The last time we spoke was a mumbled hello at Carole's funeral. After that, the Brill Brothers started finding it harder to make the charts. Ian gave up pop music and Ray was never much use on his own. He'd lost his way and I can't say I shed any tears for him.'

'What about Benny? Do your paths ever cross?'

'Now and then. I worked for him for another couple of years after Carole died, but then I got married and found a job that paid better in an advertising agency. That was where I met Bob, years later. He was a bookie in a small way of business then, but by the time he died he had this whole chain of shops and was worth the thick end of two million.' She gave him a grim smile. 'So maybe it all turned out for the best as far as I was concerned.'

'Though not for Carole.'

'No, not for Carole.' She looked at the linoleum floor for a few seconds, then said, 'Well, Mr Devlin, I think you've had more than the half hour I promised, though I can't believe what I've said has been of any use.'

'Don't you believe it. I'm grateful for your time.'

She led him back into the public area. A punter was complaining to one of the girls at the counter that he hadn't yet been paid out on the last race.

'Wait a moment, will yer?' the girl asked. 'The horse is still sweating! Besides, they haven't completed the weigh-in yet.'

Shirley Titchard turned to Harry and said, 'No patience, you see. Just like Carole. She wanted to have everything and to have it right away. Whoever she hurt in the process.' She folded her brawny arms again and gave him a direct look. 'And look what it got her - her own tombstone before she was seventeen.'

Conscience prompted him to call in at the office to see if there were any messages before his next trip. At the door of New Commodities House he bumped into Jock from the Land of the Dead. The archivist had a batch of old files under his arm and gave him an eager welcome.

'Harry! Just the man! Kim Lawrence has been telling me that now it's absolutely certain that Edwin Smith wasn't the Sefton Park Strangler. I wondered if you had any more ideas about how to discover who really killed the girl.'

'One or two, but nothing definite yet. I'm still asking myself whether the burglary here had anything to do with the case. The alarm system is sophisticated, as you well know. It certainly cost us enough. I can't fathom why anyone would go to the lengths of disabling it and rifling through my room but then take nothing.'

'Perhaps he or they were disturbed.'

'Who by? No, I can't help believing the burglar was after the old Tweats file, mistakenly thinking it contained incriminating evidence. I hope no-one's disturbed you down in the Land of the Dead?'

Jock put a hand on his shoulder. 'No need to worry. It's as safe as Fort Knox.'

'Even so, I still reckon Miller told Ray Brill that I'd found the file.'

'You don't believe Ray was the burglar?'

'I don't know what to believe. The likeliest explanation to me still seems to be that Ray knows much more about the death of his girlfriend than anyone realised at the time. Besides, I've now learned that he might have had a motive for killing her.'

Jock's eyebrows rose. 'Such as?'

'According to her friend Shirley, Carole had become involved with another man. She'd given Ray the old heave-ho.'

'I dunno. What about Ray's alibi? Surely the police must have checked it out at the time.'

'So they claim. Come inside and I'll fill you in on the latest.' He led the little Scot to his room and, pushing a sheaf of telephone messages off his chair, recounted what he had learned. Jock listened carefully and, when Harry had finished, plucked at his beard for a few moments before speaking.

'Suppose it was the other way round?'

'How do you mean?'

'Suppose instead of Ray killing Carole because of jealousy, the new boyfriend murdered her because she'd become too possessive. Doesn't that solve the problem with the alibi?'

'You're thinking of Benny Frederick?'

Jock shook his head decisively. 'I can't imagine he would have fallen for her. Surely Clive Doxey is a better bet? He was an up-and-coming lawyer and politico. Carole was a child - and the child of a close friend, to make matters worse.'

Harry thought about it. 'No-one knows what was said between them when he called round at the house that day,' he said slowly. 'They might have arranged an assignation in the park.'

'Exactly! And then they might have had an argument. God knows what she might have threatened to tell Guy. He might have panicked, not realised what he was doing...'

'You may have something.'

'The worst of it is,' said Jock, 'you'll never prove whether I'm right or wrong. Not after all these years. Let's face it, there's no forensic evidence and a man like Doxey is hardly likely to confess. It will be so easy to say that Renata must be mistaken - or that, even if Smith is now in the clear, some passing maniac must have murdered Carole. We'll never know for sure.'

Again he was right, Harry thought: the theory of Doxey's guilt was appealing, but it amounted to little more than elementary guesswork. But he could not let matters rest there - not yet awhile. 'I reckon Miller believed he might be able to learn the truth,' he said mulishly, 'and don't forget his unknown visitor. Assume for a moment it was Doxey - why would he have called for an odd old German if he felt he had nothing to hide or fear?'

'That visit could be a coincidence. And in any case, it seems clear from what the police told you that Miller died of natural causes. He wasn't silenced because he'd stumbled on the truth.'

'But he might still have had the same idea as you ' insisted Harry. 'One thing's for sure. I need to speak to Ray Brill find out what he had to say when Miller came to call.'

'So you're carrying on with the investigation?'

'Of course. To me, it's more than just a game. I'll give Ray's number a try now to see if I can arrange a meeting.'

He turned to the photocopy of Miller's list which he now kept in his drawer and dialled the Southport code while Jock, tense with excitement, watched on. But the phone kept ringing out and eventually he had to admit defeat and hang up.

'I'll try again tomorrow or even go up there on the off-chance if I don't have any joy on the phone. Kathleen Jeffries doesn't live far away from him.'

Jock sighed and said, 'Killing two birds with one stone, eh?'

'Something like that. But now I have an even more important call to make.'

'What's that?'

'I need to tell an old lady that her son was never a murderer.'

The home in Woolton where, according to Miller's notes, Vera Smith lived, was a double-fronted building set behind a tall sandstone wall. As he walked up to the front door, Harry took in the neatly tended grounds and recently painted signboards which proclaimed the place as a superior residential home for the elderly, approved by all the right organisations. So the family money had lasted long enough to keep the old woman in comfortable surroundings, even if it had not been enough to achieve an acquittal from the court in the face of her son's persistent death wish.

Harry imagined that Edwin must always have been conscious of being a disappointment to his parents. All that money and still he'd had nothing to show for his life but a storeman's job and a couple of minor convictions. The debacle of his attempted seduction of Renata must have snapped the last thin thread of his self-esteem. No wonder he had been sufficiently mixed up to confess to murder.

So what would Mrs Smith make of the news?

He pressed the bell at the entrance porch and a young dark-haired girl opened the door.

'You have a resident here, a Mrs Smith.'

'Do you mean Vera?' she asked, studying him with care.

'Yes, that's right. A Mrs Vera Smith.'

'Are you - are you a relative? I'm sorry, we weren't aware of anyone apart from the people down in Shrewsbury.' She shifted from one foot to the other and there was an embarrassed note in her voice.

'No, I'm not a member of her family. But I would like to have a word with her if possible. It is important, I can promise you. My name is Devlin and I'm a solicitor.'

The girl flushed and said, 'You'd better come in for a moment.'

He followed her into a large hall with walls adorned by summary landscapes. He had visited old people's homes before and found several of them as dark and depressing as something from the pages of Sheridan Le Fanu, but this place was bright and airy. Yet the girl's manner made him uneasy.

A woman in a matron's uniform approached them. 'What is it, Lynsey?'

'A Mr Devlin to see Vera, Matron,' said the girl in a low tone, 'He's a solicitor.'

The matron turned to Harry and to his astonishment clasped his hands. 'I am sorry you have had to call here in such circumstances, Mr Devlin. I suppose you came over here as soon as you heard the news. Is it about the will?'

'The will?'

The woman paused and took in Harry's baffled expression. 'Oh, I am sorry. I thought Lynsey must have told you. I have some bad news, I am afraid. Vera passed away at half past two this afternoon.'

Chapter Eighteen

hoping that luck would be on my side.

No more 'if onlys'. The old resolution echoing in his head sounded hollower than ever to Harry as he drove away from Woolton. If only he had thought of Vera Smith first and called at the home in Woolton in the morning, she would at least have known the truth about her son before her death. According to matron, the old woman had complained of chest pains shortly before lunchtime and collapsed and died a few minutes later. Her heart had simply given out. There was no point in self-reproach, he knew, but he could not help it. If only he had thought first of the innocent rather than of those who might be guilty. If only.

By way of penance, he returned to Fenwick Court and picked up a dictating machine and an armful of files that Lucy had told him were screaming for attention. Challenging stuff like a row about a second-hand car and a couple of disputes between neighbours. Once at home, he made himself a boil-in-the-bag meal and weakened to the extent of dialling Ray Brill's home number. No answer came and he had no excuse for not devoting the rest of the night to catching up on the backlog.

He fell into bed at one o'clock and awoke the next morning with his determination to keep looking into the Sefton Park case renewed. More than likely, Jock was right and there was no prospect of his ever being able to identify the strangler. But the least he could do for Vera Smith now was to see if it was possible to discover the man for whom her son had died in vain.

He was at the office by eight. The news vendor round the corner was flogging the latest instalment of Jeannie Walter's heart-warming story of her triumph over the system and again he hurried by. Jim, a tediously virtuous early riser, was already at his desk. He seemed distracted when Harry wandered in to say hello.

'Benny Frederick's due here to talk about the marketing video this afternoon, right?'

'What?' Jim asked. 'Oh, yes, that's right. Four o'clock, I think we agreed.' He paused and added, 'And no cracks about Cinerama, please.'

After seeing clients during the morning, Harry set off up the coast to Southport, the resort where both Kathleen Jeffries and Ray Brill lived. It was inevitably a speculative trip. He had tried phoning Ray again without success and had decided against calling the dead girl's mother to make an appointment. Everything he had learned about her convinced him that she would be reluctant to assist a stranger to revisit the past. He had the impression of a strong but private woman: only a direct personal approach would be likely to succeed.

Kathleen Jeffries lived in a part of the town populated mainly by the elderly affluent, a place of bridge parties and golf dinners, of immaculate lawns and Sunday-washed cars. It did not take him long to find her home in a small block of purpose-built flats set at the end of a quiet cul-de-sac. He pressed the buzzer on the entryphone and a woman's voice demanded, 'Who is it?' It was a stern voice, the voice of someone who thought that no news was likely to be good news.

'Mrs Jeffries, my name's Harry Devlin. I'm a solicitor from Liverpool and I would very much like to talk to you about your daughter.'

'I have no daughter.'

Immediately he was on the wrong foot. 'I mean - your late daughter Carole.'

After a moment's hesitation the woman said, 'And why should I wish to talk to you about Carole?'

'Perhaps if you were willing to let me in...'

'I should warn you, Mr Devlin, I have a dog. A very good guard dog who takes exception to nosey parkers.'

Well, he'd always known it would not be easy. 'I promise you, Mrs Jeffries, I have no wish to distress you.'

'I'm glad to hear it,' said the woman before he could continue. 'In that case you will not be offended if I say I have no wish to rake up a past that has gone beyond recall.'

'Mrs Jeffries, I wouldn't trouble you without good reason, but I have important news for you. Edwin Smith, the man convicted of your daughter's killing, was innocent.'

A long pause followed before Kathleen Jeffries said sharply, 'That is absurd. You don't know what you're talking about.'

'Believe me, I do. A woman has now given Smith an unbreakable alibi for the time of the murder.'

'You seem to have overlooked that he confessed to the crime.'

'His confession was false. Someone else strangled Carole. I am sure you would be anxious, perhaps more than anyone for the true culprit to be found. There has been talk that there was another boyfriend in her life, someone other than the pop singer Ray Brill. I wondered if you might have any idea...'

'This is an outrage!' Even standing alone on her doorstep, he could feel the heat of her anger. 'How dare you come here and talk such nonsense! I have no intention of discussing the matter with you any further. Now be off with you, or I shall call the police.'

One advantage of having acted on behalf of so many of life's losers was that Harry had learned when to admit defeat. Quietly, he said, 'Of course I will leave, if that is what you want, Mrs Jeffries, but I can assure you my only wish is for the truth to come out. Perhaps you'll at least be willing to think it over. In the meantime, goodbye.'

She didn't answer and reluctantly he trudged back to his car. He still wanted to talk to Kathleen Jeffries, but he was equally sure that he would make no headway for the time being. The loss of a daughter to murder and a husband to suicide would be enough to harden any heart and he would need to reconsider his tactics before having any chance of making a more fruitful approach to her.

Time to try Ray Brill. He jumped into the MG and set off for the centre of the resort. In one of the side streets behind the elegance of Lord Street's shops was a clutch of large three-storey terraced dwellings, all of which had been converted into flats. The shabbiest was the one where the fallen star had landed. The salt wind from the sea had stripped much of the paint from the walls and the front garden was knee-high in brambles and bits of brick. A rusting supermarket trolley which lacked one of its wheels had come to rest on the path which led to the door.

Ray Brill's name was next to the bell of the ground-floor flat. Harry rang twice long and loud, but no-one answered. Perhaps his quarry wasn't even in town and his trip was going to be altogether wasted. He swore, but as he paused for breath the front door opened and a fat man in an anorak emerged.

'Do you know where I might find Ray Brill?'

The man had the morose air of a chocoholic on a sugar-free diet. 'No prizes for guessing, pal.'

'I'm not very good at guessing.'

'He'll be chucking his money away in the arcades, if I know anything.'

'Do you know which arcades he goes to?'

'Try the places down at the front. I only wish I had the money to throw around like that,' the man grumbled. 'Chance would be a fine thing. Do you know how much my bloody ex-wife takes off me each week? Can you guess?'

Harry escaped before the fat man could tell him and drove to the promenade. Even out of season, the resort bustled and none of the amusement arcades was crying out for the lack of customers. A handful of truanting schoolkids and a clutch of unemployed teenagers he would have expected, but he also saw plenty of adults, middle-aged men and women wearing ancient coats and glazed expressions, pushing coins into slots with such singleness of mind that he felt sure that if a bomb exploded in the Floral Hall their eyelids would scarcely flicker.

In each place he visited, the flashing lights half-blinded him, but it was the noise that made his head begin to throb. Every arcade had its own incessant cacophony of weird electronic bleeps, cascading pennies and blazing guns. He watched the punters absorb the messages of the ever-changing liquid crystal displays which shone so brightly on the machines that enslaved them. Here people spoke a foreign language and followed severe commands from inhuman masters to nudge or hold, to wait for the fair play reel or to match the bar to earn a prize. They clutched at promises of big cash jackpots and a fresh pack of cards every time, digging deep in threadbare pockets for the privilege. WIN! WIN! WIN! urged the one-armed bandits as the oranges and lemons spun round and round, but as far as Harry could tell, for all the occasional tinkling of coins in pay-trays, time after time the slaves lost, lost, lost.

He was on the point of abandoning his search when he saw a face he recognised. Ray Brill's photograph had appeared in several of Ken Cafferty's newspaper clippings: Harry guessed it was a publicity shot taken during the heyday of the Brill Brothers, perhaps by Benny Frederick himself. But Ray had become old before his time. His slick dark hair had thinned and the sallow cheeks and boxer's nose were now patterned with dark red thread veins. Although he could be little more than fifty years old, he looked as though he had long since qualified both for a bus pass and a spell at the Betty Ford Clinic.

He was juggling twenty-pence pieces in his left hand and pressing buttons on a poker game machine with his right, as absorbed in the task as a scientist engrossed in calculations of infinite complexity.

'Ray Brill?'

He spun round as if an invisible puppeteer had jerked his string. 'What d'you want? Can't you see I'm busy?' The husky tones that had once sung poignantly of heartbreak had become harsh with the passing of the years and he spoke with the faint habitual slur of a man seldom laid low by drink but never wholly sober.

'My name's Devlin. I've come from Liverpool to talk to you.'

'Oh yeah? You know who I am?'

'I have one of your records at home. "Blue On Blue".'

'What d'you want? My fucking autograph?'

'I'd like to talk to you about Carole Jeffries.'

Mention of the girl's name seemed to concentrate his mind. 'What is this? Why all the fuss about a bit of skirt who died thirty years ago?'

'You've spoken to a man called Ernest Miller.'

'What if I have?' Beneath the truculence, Harry sensed unease.

'Miller's dead, but I...'

'Dead?' He propped himself against the game machine as if in need of support. 'You're having me on.'

'I wish I were. He collapsed over the weekend. I was his solicitor and...'

'So you're a brief,' said Ray Brill scornfully. He made it sound like a confession to unspeakable crime. 'What d'you need to talk to me about Carole for?'

'Ernest Miller learned that Carole wasn't strangled by Smith, the man who was sentenced for the murder. I'd like to find the man who did kill her.'

Harry gave Ray Brill a searching glance, but to his surprise the man seemed almost to relax. It was as if he had expected the conversation might take a different turn. 'Can't help you.'

'Something's on your mind, though. What is it?'

Ray Brill gave a harsh bark of laughter. 'Nothing. Certainly not you, Mister Harry Devlin.'

'You and Carole were drifting apart, weren't you? You'd had your fun, you were getting tired of her. Did she ever make your temper snap?'

'What are you suggesting - that I murdered the little cow? Don't you know, smartarse? I had an alibi.'

'Yes, I've heard that. But are you saying you wouldn't like to find out who really murdered her?'

At a nearby machine a young boy hit the jackpot and whooped with delight. Ray Brill fiddled with the money in his hand and finally said, 'Smith did it. Everyone knows that.'

'No, Ray, he was innocent. Someone else strangled Carole, I promise you. Does that shock you? After all, there once was a time when she meant something to you.'

'If I lost sleep over every girl I've screwed, I'd never have another decent night's kip in my life.'

His sneer provoked Harry. An electronic rifle roared in his ear and he found himself shouting to make himself heard. 'She'd found another boyfriend, hadn't she? That's what really hurt you. For once, the great pop star was going to get the elbow himself. Did you hate that? Did you crack on that you were the one giving *her* the push? How jealous were you, Ray?'

The noise died down and Ray Brill gave him a savage glare. 'You're fucking crazy. There was no-one else. Now why don't you piss off out of here?'

Harry shrugged and made his way to the exit. There was no point in arguing with a man in such a mood. He already had the vague feeling that Ray had said something significant. Besides he had seen through the fury in the bloodshot eyes. No question about it: Ray Brill had something to hide.

'You've been seduced,' said Harry to his partner at the end of the afternoon. They were standing in his office, their arms full of glossy brochures. 'I never thought it would happen, but you've succumbed to the wiles of a silver-tongued charmer. Does Heather know?'

For the first time that he could ever remember, the big man blushed. He spoke hurriedly, as if to cover confusion. 'You don't seem to realise that what Benny Frederick is telling us about video as a practice development tool makes plenty of sense. We need to promote ourselves more effectively to potential clients.'

'I can't see the people I act for queuing up at the television lounge in Walton Jail to watch us.'

'I was thinking more of businessmen in the Round Table,' his partner said impatiently.

'You're saying they have pronounced criminal tendencies?'

Jim snorted. 'You simply never meant to treat this meeting seriously, did you?'

'You couldn't be more wrong. I'm glad Benny's so talkative. I'm dying to ask him about the Carole Jeffries case. Now that really is a matter of life and death. I'd just like you to get this marketing malarkey out of your system, that's all.'

A resigned sigh. 'We'd better go back. He'll be wondering what we've been talking about. I take it your answer is no, then?'

'Not so fast, I want to keep his interest. Let me handle this my way.'

'Didn't the last person you said that to get twelve years?'

Harry grinned. 'For Chrissake, he was an armed robber. Bloody lucky not to get fifteen. Now let's have another chat with Mr Frederick.'

They returned to Jim's room, where Benny Frederick was glancing around, taking in the ordered mound of correspondence as well as the framed certificates on the wall. He had darting eyes the colour of coal and Harry felt sure they would not miss much. His hair was still the same anarchic mass of dark curls it had been during his heyday as a photographer and his slim frame seemed not to carry an ounce of fat. At a distance he would have passed for a man of thirty rather than of fifty plus.

'Had a chance to talk things over?'

'We're having a spot of trouble identifying our unique selling point,' said Harry. 'Maybe we could put our cards on the table and adopt the slogan *Cheap Advice For Those Who Can't Afford Better.*'

Jim raised his eyes to the heavens but Benny simply giggled and said, 'I realise you'd need to contain costs. I'm not suggesting a remake of *Ben Hur.*'

'*Carry On, Crusoe and Devlin* might be closer to the mark. Anyway, we need to mull it over. Thanks for sparing your time and talking to us. We do appreciate it.'

'No problem. I realise it's a big investment for a firm like yours, a ...' For once, even Benny faltered, a suitably glamorous euphemism eluding him.

Harry came to the rescue. 'A niche practice?'

Another giggle. 'Exactly!' He stretched out a hand. 'Well, delighted to have the chance to meet you.'

'The feeling's mutual. As a matter of fact, there was another reason why I wanted a personal word with you.'

Jim Crusoe said hastily, 'I think I'd better be off. I have a difficult trust deed to draft tonight. I'll let the two of you - have your chat.'

He shot Harry a cautionary glance as he left. As the door closed behind him, Benny turned to Harry with an expectant look and said, 'You were saying?'

'There's a business I've been looking into and I think it's possible that you may be able to give me a little inside information.'

A crease appeared in Benny's brow but he simply said, 'Fire away.'

'It's not a current case of mine, but rather one that happened thirty years ago and it has suddenly come to life again.'

'I'm not with you.'

'You will be when I mention the Sefton Park Strangling.'

Benny stared at him. 'What on earth has that to do with you?'

The past few days had given Harry plenty of practice in explaining his interest in the killing of Carole Jeffries and overcoming people's reluctance to accept the notion of Edwin Smith's innocence. Benny heard him out in silence, occasionally pushing a hand through the black curls, as if unable to believe what he was hearing.

'Amazing,' he said in the end. 'If it's true. Even so, I don't see where I come in.'

'You employed Carole, worked with her five days a week. What can you tell me about her?'

Benny took his time before replying. 'She was a gorgeous girl. I suppose you'll have seen photographs, but even a couple I took never did her justice. Her hair was long and fine, her skin absolutely flawless. She was a child who looked like a goddess - and behaved like one. I could have sworn she was immortal.'

'But she wasn't immortal, was she?'

'No, poor kid.' He paused. 'Apart from that, what can I say? I suppose she was thrilled by glamour. That's why she joined me. In those days I was photographing all the top stars. She wasn't bothered about working in the shop - in fact, she could be a lazy little cow - but she loved the idea of mixing with the John Lennons and all the others who used to beat a path to our door. But above everything she was daring and determined. Once she set her mind on something, she wouldn't let anything get in her way.'

'You make her sound ruthless.'

'Maybe so. She had a famous father who let her run wild. He was always an easy touch where she was concerned. Whatever she wanted, she could have. I knew the family, they lived near to me.'

'I've tried to speak to Kathleen Jeffries - but she rebuffed me.'

'You don't surprise me. Her memories must be painful even after all these years, although she was never besotted with Carole in the way her husband was. I don't criticise Guy. I've never fathered children and never will, but I can imagine the joy of having an offspring who seemed so perfect.'

'Shirley Titchard didn't regard her as perfect.'

'You're a lawyer,' said Benny, mischief glinting in his black eyes. 'Would you say Shirley was an unbiased witness? After all, Carole stole Ray Brill from her. I felt sorry for Shirl, but it was a contest in which there was only ever going to be one winner. Though once she had her man, things began to change. I've known Ray since he was a kid and he always had a roving eye himself, but Carole was more cold-blooded. After a while she decided he'd served his purpose.'

'She tired of him?'

'Yes, she had great fun going out on the arm of a pop singer who could make the other girls swoon, but she kept her eye on the main chance. I reckoned that, the moment someone more appealing than Ray Brill came along, she would ditch him without a second thought. The truth is, she had the moral scruples of a chainsaw.'

'And did someone else come on to the scene?'

Benny scratched his ear. 'Maybe.'

'Was Ray jealous?'

'You'll have to ask him that.'

'When he sobers up, I will.'

'It could be a long wait.'

'I've gathered that. As well as gathering from your guarded answer to my question that Ray was the jealous type.'

A shrug. 'None of us likes to be rejected. Especially when we've come to expect adulation.'

'Was he jealous enough to kill?'

'Come on!' Benny seemed genuinely shocked by the suggestion. 'Ray wasn't delighted to be dumped, but it was no catastrophe. He's always been able to pick and choose.'

'Okay - so can you tell me who had caught Carole's eye?' He paused for a moment, watching Benny's face for a reaction. 'Was it you?'

'What in God's name makes you suggest that?'

'Am I right?'

'You're joking, aren't you? I thought my tastes were well enough known in Liverpool.'

'You wouldn't be the first person to swing both ways. You were her boss, the person giving her the chance to meet all the right people. She owed you a lot. And she was lovely to look at, even if there was a splinter of ice in her heart. I can imagine that, being with her day after day, you might have been attracted against your - shall we say, better judgement?'

The mass of curls shook vigorously. 'You're right, I did find her attractive. I'd have had to be neuter not to sense her appeal, but it went no further than that.'

'Then who?'

Benny sighed. 'I've never discussed this with anyone before.'

'There's always a first time.'

'Are we speaking in confidence?'

'I can't force you to tell me anything,' said Harry. He thought it a good politician's reply.

'You give me the impression that you won't take no for an answer.'

'Too many people have died not knowing how this whole sorry mess would end,' said Harry. 'Edwin Smith, in '64. Ernest Miller, the man who put me on to the case originally. Smith's mum, only yesterday. To say nothing of Carole herself, and Guy, who couldn't face continuing to live without her. I think they all deserve to have someone who's willing to work to bring the truth to light.'

'Okay, I'm convinced,' said Benny. 'So I'll let you into the secret. Carole had fallen head over heels for Clive Doxey.'

Chapter Nineteen

People talk about justice

After Benny had left, Harry returned to his own room and asked himself whether it mattered a light that Carole had claimed to have been in love with her father's best friend.

'How do you know this?' he had asked Benny.

'Because she told me on the day she died.'

After her quarrel in the shop with Ray Brill, Benny explained, he had asked her to come into the back room and have a coffee and a chat with him. When he'd chided her about her treatment of Ray, she had tossed her head like a blonde Scarlett O'Hara and said that she did not care if she never saw the singer again: she wanted to spend her life with someone who was twice the man that Ray was. She was a girl who always loved to shock, said Benny, and she had not been able to resist the temptation to tell him the news she had been hugging to herself.

'Listen, no-one knows this but you. Clive is coming round to our house in an hour's time. Mum and Dad will both be out. And I'm going to ask him to marry me.'

He could not believe it. 'What did you say?'

'It's Leap Year Day, silly, didn't you realise? The one chance I have to pop the question.'

'You're pulling my leg.'

'Believe me, Ben, I'm deadly serious.'

'But you're only sixteen.'

'Old enough.'

'Not if your parents object. For God's sake, you're not planning to elope to Gretna Green, are you?'

'It's a lovely romantic idea, Ben, but it won't be necessary.'

She had been supremely confident, he recalled. There would be no problem, she insisted, she would tell her father what she wanted and that would be that. He would not refuse her, could not refuse her. Benny had not attempted to argue further, even though he still found it all incredible. He was well aware of Doxey's relationship with Guy, but despite being himself an incurable nosey parker - as he made the admission, he smiled sweetly at Harry - he had never had a clue that there was anything between Doxey and Carole. Yet the way she giggled with delight at his disbelief did more than anything to persuade him that she was telling the truth. She had no need to lie: she was certain that Clive was captive to her charm and that when she put her question, his answer would be yes.

And that, said Benny, was the last time he'd ever seen her. Carole had gone home to meet Clive and, later, her terrible fate. He had left Shirley in charge of the shop while he went to Anfield to watch the big match. An FA Cup tie which Liverpool had lost to Swansea: a day to remember for every Welshman, and one of the most famous matches in the history of both clubs. Harry had heard his own father talk about that game and shake his head at the recollection of the Swansea goalkeeper's heroics and the missed penalty kick that cost the home side the match, but he knew that Benny was telling him about it for a reason: to give himself an alibi. When he said that, at the full-time whistle, no-one present could credit that Liverpool had been knocked out of the Cup, he was also saying that no-one in their right mind could credit that he had had either the time or the inclination to go straight from the ground to Sefton Park and strangle Carole Jeffries.

'You seem to have good recall of the events of thirty years ago,' Harry had suggested.

'It isn't every day someone you know well and like is brutally murdered,' was the soft reply. 'These things are apt to stick in your mind.'

'Carole wasn't the only such person, of course, was she? You knew Warren Hull as well, for instance. The man who was killed a few weeks earlier.'

Benny seemed to choose his words with more than usual care. 'Yes, I knew Warren. People said he was murdered by a kid he picked up but nothing was ever proved. Why do you mention him?'

'He was Ray Brill's manager.'

'What are you getting at? Surely you're not suggesting Ray murdered him?'

Harry let it pass; the coincidence of Hull's death bothered him, but he could not explain why, even to himself. Instead he asked why Benny had said nothing until now about Carole's avowed intention to propose to Clive Doxey. He received a simple answer. The murder had come as a shocking blow, Benny said, and there had never been any reason to believe that her apparent involvement with Clive had any bearing upon it. It was obvious from the start that a sicko must be responsible. By the time the police spoke to him, Edwin Smith was already under arrest and there seemed to be no need to embarrass Doxey or hurt the Jeffries by breaking the dead girl's confidence. Besides, it was just possible that she had been talking out a fantasy. The next time Doxey came into his studio, Benny had spoken to him about the killing but received no hint that he had regarded her as anything other than the daughter of dear friends. They had both agreed it was a terrible tragedy - and left it at that.

Finally, Benny had given Harry a wry glance and said, 'So if you're right and Smith didn't strangle Carole, who do you think was responsible?'

The question had been put amiably, but Harry had felt sure that Benny was watching closely for his response. He had simply spread his arms and said he wished he knew.

Now, sitting alone in his office, he admitted to himself that he would never be able to prove the identity of the culprit. Jock had pinpointed the problem: there was no chance at this late date of finding evidence to convict that would satisfy a court beyond reasonable doubt. Yet, after all the parents of Edwin Smith and Carole Jeffries had suffered, he told himself, he must make one last effort at least to satisfy himself that Carole's killer would not go to the grave with his guilt unknown to anyone.

Ernest Miller had talked at their first meeting about the perfect murder. The old man had been shrewd: was it possible that he had managed to identify the culprit - and perhaps had even asked him round to Mole Street last Saturday? Tantalised by the thought, Harry found himself wishing that, if Miller had had to die, he had been killed by his visitor rather than succumbing to the asthma that had dogged him over many years: then at least there might have been a crime for which the murderer could be put away. He had ascertained in casual conversation before Benny left where he had been at the time of Miller's death. At a video industry conference in Mayfair had been the easy reply. It had lasted until lunchtime on Sunday, Benny claimed. If he thought he was being quizzed for a purpose, he gave no sign of it, but Harry had already decided that Benny Frederick was nobody's fool. Never mind the openness of his manner: if he had anything to hide, he would hide it well.

Would the same, he wondered, be true of Clive Doxey?

He spent so long mulling over what he had learned that he was almost late for the meeting of the Miscarriages of Justice Organisation. When he finally arrived, Kim Lawrence was chatting to a girl who sat behind the desk at the door of the conference room in Empire Hall. Next to them stood a noticeboard bearing MOJO's logo of a pair of handcuffs that had been snapped in two and in huge red letters the legend TONIGHT'S LECTURE -

WHY THERE MUST NEVER BE ANOTHER WALTERGATE, BY PATRICK VAULKHARD.

'He'll be talking himself out of a job if he's not careful,' said Harry.

'No danger of that in this bloody society,' said Kim with a wry smile. To his surprise she bent her head forward and brushed his cheek with her lips. 'Glad you could make it anyway.'

'Thanks for inviting me,' he said, as he tried to guess if the kiss meant anything more than a simple social greeting. 'Sorry I only made it at the eleventh hour.'

'No problem.' She gestured towards the rows of empty chairs in front of the vacant speaker's podium. 'We need all the support we can get. We're due to start in a minute and the place is three-quarters empty.'

'It was a mistake to fix a date that clashed with Everton's replay.'

'Are you suggesting soccer fans are connoisseurs of injustice?'

'Have you never heard them complain about dodgy refereeing decisions?'

She laughed. 'How did I get into this? I can never tell whether you're being serious or not.'

'I promise you,' he said quietly, 'I am serious about genuine injustice. Whether it occurred thirty years ago or yesterday.'

'Any more news about the Sefton Park case?'

He nodded. 'I'll tell you later.'

'I think,' she said, 'Edwin Smith would have been glad of you as a champion in 1964. Just as the Walters were lucky to have you - as well as Patrick.'

'My ears are burning.' said the barrister's voice.

'Hello, Patrick,' said Kim. 'Ready to wow them?'

'I crave only your approval,' said Vaulkhard, bending to kiss her hand. Harry told himself it was a gesture she endured rather than enjoyed. 'Lovely to see you, Kim. As well as to find you've roped in young Mr Devlin here. Not noticed you at any of these meetings in the past, Harry.'

'Pressure groups aren't usually my cup of tea. Compulsory membership of the Empire Dock Occupiers' Association causes me enough hassle. It's like belonging to the Mafia but with rules more elaborate than the Law Society's. Anyway, I couldn't miss this one, could I?'

'It was a hell of a case,' said Vaulkhard. 'Sorry I seem to have hogged the publicity.'

'Hardly, in comparison to our Jeannie.'

A foxy grin. 'When they made Jeannie Walter, they broke the mould.'

'Thank God,' said Harry.

'I see Sir Clive is giving me meaningful looks,' said Kim. 'Perhaps we'd better make a start.'

She led Vaulkhard to the podium and Harry stole a glance at Doxey. He always found it strange to see in the flesh people he had come to know through television. So often they seemed smaller in real life and much less august. Sir Clive Doxey, however, was an exception to the rule: an imposing figure even when seated, a man whose silver mane had not a single hair out of place. His lips were pursed, as though he was unaccustomed to being kept waiting and it was a habit he did not intend to acquire. Even the way his arms were folded seemed to exude distinction and to make the statement that this was a rare man, a man of principle. It was impossible to remain indifferent on a first encounter with someone so formidable. For Harry, it was a case of deep dislike at first sight.

Patrick Vaulkhard began to speak. He had mastered this particular brief long ago and he glided with ease through the facts of the Walter case, conserving his energy for a scathing and comprehensive attack on those whose misdeeds had led to the original false conviction and those whose contempt for truth had caused them to keep Kevin inside, even after it became clear that he had not committed the crime for which he had been imprisoned. In passing, he paid tribute to Harry's efforts on his client's behalf, as well as expressing his admiration for everything that Jeannie had done - 'although,' he said with a faint smile, 'I could never be as eloquent an advocate on that particular subject as she herself has proved to be in the splendid newspaper serialisation about her campaign.' Occasionally, Harry noticed Kim shooting him a glance, her expression conveying amused annoyance. His lack of concentration must be showing. He guessed she must realise that his thoughts were drifting back to a miscarriage of the distant past.

He found himself beginning to chafe with impatience until the talk finally came to an end and Vaulkhard dealt with questions that ranged from the earnest to the absurd. Kim offered thanks and the small audience gave ragged applause. Harry jumped to his feet, anxious not to miss the chance to buttonhole Clive Doxey, but he need not have worried. Kim gently manoeuvred Doxey through the throng and towards where Harry was standing.

'Clive, I'd like you to meet a professional colleague of mine, a partner in another firm in the city centre. Harry Devlin, this is Sir Clive Doxey.'

They shook hands and Kim added, 'As you will have gathered, Harry instructed Patrick Vaulkhard on Kevin Walter's behalf.'

'A disgraceful episode,' said Doxey. 'It shows how appallingly easy it still is for miscarriages of justice to occur.'

'Very true,' said Harry, 'and another case I've been looking at over the last few days bears that out. As it happens, I wondered if I could bend your ear about it, since I'm sure that you can cast light on one or two aspects that have been troubling me.'

Doxey gave a tolerant smile. 'Well, I don't need to be off home for another half hour, but I think from the expression of the caretaker standing at the back there that we may have to move elsewhere.'

'There's a bar next door. Perhaps you'd let me buy you a drink. You too, Kim, unless you have to dash off this minute.'

'I'd love to come,' she said. 'Harry's told me a little about this case, Clive, and although it's an old one which wouldn't fall within MOJO's sphere, I'm sure you'll have a special interest in what he's uncovered.'

'I am intrigued,' said Doxey. 'Shall we adjourn?'

They found seats in the Empire Bar on the first floor, looking out over the black Mersey to the lights of the Wirral peninsula beyond. Harry brought the drinks over and then settled down in a chair facing Clive Doxey. Doxey was amiable and relaxed, unwinding after a long day. He had asked for a Southern Comfort; Harry was drinking beer, Kim a glass of aqua libra.

'Now then, Mr Devlin, how can I help you?'

'I'd like to take you back in time,' Harry said. 'To 1964, in fact.'

'The world was very different then,' said Doxey reminiscently, 'and I was a young man, still full of illusions about political progress.'

'Which you shared with your good friend Guy Jeffries.'

Doxey gave him a sharp look. After a brief silence he said in his most equable tone, 'Yes, that's right. Dear Guy, I believe he had the finest mind of our generation.'

'And yet he died a broken man.'

'He had - personal problems. His daughter died, you know.'

'Yes, I do know. Her murder is the reason I wanted a word with you. It turns out that the man convicted of the crime was innocent after all.'

No actor could have feigned the shock on Doxey's patrician features. 'What on earth are you talking about?'

Harry told him. From his first meeting with Ernest Miller to his conversation with Renata Grierson, he missed out none of the essentials, but he decided to say nothing for the time being about Benny Frederick's claim that Carole had fallen for Doxey. The great man listened intently, not interrupting; if he had been incredulous at first, he seemed gradually to absorb the enormity of what Harry was saying - that if Smith was innocent, Carole must have died at the hands of someone hitherto unsuspected. When the story was complete, he stroked his jaw thoughtfully before speaking.

'An extraordinary tale, Mr Devlin. Assuming you are correct, of course.'

'I believe Renata was telling me the truth. And I'm sure Miller was on the right track.'

'You're not suggesting he was murdered for his pains, I gather. That really would be storybook stuff.'

'No, I spoke again to someone I know in the police before I came out tonight. They're positive that Miller was not killed by anyone. It was an accidental death. All the same, I am intrigued by his Saturday visitor. Who can it have been?'

'Well,' said Doxey with a heavy sigh, 'I'm afraid I cannot help you there.'

'That may be, Sir Clive, but you knew the Jeffries family as well as anyone. I would be grateful if you could tell me a little more about them.'

Doxey glanced at Kim and Harry sensed that, had she not been there, he would have made some excuse and left. But he had made a name for himself as someone prepared to delve into any case that carried the faintest whiff of unfairness. He could not escape just yet. So he took refuge in a display of candour.

'You understand, Mr Devlin, this is painful for me. The killing of Carole Jeffries was not like any other case. I knew her well and Guy and Kathleen were old and dear friends.'

'Tell me about them.'

Doxey made a show of casting his mind back in time before saying, 'They first met at the University as students, as I recall. This was before I knew them, but I gather that both were thought to be destined for brilliant careers. Kathleen was as formidable a mathematician as Guy was a political philosopher. Things didn't work out quite as they planned and Kathleen fell pregnant with Carole.'

'So there was a shotgun wedding?'

'You imply that Guy was reluctant to marry, which I think was far from the case. He adored her in those days - as he adored his daughter from the moment she was born. But there were complications with the birth; I never knew the precise details, but Kathleen had gynaecological problems from that day on and having another child was never on the agenda. She suffered from ill health and her career took a back seat while she brought Carole up.'

'Did she resent that?'

'Like many mothers, I suppose she had mixed feelings.'

'And her relationship with Guy when you knew them?'

'Oh, as I said, he was devoted to her.'

'Come on,' said Harry impatiently. 'You were talking about the time they first married. Did they drift apart later? I gather he once had a reputation as a ladies' man.'

Doxey seemed on the point of objecting to Harry's bluntness, then changed his mind. 'Yes, Guy was a good-looking fellow, of course, sociable and outgoing. He didn't see it as his role to stay at home lending moral support whilst his wife brought up their child. He was out most nights, giving lectures or attending political meetings, and when he stayed at home he would be closeted in his study, working on a book or an article.'

'But that changed after Carole died, didn't it?'

'Yes, he went to pieces. Nervous breakdown; drink; drugs too, I suspect. Certainly he died of an overdose. In the weeks and months after the murder, I called on them several times. I was as shell-shocked by what had happened as anyone.' He paused, as if debating exactly what to say next. 'In a sense I thought Carole's death might have brought us all even closer together, but Kathleen was fiercely protective of Guy and, however selfishly, I began to feel excluded. As for Guy, he seemed for a time to have lost the will to live, but she helped him survive for another fifteen years. Long before then, he was lost to the Labour cause: even on election night in the October of that year, he stayed at home with Kathleen and refused every invitation to join the rest of us as we celebrated our victory.'

Doxey shook his head. 'He started working again eventually and wrote the occasional article. But the spark had gone. It was as if almost overnight a young Turk had transformed into a weary elder statesman. I sat in on one or two of his public lectures during the late sixties and early seventies, but he'd become rambling, forgetful and bereft of ideas. Harold Wilson's people were dubbed Yesterday's Men, but the description fitted nobody better than Guy Jeffries himself. I last saw him during that dreadful winter of '78-'79, with rubbish piled high in the streets and the dead left unburied. So much for our socialist dream, I said to him. Both of us realised the Tories were likely to regain power and the prospect proved too much for poor Guy. His health was ruined, he had nothing left to live for. Suicide must have seemed the easy way out.'

'And Kathleen? How did she cope during those difficult years?'

'I don't think I'd claim I've ever really understood her. She's strong, but quiet, and I've never seen her face betray a single emotion in all the years I've known her. I'm sure she was shattered by Carole's death, but I've never heard her utter the girl's name from that day to this. I think it was her way of blocking the tragedy out of her mind. Yet I will say this, Mr Devlin. I have always admired her.'

Doxey exhaled and sat back in his chair. He had seemed tense throughout their conversation but now he was beginning to relax. He reminded Harry of a politician who has seen off the sharpest questions at a press conference and has started to wax lyrical about the contribution made to his success by a devoted wife and family. The time had come to discard the velvet gloves.

'But not quite as much as you admired Carole?'

Doxey stared at him. 'I'm not sure I follow your meaning.'

'She was in love with you, wasn't she? I presume she didn't lack encouragement.'

'That is an outrageous suggestion! She was only sixteen!'

Harry was aware of Kim giving his shins a warning kick under the table, but it was too late to change direction. 'I'm sorry you see it like that, Sir Clive. I'm not accusing you of discreditable conduct. But I am told that, on the day of her death, Carole Jeffries had intended to propose to you.'

'Enough!' Doxey rose clumsily to his feet. 'I'm not prepared to listen to any more of this! Kim, I'm sorry, but I must wish you goodnight. It is late and I must return to my hotel.' He turned to Harry. 'As for you, Mr Devlin, I applaud your intentions. I have no doubt you mean well. But in my view that does not entitle you to make offensive insinuations about my personal conduct.' And with that, he strode briskly away.

Harry gave Kim a rueful grin. 'A picture of injured dignity, wouldn't you say?'

'I hope you know what you're doing.'

'My sources, as the journalists would say, are impeccable. Let me buy you another drink and I'll tell you all about it.'

He brought her up to date with the latest developments and was rewarded by the absorption with which she listened. When he had finished she asked what he made of it all.

'I don't believe your friend Sir Clive. I think he was involved in some way with Carole Jeffries.'

She leaned closer to him. 'And what do you deduce from that?'

The crowd in the bar was thinning out. He glanced at his watch and said awkwardly, 'Look, we're going to be chucked out of here soon. My flat's two minutes away. Would you like to come round for a coffee and I'll explain the way my mind's working?'

She smiled and said, 'You make it sound like an offer no woman could refuse.'

He felt himself blushing. He hadn't meant to proposition her; his head was already spinning as a result of what Doxey had said, for he thought he was close to understanding the reason for Carole's death.

A few seconds passed as Kim watched him with a wry look on her face. Then the pager in his pocket began to bleep. He fumbled for it and, with a stammered excuse, hurried to the payphone next to the exit door. When he returned a couple of minutes later, it was with an overwhelming sense of despair.

'What's the matter?' she asked.

'Patrick Vaulkhard had better tear up his script,' he said bitterly. 'He won't be needing it again. The call was from Jeannie Walter, she wants me to go over and meet her right now. Kevin is in hospital with a police guard ringing the operating theatre. A couple of hours ago, he fell through a skylight while taking part in an armed robbery at a Customs warehouse.'

Chapter Twenty

divine retribution.

Tears had streaked the mascara on Jeannie Walter's ravaged face and the damp marks glistened under the harsh fluorescent lights of the hospital waiting room. She was pacing back and forth across the linoleum floor and chewing her fingernails with a desperate savagery. The police had called her away from a party and underneath the fur jacket she had bought on the day of the courtroom settlement she was wearing a tight black cocktail dress and little else. In this place of draughty echoing corridors her presence was as incongruous as that of a fan-dancer at a funeral.

'He's got less brain than a fucking sparrow,' she said. 'He had no need to do it, no need at all.'

She had been saying the same thing since Harry's arrival. He had forborne to suggest that Kevin could not help it, that crime was in his blood, that he could no more give up wrongdoing than a junkie could forsake his needle. A few minutes earlier he had spoken to the policemen who were waiting for news of Kevin's injuries. They were in confident mood: the operation to catch the warehouse thieves in the act had been a complete success. That one of those involved had sustained serious injuries while scurrying across a rooftop in a vain attempt to escape was scarcely cause for concern - especially once he had been identified as Kevin Walter, so recently the scourge of the South West Lancashire Major Enquiry Squad.

Apparently the police had received a tip-off: the job had been planned for months and presumably Kevin had not regarded the outcome of his court case as any reason for pulling out at a late stage. They even wondered if their informant had been jealous of Kevin's success in the legal lucky dip. It didn't matter - as well as him, they had six more of the city's toughest career criminals under lock and key.

A doctor approached them. His manner was grave and he spoke in a sympathetic murmur. 'Mrs Walter? My name's Iqbal. I have just come down from the theatre. Can I speak to you in private for a moment?'

'What's the matter? Where's Kev? What state is he in?' Jeannie was on the point of seizing him by the lapels of his white coat.

The doctor put a restraining hand on her arm. 'Mrs Walter, this is a difficult time for you, I realise. Please, let us find a room where we can talk together.'

She turned to Harry. 'For Christ's sake, why won't they tell me anything?'

Seldom had he felt so helpless. Gently, he said, 'Talk to the doctor, Jeannie, he'll tell you as much as he knows.'

She bit her lower lip and said, 'All right. But don't go, will you? Promise you'll be here when I get back.'

'I promise,' he said, although at that moment he would rather have been anywhere else in the world.

Leaning on Iqbal's shoulder for support, she tottered down the corridor and out of sight. Harry sat down on a hard black plastic chair and took a last sip from his polystyrene cup of vending machine coffee. The silence was broken only by the occasional trudge of weary night staff and the squeaking trolley wheels that set his teeth on edge. He closed his eyes, not daring to imagine how badly hurt Kevin might be. Come what may, it would be a long time before his next robbery. The stupidity of so many of his clients kept Harry in work, but he cursed Kevin's greed, all the same. Why were people never satisfied, why did they always want more, why did the rich man take pleasure in dodging a little income tax?

'Having a rough night?' asked a voice he recognised.

He glanced up and saw a tall blond-haired man whose hands were sunk deep in the pockets of his raincoat. 'Hello, Pete, I didn't expect to see you here. And to answer your question, yes, I have had better evenings.'

Detective Sergeant Peter Olson gave him a grim but not unsympathetic smile. 'I don't like to kick a man when he's down, but you may find things soon get worse.'

'I doubt it. My client's seriously injured and likely to go down for years when he finally recovers. His wife's hysterical and I'm sitting here unable to do anything to offer her consolation. How can things get worse?'

'You acted for Kevin Walter in his compensation claim, didn't you?'

'Yes, and I don't suppose the people from the old Major Enquiries Squad will be heartbroken by tonight's events.'

'Not just tonight's events, Harry,' said Olson softly.

'What else?'

Olson sat down next to him. 'I shouldn't be telling you this yet awhile, perhaps, but I don't see that forewarning you will change anything. Fact is, a woman has come forward. Her name is Gaynor and she used to be a prostitute on the Falkner Square beat. She's accused your client of raping her.'

'Wonderful,' said Harry through gritted teeth. 'When is he supposed to have done that? During his period of wrongful imprisonment?'

Olson smirked like a gameshow host about to reveal the night's star prize. 'Five years ago, on the ninth of March to be precise.'

Harry stared at him. 'Are you kidding? That was...'

A complacent nod. 'The same date as the robbery of the jeweller in Southport, yes?'

'It's impossible!'

'All too possible, Harry, I can assure you. She tells us he picked her up that night, but didn't want to pay for what she had to offer. There was a struggle and he finished up beating the shit out of her as well as raping her against an alley wall.'

'Come on now. This is the first anyone's heard of it.'

'She never reported it at the time, of course. Prostitutes often don't, as you well know. They seem to regard an occasional battering as all part of the job and, rightly or wrongly, they don't expect to receive much sympathy from us. Besides, she saw in the newspaper that Kevin had been picked up for the Southport job. She knew he was innocent of that, but it seemed to her that he'd got his just deserts.'

'And is there any evidence to support her story?'

'Several people can vouch for it. We've done our homework, we have to in a case like this. Wouldn't want to be accused of harassing an innocent man, acting out of spite as a result of his court case, would we? We've spoken to other girls who were out that night, including one who can remember seeing Kev pick up her mate. They operate their own mutual security system, jotting down the numbers of punters' cars, just in case anything nasty might happen. And there's more.'

Harry groaned. 'Break it to me gently.'

'This afternoon we traced the cleric who found her lying a few yards away from the Cathedral and helped wipe the blood and tears away. He'd urged her to report the attack to us, but respected her right to keep silent. Short of serving a subpoena on God, I'd say he's as close to a perfect witness as I'll ever meet.'

Olson had an answer for everything. 'So why has Gaynor suddenly decided to speak up?' Harry asked heavily.

'Because of all the fuss on the telly about bloody Waltergate, of course. The sight of Jeannie portraying Kev as the innocent victim got right up Gaynor's nose. And I suppose she thought the media might be interested in her story too. She's a reformed character, you know. Married one of her punters who runs an estate agency - from one kind of exploitation to another, eh?'

'Holy shit.' Harry shook his head in dismay. 'No wonder Walter had trouble providing the South Lancs boys with an alibi for the crime he didn't commit.'

'Funny the way things turn out, innit?' said Olson happily.

'Hilarious.'

'Don't look so glum. I'm sure you were well paid for the case you brought against the Squad. And you ought to be rubbing your hands at the prospect of all the extra business. Though even a lad with your imagination may find it hard to persuade the court that Kev took part in the robbery while the balance of his bank account was disturbed.'

'I suppose I ought to say thanks for tipping me the wink,' said Harry, 'but frankly, I preferred blissful ignorance.'

'Ah well,' said Peter Olson, 'you can't win 'em all. Be seeing you.'

Even before the detective's revelations had sunk in, Harry heard the click-click-click of Jeannie's heels coming back down the corridor. He had thought himself proof against any further shocks that night, but the expression on her face caused his stomach to lurch. Never had he seen such naked despair.

He stood up and as he took her hand, another single tear rolled down the ruin of her cheek. 'Have the police spoken to you?' he asked.

'Police, police?' she answered vaguely. 'No, I've been with the doctor. He's been explaining the situation to me.'

He felt a sick certainty that he knew what was coming. Yet he had to ask. 'And - what is the situation?'

'Kevin's broken both his neck and his spine. He'll be lucky to survive the night, but if he does, one thing's for sure. He'll never walk again. He'll be a bloody cripple for the rest of his days. My Kev - confined to a fucking wheelchair!'

Harry tightened his grip on her hand but said nothing. There was nothing to say.

The blotches on her skin darkened and when she spoke again her tone was as hard as an asphalt road. 'That bloody warehouse, it was criminal what they'd done! The window frames around that skylight were rotten through and through. No wonder Kevin fell. I tell you one thing - we're going to sue them for every penny they've got!'

As dawn approached, he unlocked the door to his flat. His limbs were aching and he felt exhausted, but knew he would never be able to sleep after such a night. Stumbling into the shower, he let the jet of hot water burn his skin and wash fatigue away. He had left Jeannie Walter talking to Iqbal about her husband's condition: the only sure thing was that it would be some time before he was fit enough to be questioned by the police. Harry had said nothing to Jeannie about Gaynor's allegations: she had enough on her plate. Phrases from Vaulkhard's talk about the unending quest for justice kept surfacing in his brain and he wondered grimly whether the tabloid which had serialised the Waltergate story had put a clause in the deal to claim its money back if the truth about Kevin proved to be worse than the fiction dreamed up by the crooked cops of the Major Enquiry Squad.

Forget it, he thought as he towelled himself dry, *what about Carole Jeffries? Who should have taken Edwin Smith's place in the condemned cell?* During the long chilly hours in the hospital, ideas about the Sefton Park Strangling had jostled around in his head like schoolkids in a bus queue. He simply did not believe Clive Doxey's denial of involvement with the girl. Yet what could he prove? And would even the existence of a relationship establish a credible motive for murder? So many things still bothered him: the lurking suspicion that Ray Brill had told him something significant was one thing, the old pieces of paper Ken Cafferty had shown him another. He believed he was coming within a touch of the truth, yet still the curtain of time divided him from the murder and made it impossible for him to see precisely what had happened thirty years ago.

By half past five he was at his desk in Fenwick Court, battling through the backlog of paperwork that had accumulated over the past few days. It was a bitterly cold morning, but free from interruptions of clients and staff, he tried to concentrate on the mundane trivia of court correspondence and instructions to counsel. Yet hard though he tried, he could not drag his thoughts away from Carole's death.

On the stroke of seven he rang Ken Cafferty's paper in the hope that the reporter was on the early shift. 'You're in luck,' the girl at the other end said. 'Who shall I say is calling?'

'Are you a mind-reader?' demanded Ken when he came on the line. 'How did you know I wanted to speak to you? Is this rumour about Kevin Walter being under arrest true?'

'So you've heard?'

'I take your answer to mean that it's gospel truth. Fine, you don't need to say another word.'

'Listen, I wasn't calling about Waltergate. It's the murder of Carole Jeffries that is really bugging me. Can you spare me a few minutes? We could have breakfast together at The Condemned Man. Would you meet me there in half an hour?'

'I can make it sooner if you're so keen.'

'I was allowing you time to dig out the old cuttings on the Sefton Park case again. I'd like to take another look at them.'

'You never give up, do you? Okay, let me just have a word with the newsdesk and I'll see you at Muriel's.'

'What's so interesting about the blacks?' asked Ken in between mouthfuls of Cumberland sausage.

Harry was bemused. 'The blacks?'

Ken gestured to the flimsy sheet of yellowing typescript in Harry's left hand. 'That's what we used to call it. After carbon black, you know. Until the new technology came in, all the files would contain their share of blacks. Of course, they contained a lot of stuff that never saw the light of day.'

'Yes, I can see discrepancies between this and the cutting that is evidently based on the same report.' Harry traced a finger along one line from the black, where Guy Jeffries was quoted as saying *I could never have let her go.* 'But I don't understand the reason for them.'

'What you have there is the story the journalist wrote. The sub-editor would have marked the top copy, cut it down to size and crossed out all the split infinitives as well as striking a line through everything libellous. And that bowdlerised version is the one Joe Public would read.' He took the paper from Harry and glanced at it. 'This is the first report for the Monday edition after the story broke. Compare it to the clipping that actually appeared. See how the sub has toned down the quotes. In the original you can almost hear that poor bastard Guy Jeffries sobbing in despair; in the final story, he is simply described as distraught and uttering a few platitudes about what a wonderful girl his daughter was.'

Harry took back the sheet. 'I see he never actually uttered precisely those sentiments.'

Ken tutted. 'Yes, a bit of sympathetic imagination there, I reckon. I suppose the sub thought that was what Guy would have wanted to say if he was thinking straight.'

'As a matter of fact, if you look down the page, you'll notice that the quote extolling Carole's virtues came from Clive Doxey - described here as a close friend of the family.'

Craning his neck, Ken said, 'Well, there you are then. Spot of journalistic licence, that's all.'

A heavy hand clamped down on Harry's shoulder. 'What's this I hear about Kevin Walter?'

'Been a bad lad, hasn't he, Muriel?'

'I hear he's in a shocking state.'

'He won't be raiding any more warehouses for the foreseeable future, that's true.'

'And what's this about some trollop crying rape?'

Harry stared at the huge woman in fascination. 'How do you know about that?'

She tapped her nose with a finger as thick as one of her own sausages. 'A little bird told me.'

'Rape?' asked Ken, his nose twitching. 'What's the crack?'

Harry groaned and pushed his knife and fork to one side. 'It's a long story and I haven't got time to tell you right now. Soon, though, I promise.'

'Listen,' said the journalist, 'you owe me.'

'More than you think,' said Harry. 'I forgot my wallet. Can you settle up with Muriel?'

His next stop was at the Land of the Dead. Officially, the place only opened at nine, but as always, Jock was in early. The little Scot was gulping down a cup of black coffee as Harry walked through the door and huddling up to a twin-bar electric fire which made little impact on the freezing chill of the underground lair. His eyelids were heavy and he looked as though he had not slept.

'Heavy night?' asked Harry. 'You look as bad as I feel.'

'You know how it is,' said the archivist with a tired movement of the shoulders. 'What can I do for you?'

'I'm on the same mission as before. Can I have another look at Cyril's file on Edwin Smith?'

'Surely.' He led Harry through the maze of relics and rubbish to the place where the old folder was stored. 'What's the latest?'

'You'll make a gumshoe yet. You were right about Clive Doxey. I'm sure he knows more about this particular miscarriage of justice case than he's willing to admit.'

'You've spoken to him?'

'Last night. And what's more, I've been told that on the day of her death, Carole told Benny Frederick that Doxey was the man she wanted to marry.'

'You're kidding!' Jock looked startled, but then a faint grin began to slide across his face.

'Doxey denies it, but I don't believe him. However, some pieces don't fit. With an effort, I can picture elegant Sir Clive turning up at Mole Street to confront Ernest Miller, but I simply can't see him breaking into my office to steal the file you have in your hand - even if he'd previously spoken to Miller and was afraid there was something in the old papers that might incriminate him.'

'Perhaps he hired someone to commit the burglary.'

'A hell of a risk.'

'Not necessarily. His work must have brought him into contact with the criminal classes over the years. I'll bet he must know suitable people.'

'The other possibility, of course, is that the burglary had nothing whatever to do with my asking around about the Sefton Park case.' He began to leaf through the file, but when Jock asked if he was looking for anything in particular, he shook his head. 'I simply wanted to reread some of the statements. What Guy had to say about Doxey, for example. I wondered if there might be a clue there.'

Jock read the statements over his shoulder and eventually said, 'One thing that comes out loud and clear to me is a father's terrible distress at the loss of his daughter. You know, Harry, this is all fascinating, but I wonder if we're ever going to get any further. After all, how are we ever going to be able to prove that Doxey killed the girl? He's no fool, he'll never admit it.'

'Come on,' said Harry. 'I thought you at least understood why I want to learn the truth. You're not suggesting that I give up now?'

'Think about it for a moment. If you're right, you're dealing with someone who has killed at least once before. A rich man who could afford to have anyone who came too close to him taken care of.'

Harry laughed and in the vast underground chamber the sound bounced back at him like an eerie warning. 'Sir Clive Doxey, tribune of the ordinary working man, pay someone to rough me up or worse? You must be joking.'

But when he looked into the other man's eyes he saw apprehension rather than the customary good humour, and he realised that right now Jock was not joking.

Walking back to the office, he swung his arms to keep warm as the first flecks of snow began to fall and wondered if he would be wise to heed Jock's words of caution. He knew he must take care, for the ideas he now had about the case were so shocking that he had explained them to neither Ken nor Jock. But there was no question of his giving up his search for the truth about the death of Carole Jeffries. He had come to believe that he owed it to her as well as to Vera Smith and her son to keep going to the bitter end. The dead deserved justice as much as the living.

Once at Fenwick Court, he briefed Ronald Sou about the latest twist in the Waltergate saga. The news of Kevin's misdeeds prompted even the inscrutable clerk to shake his head, the equivalent of a fainting fit in many another man.

'I don't expect rapid developments today, but keep an eye on things. I'm driving up to Southport shortly and I may not be back for a while.'

The phone buzzed and he snatched it up in irritation. 'Suzanne, I don't have anything on in court this morning and I'm likely to be out until lunchtime.'

'There's someone to see you,' came the smug reply. 'Reckons it's important.'

'I told you that I would ... who is it?'

'Name of Doxey,' said the girl. '*Sir* Clive Doxey, so he says.'

Chapter Twenty-One

Yet I have concealed a most terrible crime

'I came to see you,' said Clive Doxey, 'because last night your questions startled me and provoked me into an unwise lie.'

'And now you propose to make amends?' asked Harry. He gazed sceptically at the most distinguished visitor ever to fill the client's chair. 'Why the sudden change of heart?'

'Because on reflection I decided you were a man unlikely to take no for an answer, Mr Devlin. Very late last night I telephoned Patrick Vaulkhard at his home and he confirmed my impression. So here I am. Good of you to see me without an appointment.'

Doxey rested his palms on the battered old desk and gave a glimmer of the self-assured smile so familiar from a hundred current affairs programmes. But Harry's instinctive reaction had always been to switch to the soccer highlights on another channel, and now he sensed that Doxey's lines were as carefully rehearsed as the we're-both-men-of-the-world manner. *He must be worried*, he thought.

'So you've come to tell me that you were involved with Carole Jeffries, after all?'

'I wonder who gave you that idea?'

'Someone in whom Carole confided her plan to propose to you on Leap Year Day.'

Doxey closed his eyes for a second before replying. 'Well I suppose it was foolish for me to deny it. Carole and I did fall for each other. She was only sweet sixteen and I was close on thirty, but that didn't matter. I wasn't a dirty old man bent on adultery. I'd been living with a girl who lectured at the Polytechnic, but we'd split up around the Christmas of 1963. I was unattached and ready for a new relationship.' He gave Harry a direct look. 'It was nothing to be ashamed of.'

'Did Guy or Kathleen know you were smitten?'

A shake of the head. 'They had no idea that we were seeing each other, far less that marriage was a possibility.'

'And was it?'

'Yes, your informant was quite correct. On the day Carole died, she did propose to me.'

'Did you accept?'

Doxey seemed for a moment to measure pros and cons, as if wondering whether a lie would serve him better than the truth. 'Yes,' he said finally. 'I was glad to do so.'

'So you were keen to marry the girl?' Harry frowned, uncertain whether to believe what he was being told.

'I was crazy about her,' was the calm reply. 'She had that effect on people, you know. Intoxicating.'

'And dangerous.'

A brief pause. 'I suppose you're right. But on the day of the murder, I told her I felt the time wasn't right to explain to her parents that we were in love. As it proved, in the end there was never a right time.'

'Even after her death you said nothing?'

'It hardly seemed relevant.' Doxey began to shift around in his chair. He seemed uncomfortable with the admission. 'They had suffered a dreadful blow. I didn't think it would help them to learn that their girl had become involved with a friend closer to their age than hers.'

'And they never guessed?'

'I did wonder,' said Doxey, 'if they might have gained an inkling. After the murder, I sensed that something had died in our relationship also, though nothing was ever put into words.'

'As if in some way you were to blame for what had happened to Carole?'

'A ridiculous idea. How could I have been?'

We'll come back to that, thought Harry. Aloud, he said, 'I'd like to know more about Carole. Would you mind telling me how the two of you got together?'

Doxey licked his lips. 'I'd always been fond of her, through all the years I'd been spending time with Guy and planning on how we could change the world. She was a pretty child who soon grew into a gorgeous teenager - and she was a terrible flirt. I'd never thought of her in a sexual way, you'll have to take my word for that, but after I'd finished with my own girlfriend, I suddenly saw Carole through new eyes. She was more than an attractive little thing who happened to be the daughter of a man I liked and admired. I realised she was a desirable young woman. And all at once - I desired her.'

'Did she respond?'

'Oh yes. I started turning up at the house on the flimsiest pretexts. And one day, I found my luck was in. I called unexpectedly in the middle of the afternoon, and she told me that both her parents were out but that it was a shame for me to have made a wasted journey and would I like to come in for a cup of coffee? I hardly need go into the details. Suffice it to say that we finished up in bed and I overstayed my welcome so long that I'd barely got my trousers back on by the time Guy and Kathleen returned.'

'And after that?'

'We made love at every possible opportunity,' Doxey said. His tone was defiant, perhaps even, Harry thought, a touch boastful. 'I will be candid with you - I realised I must be when I decided to talk to you again this morning. She was insatiable: we both were. I didn't feel as though I was exploiting her. No, I am *sure* I never exploited her. She was young, I can't deny it, but she had an old head on her shoulders and she knew what she wanted. I was only glad it was me.'

'And what about Ray Brill?'

Doxey flapped his hand in a dismissive gesture which sent Harry's desk tidy spinning to the floor and scattering paperclips all around. 'He was a passing phase in her life, no more. She'd been bowled over by the idea of going out with a pop singer, she admitted as much to me. He was a charmer, even though he was never going to be a second Paul McCartney. But Carole was no fool. She was much brighter than Brill and she knew that he wasn't a long-term bet.'

'Did she realise he might not take the same view?'

'She didn't worry about giving him the push. Why should she? For a man like that, there are always plenty of girls around.'

'I'm told Carole had a secretive streak. Did she relish the intrigue and hiding your love from her parents?'

'Yes, she did love to be mysterious. It was part of her appeal. But she disagreed with me about keeping our engagement quiet for a while. She was adamant that her parents should be told. We would have needed their consent for a wedding, of course, but I felt it was a question of tackling them sensibly, waiting for an opportune moment. Carole at least agreed with me that, provided he was in the right mood when I tackled him, Guy might be more sympathetic than Kathleen.'

'Despite his own devotion to his daughter?'

'If he loved her - as I am sure he did - he must have wanted her happiness most of all.'

'But you decided not to stay around and broach the subject with him yourself that afternoon?'

Doxey shrugged. 'You might call it lack of nerve, Mr Devlin but...'

'And you claim you never saw Carole again after you left the house?'

Doxey's tone hardened. 'I did not lurk about, if that is what you are implying, and follow her into Sefton Park.'

'Did you quarrel about whether or not to break the news to Guy and Kathleen?'

'Not at all. I cannot say I care for your insinuations, Mr Devlin. I would sooner have killed myself than seen a hair on her head come to any harm.'

'I accept that you found her attractive,' said Harry, 'but I only have your word for it that you agreed to marry Carole. Suppose her proposal horrified you. After all, you were a rising star of the radical left. An affair with the teenage daughter of your closest colleague might have done you untold harm if it had come to light. Perhaps for you it was only a fling.' He paused deliberately. 'If you'd turned her down and she then threatened to go public, wouldn't that have been a motive for murder?'

Doxey's plump cheeks were drained of all colour and he was gripping the edge of the desk as if in need of support. When he spoke his voice was choked with anger as well, Harry thought, as with a touch of fear. 'What you suggest, Mr Devlin, is entirely misconceived. I came here this morning in good faith, hoping to clear up last night's little misunderstanding. I gather you have a reputation for doggedness and I appreciate that even after thirty years, my relationship with Carole might in some quarters still be seen as providing cause for criticism. The press is never happier than when it is questioning the morals of people in the public eye, and I have made one or two enemies over the years. You can embarrass me, I accept, but you have no grounds whatsoever for accusing me of murder.'

'So you say.'

'And I can prove it!' Doxey raised his voice. He was beginning to look his age: still smart and well groomed, but undoubtedly sixty plus.

Harry gave a sceptical nod, confident now that he had unsettled his man. 'Really? And how can you do that?'

'A check on my medical records should suffice. You see, Mr Devlin, two days before Carole was killed, my right wrist was put into plaster. I had slipped on ice the previous day and fractured it when I tried to break my fall. On Leap Year Day in 1964, I could no more have strangled Carole Jeffries than made love to her to celebrate our betrothal.'

After Doxey had gone, Harry sat for a while at his desk, with his phone off the hook. His mind was working furiously. At last he felt sure he could see the sequence of events leading up to Carole Jeffries' death, rather than the blurred image presented by press cuttings and Cyril Tweats' old file.

He had a sense of events moving towards a crescendo during the first few weeks of 1964. Carole had been reckless. After stealing Shirley's lover, she had grown tired of him and turned to an older man. Her contempt for Edwin Smith had mirrored her treatment of Ray Brill. The golden girl of shock-horror news coverage had been tarnished by her unrelenting pursuit of pleasure. And what, he wondered, did her parents make of it all - the adoring Guy and the stern Kathleen? How would they have reacted had they learned that their daughter had fallen in love with a family friend, a man almost twice her age?

The press picture of Carole came into his mind. Over the last few days he had come to understand her and now he believed he knew the reason for her death. He had so desperately wanted to know who had strangled her, and why, and now that he had his answers, his principal emotion was sadness rather than satisfaction. With murder, he reminded himself, there were no slick solutions, just the desolate reality of human behaviour as weak as it was wicked.

Soon he was on the road and heading north. As he drove he tossed around various ideas on how he might obtain confirmation for his hypothesis about Carole's murder, but in the end he decided he must trust to luck. Even as he was parking once more outside the block of flats where Kathleen Jeffries lived, he had no more than a vague plan for persuading her to talk to him. All he could do was make her realise that the truth could not be buried forever. It must be acknowledged: Vera Smith deserved nothing less.

He pressed her bell and when he heard her sharp voice through the entryphone, he said, 'This is Harry Devlin again. I really do need to talk to you about Carole.'

He could imagine her compressing her lips in cold anger - and, perhaps, apprehension. 'I have nothing whatever to say to you.'

'Mrs Jeffries, please listen to me. I know what happened on that Leap Year Day. I know who strangled your daughter. And what's more, I strongly suspect that you know too.'

'You're talking nonsense! This is most offensive - an impertinent intrusion on private property. If you are not away within the next two minutes, I shall not hesitate to call the police.'

'It won't do any good,' said Harry. 'And besides, the police will need to be told about the mistake they made thirty years ago. Isn't it better for us to talk?'

'Why on earth should I wish to talk to you, you foolish young man?'

'Because,' said Harry patiently, 'you have kept a terrible secret for so long and now it's a secret no more.'

'I don't know what you mean.' But there was no disguising the dismay in the disembodied voice.

'I think you do, Mrs Jeffries. Let's face the truth together. We both know that Carole was killed by her own father. Your husband, Guy.'

Chapter Twenty-Two

and I may succeed in carrying my secret to the grave.

'Guy idolised her,' said Kathleen Jeffries, 'that was half the trouble. And for all his faults, I idolised him.'

Harry nodded. They were sitting in her lounge, a large austerely furnished room which boasted a narrow balcony and a view across the dunes to the distant sea. The dry heat of underfloor central heating made the room warm but somehow far from cosy. Her mantelpiece was bare of family photographs and bric-a-brac; her shelves were crammed with nineteenth-century classics rather than with her husband's books. Curled up in a corner was the old Labrador that had been her sole companion during the years since Guy's death. After half an hour of conversation, he felt he had begun to win her confidence and she had even thawed to the extent of making him a cup of tea. In response to her final angry questions, he had explained how he knew that, if Smith was innocent, then unless Carole had fallen prey to a passing maniac, the only person who could have murdered her was Guy.

'Benny Frederick, like Ray Brill, had an alibi. Clive Doxey had broken his wrist and was scarcely in a fit state to strangle anyone. Who else could have been guilty?'

'So you followed a simple process of elimination?' she asked, the hint of scorn in her voice making her sound like an elderly schoolmistress despairing of a pupil's haphazard ways.

'No, there was much more to it than that.'

He'd explained that he had puzzled over the dedication at the front of *Our Sterile Society. To Carole, whom I adore?* I've never been a parent and I'm sure if I ever did have a child I might worship her, but I doubt I'd wear my heart on my sleeve in quite the same way.

It was obvious from that, and from everything I'd been told, that it was an exceptionally close relationship. Perhaps unhealthily so.'

Yet his ideas had not crystallised until he considered the discrepancy between the newspaper's published account of an interview Guy gave immediately after the discovery of Carole's body and the original version preserved in the file on the black. His exact words had been *I could never have let her go*, but in print he had been quoted as saying *I should never have let her go*. Presumably a long-forgotten sub-editor had regarded the change as an improvement which seemed to make more sense: yet when one realised Guy was an obsessively devoted father whose only child was about to marry his best friend, a man almost twice her age, the words he actually used took on a sinister significance. Even in the bits and pieces of the old Cyril Tweats file, Guy came over as a man not merely shocked by his bereavement but horrified by it - and, perhaps, filled with self-loathing. It had dawned on Harry that in suspecting Doxey, he had been looking at the wrong man

Kathleen Jeffries peered at him over the half-moon spectacles which perched on the end of her long nose. She was a tall grey-haired woman whose mouth seemed to Harry to have a natural curve of disapproval. Again he felt like a schoolboy awaiting chastisement for some juvenile idiocy. 'But why have you sought to rake up the old business? I don't understand why you...'

'Should poke my nose into other people's affairs, when there is nothing in it for me? Blame my curiosity, Mrs Jeffries, everyone else does. But I also think of Edwin Smith's mother, who died with her pathetic son's name still not cleared. You were a mother, too; perhaps you will agree that she would have been glad for someone, at least, to vindicate her faith in him.'

'I was not a good mother,' said Kathleen Jeffries and Harry realised that, for all her severity of manner, she would judge herself most harshly of all. 'Had I been, perhaps my daughter would still be alive today.'

He guessed that she had been waiting for thirty years to unburden herself of the truth. Those three decades of accumulated guilt, horror and fear were drawn in the lines that furrowed her brow. Yet her back was straight and her voice calm. She must, he thought, have been very strong to survive so much for so long.

'Tell me about Guy,' he said gently, putting his teacup down. 'You met him when you were both students, I believe?'

'Yes, for me it was love at first sight.' She sighed and leaned back in her leather chair. 'I'd had little experience of men - we're talking of the years immediately after the war, long before women could claim to be liberated. Guy and I hit it off at once and I must confess I was flattered by his attention. He was an exciting man, clever and ambitious as well as handsome. Even then it was clear that he would make his mark. He introduced me to politics and I became as enthusiastic as he was for social change. We believed that with the war over, we could help to change the world.'

She moistened her lips. Harry said nothing, content to let her take her time. 'Things didn't work out as we had expected, but then the lesson of life is that they never do. I became pregnant - a terrifying prospect and yet one I found strangely exhilarating. Guy panicked when I broke the news and I half expected him to press me to find some back street abortionist or simply leave me in the lurch. But to his credit, he did not. In later life, I've often remembered that and told myself that in our early days together, my passion for him must have been reciprocated.'

'So you married...'

'Hastily, yes. And I had the child. I had been well throughout the pregnancy and I expected the birth to be straightforward.' She closed her eyes for a moment. 'How wrong I was. My midwife was inexperienced, mistakes were made. Carole was fine, but I nearly died and I was told that a further pregnancy would be dangerous. Today, perhaps, one would have sued, but in the post-war years, medical negligence was as much a taboo as teenage sex. So I just got on with my life, and looking after my husband and child.'

'You gave up your career?'

'I didn't regain my health for over a year. And afterwards, caring for Carole seemed to take up all my energy. Looking back, I realise that despite everything Guy used to say and write about women's rights - he was ahead of his time, the feminists would have been proud of him - he was as emancipated at home as a ruddy-cheeked Tory squire. But I didn't see it like that; I was proud of him and as desperate for him to succeed as he was himself. So I contented myself with my domestic responsibilities and baked and dusted with as much determination as any suburban housewife.'

'While Guy's star rose?'

'Yes, and naturally I enjoyed my share of the reflected glory. Guy rapidly earned a reputation for radical and creative thought. During the fifties, the long years of opposition offered him the ideal opportunity to expound his views with conviction and flair.' She gave a grim smile. 'It is easy to put the world to rights when one does not have the responsibility for doing more than delivering a lecture with wit and verve or checking the proofs of an article which excoriates the dullards in power.'

'But you did not see Guy in that light then?'

'Of course not, although it is true that after Carole's birth I had lost much of my original interest in sex. It became more of a duty, less a source of uninhibited delight.'

Harry fiddled with his tie. He felt uncomfortable, but he had to ask the question. 'And - what about Carole?'

She looked him in the eye. 'Do you really believe that he was her lover?'

'It would explain...'

'It would explain nothing, Mr Devlin. I understand what you are thinking, but I am quite sure you are mistaken.' Sensing that he was not convinced, she continued urgently, 'Of course Guy was besotted with Carole from the moment he first saw her in the hospital, but I never had cause to suspect anything other than the intense devotion of a father to his only child. We often quarrelled about the way he spoiled her. I said it would do her no good in the long run, but Guy always argued I was far too strict.'

'A battle you could not win?'

'Precisely. Carole was no fool. Soon she learned how to take advantage of him, how to play the two of us off against each other to her own advantage. There was very little I could do about it. By the time she reached her teens, she was running wild. It appalled me - but I felt powerless. Whatever she wanted, Guy allowed her to have. She was clever enough to have stayed on at school, to have done well at university, but when she decided to throw it all up, he insisted it would be wrong to impose our views on her. And so she left - to start work behind a shop counter, for Heaven's sake!'

She glared at Harry, still furious at the memory. 'That incident led to our bitterest row. I simply couldn't believe he was prepared to let her throw her education away, but he brushed my protests aside. He said I was jealous of her, that she was doing all the things I would have liked to do in my own youth. And - who knows? - perhaps he was right.'

'Did you know she was going out with Ray Brill?'

'That loathsome pop singer? Yes, of course I did. She gloried in the fact that she'd stolen him from the girl she worked alongside.'

'What did Guy make of Brill?'

'He said it was only a passing phase, that she would soon grow out of him and find someone more mature.'

Harry bit his lip. 'I'd like to ask you about the day of Carole's death. Forgive me, I'm sure it must be painful for you.'

Her mouth a tight line, she said, 'Compared to everything that has happened in the past, Mr Devlin, I don't suppose it matters a jot. When I returned home that evening, I found my husband in a state of complete collapse. I could not understand it: he seemed to be over-reacting absurdly to the fact she had gone out for a short walk but not come back as quickly as expected. I supposed there would be some simple explanation, but Guy's attitude convinced me that we should call the police. As time passed, my own nerves began to fray, but the news that her body had been discovered came as a quite devasting blow.' She bowed her head. 'Carole was, after all, my daughter and despite the friction between us, I did care for her. However, I can't deny that I had come to resent her as well. I resented the way she defied me and I resented her for being the apple of her father's eye.' She gave him another stern schoolmistressy look. 'Do I shock you, Mr Devlin?'

He shook his head. 'It takes a great deal to shock me. I wonder, how did you find out your husband had killed her? Did he confess?'

'No, at least not there and then. Those terrible days after Carole's death are no more than a blur in my memory. I can remember a vague sense of relief that the police had been quick to pick up her killer. I had never cared for Vera Smith's boy, a wretched inadequate, although she was an indomitable character and her late husband had been a forceful businessman. Yet I found it impossible to hate Edwin for what I thought he had done. The murder drained me of all emotion, and Guy was in a terrible mess. It wiped him out and soon he was undergoing psychiatric treatment.'

'So when ...?' He let the unfinished question hang in the air.

'I can't give you a time and date when I realised that Guy had murdered our daughter. It was simply not like that, but in time I began to realise that the breakdown he suffered was caused by something more than grief. He used to talk jumbled nonsense in his sleep, and slowly it dawned on me that what was crucifying him was guilt. Not just the natural guilt that we all suffer at a time of bereavement, when we wish desperately that we had not said and done certain things, but remorse more deeply rooted than any I could have imagined. When Smith committed suicide, I thought time would start to heal the wounds, but it did not. Guy would not explain what was wrong, we were scarcely able to communicate at all, and so I searched around in my mind for an explanation.'

'Did you confront him?'

'Yes, finally I summoned up the courage to ask him what had really happened. By then I was certain that he had not been telling me the truth. I dreaded the thought of what he might tell me, but nothing was worse than not knowing. His resistance was token. When I pressed the point, he came straight out with it. Yes, he had strangled her. She had tormented him and he had reacted instinctively, with ferocious violence.'

'He was jealous of Clive Doxey, wasn't he?'

'How did you guess that? Yes, Carole had been all too aware of her power over him, had known how to exploit it to best advantage. She was no innocent - I already knew that - yet Guy swore to me that he had never interfered with her in any way.'

'And did you believe him?'

'Yes,' said Kathleen Jeffries. She threw her head back defiantly and her dog lifted its head and growled softly, as if warning Harry not to challenge his mistress. 'You see, I knew my husband. I knew when he was keeping something back about our daughter's death - but I also knew when he was telling me the truth. I can assure you, Mr Devlin, if he had been sleeping with her, I would have squeezed an admission out of him.'

'The way I imagined it,' said Harry slowly, 'Guy did not envy a boy like Ray Brill; he was confident a pop singer was just a teenager's passing fancy. But when she told him she was in love with an older man who happened to be Guy's closest friend, a man she wanted to marry, he found that far too much to take.'

She nodded. 'He realised that Carole's feelings for Clive were genuine and he could not face the prospect of losing her. She had outgrown her father's love and wanted to make a life of her own. Being Carole, she was not prepared to wait. The silly fool had proposed to Clive and he had accepted. She was determined to marry and that meant she needed parental consent. Guy refused - and that proved disastrous for all of us.'

'She threatened him?'

'Child abuse was not a subject people talked about so much in those days, Mr Devlin, although I expect it was no less prevalent then than it is today. But Carole was ruthless - as well as shrewd enough to know that a lie told with conviction will often be believed. "No smoke without fire" is, I have always thought, the wickedest phrase. Guy told me how she put it: "Think how the Tory Press will lap it up. A leading Labourite screwing his own daughter - imagine what he would do to the economy!" She said it would make a bigger stir than the Profumo scandal. If he didn't change his tune before I came home, she said, she would tell me that he had seduced her and then call the police. Even if the newspapers did not print the story - they they were more timid in 1964 than today, or perhaps more responsible - the damage would have been done. She said she would go out for a walk in the park to give him a chance to think it over.'

Both of them said nothing for a little while. The Labrador had lapsed back into sleep and Harry could hear the gentle sound of its breathing. He pictured the scene in his mind: the wild and wilful girl, the father tortured by fear and jealousy. Glancing back at Kathleen, he saw that the mask of severity had finally slipped. In her weary features he saw despair written more clearly than any words could have told. Suddenly she seemed old and frail. Keeping the secret for thirty years had drained every ounce of her strength.

At length she said, 'Guy walked out of the house and followed her in a state of panic. He caught up with her and begged her to see reason, but she simply laughed in his face. She was no fool, she knew when she had the upper hand. He took hold of her, wanting to shake some sense into her, but she struggled and told him he was dirty, he disgusted her. Her own father and he had taken advantage of her, abused her for his own vile pleasure.'

Harry stared at the floor, unable to meet her gaze as she described the day which had destroyed so many lives. Her voice began to crack as she said, 'He could not remember strangling her with her own scarf. All he knew was that her body went limp in his hands and he suddenly realised what he had done. Frantically, he tried to revive her, but it was no good. He was feverish, not knowing what to do. He dragged her body into the bushes and staggered back to the house. He had been outside for less than a quarter of an hour: no-one had seen him leave the building. His only thought was that the truth must not come out.'

'When he had told you all this,' said Harry after a little while, 'what did you decide to do?'

She cast her eyes down. 'Not what I should have done, that goes without saying. I showed no courage. I had lost a daughter and I could not contemplate losing Guy as well. Despite everything that had occurred, stupid and inexplicable as it may seem - I loved him. Edwin Smith was dead and I could not save an innocent life by speaking out. Guy was a sick man; it was plain to me that he would never recover from what he had done. The guilt he carried with him to the grave was punishment enough. I said no-one else would ever know.'

'And Mrs Smith, what of her?'

'I acted wrongly, I do not deny it. But we all have our weaknesses, Mr Devlin. Guy was mine.'

'So you stayed with him and kept your promise?'

'You sound horrified, but I felt I had no choice. Guy was like a lost soul for those last fifteen years. He could never bring himself to tell the psychiatrists the truth and in the end they all gave up on him. We broke off with our friends in the Party. Guy did a little writing as well as assignments for the University, but all the passion was spent. There had been talk of a Chair, but of course that came to nothing. Clive tried to stay in touch, he was hurt and bewildered when we rebuffed his approaches. But that was inevitable. He had been the unwitting catalyst for our family tragedy.'

'And Guy's suicide?'

'It was not his first attempt, far from it. There had been other incidents with whisky and sleeping pills, but I had managed to hush them up. I'm afraid I've been rather too good at hushing things up, Mr Devlin. Frankly, when the end came, it was a merciful release. Everyone felt sorry for me, but no-one knew the burden I had had to bear since Carole's murder.' She gave Harry a wry smile. 'Do you know, I think there may be a grain of truth in that old cliché about a trouble shared. For so long I have been bowed down by my own sense of complicity in the crime. I would never have believed it, but I am glad you've been willing to listen to me. May I ask, now that you know the worst, what you intend to do with your knowledge?'

Harry thought for a minute or two before he spoke. The Labrador stirred and considered him with questioning eyes while Kathleen studied her short unvarnished fingernails. 'What can I do? Ernest Miller, the man who first urged me to believe that Edwin Smith did not kill your daughter, is dead. I've turned up several stones during the last few days and I haven't always liked what I've found underneath them. I can't see how anyone would gain if I were to broadcast what I have learned. Don't misunderstand me· I can't guarantee that the truth will never come out. Plenty of people are aware of the enquiries I've been making and someone may be able to put two and two together themselves. But I don't see why I should encourage them to do so.'

Kathleen turned her gaze on him and he saw a flicker of hope in her pale grey eyes. 'So you are willing to let sleeping dogs lie?'

'What matters most of all to me,' he said, 'is that at last Vera Smith can rest in peace.'

So that's that, he thought, as he unlocked the MG. Guy killed Carole and, although he escaped the law's net, he was tortured by remorse until the day of his death. A perverse kind of justice had in the end been done. Ernest Miller's speculation had been spot on: had that strange old man not set the enquiry in motion, Kathleen Jeffries might have gone to her own grave bowed down by the weight of her unshared secret. It was too late for her to rebuild her life, but at least she too might now have the chance to find a sort of peace.

A thin layer of snow lay on the pavements and his tyres threw up spray as he pulled away from the trim block of flats. Only two questions were left in his mind, yet Harry knew they would nag at him if he did not seek out the answers. First, who was Ernest Miller's last visitor? Of course, he could now imagine no sinister motive for that unusual house call: Miller surely could have had no idea that Guy was Carole's murderer and even if he had guessed, no-one had a motive to stop him broadcasting it to the world. Maybe it was simply an unimportant coincidence, like the break-in at Fenwick Court. The second question was something and nothing, really, but he wanted to put it to Ray Brill. Since he was in the neighbourhood, why not call? He decided to see if Ray was at home: he did not relish another trawl of the resort's amusement arcades.

As he turned into the street where Ray lived, he found himself swerving to avoid a group of passers-by who had strayed from the pavement. He didn't have time to swear at them: he was distracted by the scene that had captured their attention. A police van with flashing blue lights was parked fifty yards away and the narrow road had been cordoned off. He slammed down on the brake and came to a halt just short of the barrier. A uniformed constable approached and he wound down the window. He could hear walkie-talkies crackling, could see the sombre expression on the constable's face.

'What's going on?'

'There's been an incident overnight, sir, I can't say more than that. Now if you'd be good enough to turn around, you can find your way to Lord Street down the next road.'

But Harry wasn't moving. The van stood outside the house he had called at before. The front of the building was blackened and all the windows had caved in. As he absorbed the implications of the scene, he groaned.

'So there's been a fire? What about Ray Brill - has anything happened to him?'

The constable leaned forward and spoke in an urgent tone. 'You knew the gentleman, sir?'

His use of the past tense struck Harry like a physical blow - as did the sudden realisation that if Ray was dead, perhaps he had not yet solved the puzzle posed by Ernest Miller after all.

Chapter Twenty-Three

For the record

Within an hour he knew as much about Ray Brill's death as the police - but that was very little. His stroke of fortune had been to catch sight of a familiar figure coming out of the police van. He was a sergeant, universally known as Wedding Cake because he had been married three times, and he was not only a neighbour of Jim Crusoe but also one of Harry's most dependable divorce clients. Wedding Cake blamed the stress of the job for his matrimonial disasters, but everyone else put it down to chronic lust.

According to Wedding Cake, the alarm had been raised at eleven the previous evening. The fat man whom Harry had met on his first visit here had arrived home from the pub to be confronted with the acrid smell of smoke the moment he walked down the path to the door. The fire brigade had arrived within minutes, but by then the blaze had already taken hold. They had broken into the building to find the burnt remains of Ray Brill sprawled across the floor of his bedroom.

'Overcome by the fumes?' asked Harry.

'We'll have to await the post mortem to be sure,' said Wedding Cake primly.

'Come on. If it wasn't for me, you'd be funding the Child Support Agency single-handed.'

'All right, but this is strictly off the record, mind. All the indications are that it's a put-up job and a pretty amateurish one. We reckon someone slugged Brill, then torched the place to cover his tracks, trying to make it look as though a carelessly tossed away cigarette butt was the cause of it all.'

'Any leads?'

'Nothing yet, but it's early days. We're going over the place with a fine toothcomb and my bet is that we'll find some useful forensic before we're finished. Having said that, right now, you're probably our prime suspect.'

'Thanks.'

Wedding Cake smirked. 'We have to look at every possibility. You say you wanted to talk to Brill, but I still don't know why. I appreciate you may have been a fan, but shouldn't you be at work?'

'Jim would certainly say so and no, I'm far too young to have been a fan of the Brill Brothers. As for my interest in Ray, it's a long story.'

'I've got plenty of time to listen.'

As Harry gave an edited account of his enquiries into the Sefton Park Strangling, Wedding Cake's eyebrows rose and when he finally paused for breath, the policeman did not disguise his amazement.

'No wonder you're so slow at replying to telephone calls. You're constantly running round poking your nose into murder mysteries.'

'I suppose someone's got to do it.'

'Ha-bloody-ha. Now listen, do you think there is any connection between the waves you've been making and the murder of Ray Brill?'

Harry spread his arms. 'Who knows? One minute I think the case is all over, the next it opens up again.'

'Exactly why did you want to talk to Brill? Simply to let him know who had killed his girlfriend of thirty years ago?'

'No, there was more to it than that. When we spoke, I felt he was holding back on me. I still believe that he was. Yet I can't understand what he had to hide.'

'Clear as mud, the whole thing. Anyway, you can leave this one to us now.'

'If you say so,' agreed Harry in his meekest manner.

Wedding Cake gave him a haughty look. 'And if you do happen to make any inspired deductions, let me know straight away. I don't want to find your corpse stretched out across the floor of your office. At least, not yet. I need to talk to you about the alimony for Sharon. I've met this lovely girl, you see, and...'

'Listen, I'll promise to tell you my hunches if you agree to have a word with me before you next propose, okay?'

'Romance is dead,' said Wedding Cake gloomily.

'No, but it's bloody expensive.'

All the way back to Liverpool, the question of why Ray Brill had been killed gnawed at him and by the time he was parking his car at the snow-carpeted Fenwick Court, an explanation was beginning to take shape in his mind. He felt sure he had learned enough over the past few days to fathom the mystery, but one last leap of imagination still needed to be made. Unsure what to do next, he was coming back to the office with the best of intentions; at the very least he knew he ought to check his post and messages. But when he saw Leo Devaney emerging from the basement record shop, umbrella in hand, he sensed fate was about to intervene.

'God, what weather! I'm on my way back to the record fair, I mentioned it to you, remember? Have you time to look in?'

'I should be getting back to my desk,' said Harry, 'but...'

'All work and no play? Why not come over with me? Surely you can spare half an hour. Besides, you might pick up one or two rarities. There's some good stuff on the stands. Specially mine. Come on, you can share my brolly.'

'I might scout round,' Harry said thoughtfully, 'see if I can find anything by the Brill Brothers.'

'I've still not picked up anything of theirs lately, but I did see one of their albums this morning. It's in lousy condition, mind you. It crossed my mind that I might buy it for you later in the day, when things got a little less hectic and the prices a little cheaper. But if you turn up now, you can have a look for yourself and cut out my mark-up.'

'You'll never make a businessman,' Harry said as they turned out of the courtyard and headed in the direction of Dale Street. 'But perhaps if you don't know already, I can give you a good tip. If you do come across any Brill Brothers material this afternoon, it might be worth investing a few quid. I have a feeling their work is going to become much sought-after in the very near future.'

'Can't see it myself. What makes you think that?'

'Ray Brill died last night.'

Leo stopped in his tracks. 'Seriously?'

'As serious as any death is ever likely to be.'

'I can't believe it! Jesus, he is - was - my age! What was it, heart attack?'

Blinking snowflakes out of his eyes, Harry shook his head. 'The police reckon he was murdered.'

'You're kidding! He was hardly in John Lennon's league!'

'I don't think a loony fan was to blame. Someone called on him last night, hit him over the head and set fire to his flat in an attempted cover-up.'

Leo was bewildered. 'It's incredible! Who would want to do anything like that?'

'Any number of people, judging by what you told me last week. Spurned lovers, cuckolded husbands, irate fathers. He didn't go out of his way to make himself popular.'

'True enough, I suppose - but how did you bump into him?'

'I tracked him down to Southport. When I spoke to him, he was pouring cash into a slot machine. You could safely say he was on the downward slope.'

Leo thought about it. 'As soon as this news gets out, Brill Brothers records will become eminently collectable. You wait, all the old has-beens from the Cavern era will be wheeled out to sing Ray's praises and some bright spark will re-release 'Please Stay' as a tribute.'

'I can see it climbing to the top of the charts.'

'Every chance.' Leo shook his head, still trying to absorb the news. Finally he cleared his throat and said, 'What exactly was your interest in Ray?'

'I thought he could tell me something about the killing of a girl he'd once known, but I was on entirely the wrong track.'

Leo looked mystified but said nothing more as they crossed the road and walked under an archway between two old buildings. The alleyway broadened into a courtyard. At the far end was a door next to which stood a sign proclaiming RECORD FAIR TODAY. Leo nodded to the ageing hippy on the door, who waved them through with careless geniality.

'I'd have been glad to pay,' said Harry.

'No problem. I'm grateful for the tip-off about Ray. Just don't tell anyone else until I've scoured the place for his stuff, okay?'

'Where was the album you saw?' asked Harry.

'Hang on a moment while I have a word with Simon, then I'll take you there.'

Leo led the way down one of the aisles between the rows of tables on which stood box after box of records, tapes, compact discs and memorabilia. One customer was haggling noisily over the price of a Manfred Mann album and two men in their forties were recalling the merits of Northern Soul with the nostalgic exaggeration of old buffers harping on about the Dunkirk Spirit. From a pair of speakers on one stall Harry heard Mick Jagger demanding who wanted yesterday's papers, who read yesterday's news. In one corner, a bespectacled youth was studying an original Cavern Club poster for a Beatles gig as if it were a Rembrandt, while across the way, a muscular stallholder had clamped in a vice-like grip the wrist of a spotty shoplifter whose twitchy demeanour suggested that he existed on prohibited substances rather than square meals. Towards the back of the room Leo paused in front of a banner marked DEVANEY RECORDS. Sitting underneath it was his friend Simon, a pretty young boy with a neatly trimmed moustache who was clad in a white vest and denim jeans.

'How's business, love?'

'A bit slack in the last half hour. Hi, Harry, how's life in the legal profession?'

'Jim would say I ought to be back in the office right now, finding out.'

'He's such a spoilsport,' said Leo. 'Listen, love, have you heard anyone mention the name of Ray Brill while I've been out?'

Simon shook his long brown locks. 'Why do you ask?'

'Tell you later. Hang on for another five minutes, will you, while I show Harry something?'

Simon smiled indulgently and blew Leo a kiss.

'I think the Brill Brothers album was on this side of the room,' said Leo as they moved away. 'I still can't believe that Ray has been killed. Extraordinary, isn't it, how often death strikes the people of pop? For goodness' sake, even the Singing Nun finished up in a lesbian suicide pact. Did you know she and her lover were both found clutching a cross in their hands?' He took in the expression on Harry's face and said, 'Are you all right?'

'Yes, yes ... it's just that something you've said has struck a chord.'

Leo stared at him, conscious that something momentous had happened, but wholly unable to grasp what it might be. 'Come on, you've piqued my curiosity. What did you mean when you said that your questioning of Ray was on the wrong track?'

Harry rubbed his chin and pondered for a moment. All at once, his ideas were slotting into place like oranges on one of Ray Brill's favourite fruit machines. 'As you said, it's strange how often death strikes people in the pop business,' he said slowly. 'I think perhaps I should have been asking Ray about the murder of his manager, rather than his girlfriend.'

'Warren Hull? What on earth makes you say that?'

'I'm beginning to wonder,' said Harry, whether Warren Hull's death all those years ago might have been the reason why Ray was murdered last night.'

Chapter Twenty-Four

I do not regret the murder at all

L eo did not attempt to hide his bewilderment. 'Didn't I explain that to you? It was a gay killing, something the police weren't able to solve. I've always reckoned the culprit was a rent boy who turned nasty when Warren made excessive demands.'

'Maybe,' said Harry, 'maybe not.'

'What do you mean?'

'Old sins cast long shadows.' Harry thought briefly about Kevin Walter before he continued. 'I've spent the last week or so trying to discover the explanation for one crime from the Swinging Sixties, but now I think I should have devoted more attention to another.'

'I don't understand.'

'Tell me about Warren Hull. I take it most people knew at the time that he was gay?'

'Oh yes, he flaunted it.'

Something in Leo's tone made Harry ask. 'Did you know him, by any chance?'

Leo flushed. 'As a matter of fact, I did. As you know, I've always been crazy about pop, and in the early sixties I was in my teens and Liverpool was the perfect place to be. I would hang around places like the Cavern and the shops run by people like Brian Epstein and Benny Frederick and...'

'So you knew Benny, too?'

'Well, yes, he and I - we go back a long way.'

'You were close friends?'

'What if we were? Why are you asking all these personal questions?'

'And Warren Hull?' pursued Harry. 'He was much older, of course, more than twice your age. Did he take you under his wing?'

231

Leo's pale face reddened. Lowering his voice to a whisper, he said, 'If you must know, Warren was a swine.' He specialised in young boys and teenagers. I was simply one of many. For a short time he courted me, until he had his way and then - and then he moved on to his next victim. It was as if I had never existed. He treated me like dirt.'

'Did Benny know this?'

'Of course. He was - kind to me afterwards. He and I had no secrets in those days, even though he had money and I was just another young lad who was crazy about the Merseybeat.'

'What was Benny's relationship with Warren Hull?'

'Oh, he took his photograph and all that, but basically he loathed him. Most people who knew anything about Warren did. I promise you, few tears were shed when we heard that he had been murdered.'

'Sounds as if there can have been no shortage of suspects.'

Leo shrugged. 'I told you. The police never charged anyone.'

'Did they question you?'

Despite the chatter all around, it seemed to Harry that there was an almost interminable silence before Leo answered. 'What are you implying? Of course they found out about Warren and me. But I was only one of his conquests.'

'And did you have an alibi?'

'As a matter of fact,' said Leo, 'I did.'

Harry gave him a direct look. 'Do you mind telling me what it was?'

'I can't see that it's any business of yours,' said Leo sulkily. 'Aren't you taking this detective stunt rather too far?'

'I can't force you to tell me anything,' Harry agreed.

Leo sighed. 'Oh, what the hell? If you must know, on the night Warren Hull was murdered, I was staying over at Benny's home.'

Harry nodded. 'I see.'

Leo licked his lips. 'Look, it all happened a very long time ago and I can't see that any of this can have any bearing on Ray Brill's death. I think I've answered enough questions. Do you still want to have a look at that album or not?'

'Please.'

They edged through the crowd towards a set of tables in the far corner of the room. Leo pointed to a row of cardboard boxes marked '50s, '60s, '70s, '80s and '90s. 'After all this build-up, let's hope it hasn't been snapped up since this morning.'

Harry leaned over the '60s box and flipped through the tattered record sleeves with a practised hand. The Allisons, Herb Alpert, John Barry, The Beach Boys, Jane Birkin and Serge Gainsbourg, The Beatles, Pat Boone, The Box Tops and - success! - an album called *Brill Cream*.

He froze in the act of stretching out his hand for the record. What he saw on the grimy sleeve hit him like an electric shock.

'Are you all right?'

'Yes,' said Harry croakily. 'I mean ... yes, of course I am.'

'I didn't think you expected it to be in pristine condition,' said Leo, 'but there's no need to make a performance about it. You can always negotiate on the price.'

'It's not the state of the record that bothers me,' said Harry slowly.

'Then what's the matter? I've never known you act as strangely as you are today.'

'Look at the picture,' said Harry, his voice hoarse.

Leo stared at the sleeve. 'Yeah, yeah, it's the Brill Brothers. Two fresh-faced young lads singing some sugary heartbreaker as if their lives depended on it. So what? One thing is for sure. Ray Brill changed a good deal over the years. I bet by the time he died he looked like an old man.'

'Can't you see? It's not Ray Brill that I was looking at.'

'I'm still not with you,' said Leo, unable to conceal his impatience.

Harry shook his head. He was beyond speech. Echoing in his head was the lyric of an old Dionne number he had played as recently as last weekend. A line about all the stars that never were, who wound up parking cars and pumping gas. And all at once, he realised that he knew who had murdered Ray Brill - and why.

Twenty minutes later he was back in the Land of the Dead. He'd left Leo Devaney at the record fair, bewildered by his sudden urge to get away as soon as he had paid for the old record.

'It's not in great nick,' said the stallholder as he took the money.

'Doesn't matter,' Harry had said before he bade Leo a hasty farewell. From a payphone outside he made a quick call to Kim Lawrence to check one fact, then hurried through the city streets towards the river, scarcely aware of the steadily falling snow.

Once underground, he bustled through the familiar passageways. Everywhere was quiet. Jock was at his desk as usual. He looked up in surprise as Harry entered his domain and pushed the half-moon spectacles on to his forehead.

'What brings you here? Have you got some more news?'

Harry registered that the little Scot sounded exhausted. For once Jock was giving no sign that he relished the prospect of detective talk.

'Ray Brill is dead.'

'What? Good grief. How did it happen? Did he fall off Southport Pier last night in a drunken stupor?'

'No, someone called on him at home and bashed his head in, then set the place alight to make it look as if he'd died in an accidental fire.'

Jock scratched his bald head. 'Arson? I can't believe that. Surely there's some mistake?'

'No mistake,' said Harry. 'Except that the murderer got into a rut. He repeated himself once too often.'

Jock stared at him. 'You're not talking sense.

'I only wish that were true. But you see, I've finally figured out what happened. Ernest Miller lost interest in the Sefton Park case because he learned about another unsolved crime. And on this occasion, he was actually told who the culprit was. Hence he had to die. Ray Brill was the only other person in the world who knew and it was simply too dangerous to allow him to survive.'

'What do you mean?'

Harry sighed. He slipped the long-player out of its polythene bag and pointed to the photograph on the front cover. 'I mean that the moment I recognised you, I realised you must have been the one who killed Ray Brill. And realised that your real name must be Ian McCalliog - although at one time everyone knew you better as Ian Brill.'

Chapter Twenty-Five

but I have not altogether escaped punishment'

The bewilderment on Jock's face slowly gave way to fear. He half-rose to his feet, then seemed to think better of it and sank back into his chair. Harry could sense his desperate efforts to compose himself, saw his eyelids blinking as his mind whirled, trying to come to terms with the shock of discovery.

Harry looked again at the photograph on the album sleeve. Ray Brill stood with arms folded: he was acting mean and moody and not a flicker of emotion compromised his dark features. Ian Brill, born McCalliog, stood by his side, wearing a shy and boyish smile. In those days he had been as slim as a girl and his hair had been thick and wavy; his smooth chin might never once have seen a razor. But there was no mistaking him, all the same. The brown eyes had not changed and his two front teeth still overlapped.

'A long time ago,' said Jock when at last he found his voice. 'And yet I remember it as if it were yesterday.'

Harry tossed the record to one side. 'You're not the first person to find we can't escape our past.'

Jock cast a wry glance at the Ross Macdonald paperback next to his desk. 'I should have learned that from reading Lew Archer novels. Tell you one thing. I'd sooner be the detective than the detected. So how much have you worked out, how much have you guessed?'

'Enough to be sure, if not quite enough to satisfy my own inquisitive streak. Whether it will suffice for the police is a different matter. It's for them to dot every 'i' and to cross each 't'. I doubt if you've managed to kill three people without yielding a single clue.'

'Two,' said Jock quickly. 'There were only two murders. Miller died by accident. A lucky chance, as I thought at the time.'

Harry shook his head. 'I wish you hadn't told me so many lies.'

'What do you expect? I've always been a survivor. Confession is for the weak.'

'And the innocent?' demanded Harry, bitterness rising for a moment to the surface. 'People like Edwin Smith?'

Jock shrugged. His confidence seemed to be returning and he ventured a small smile. 'Pity he didn't cough to the murder of Warren Hull whilst he was at it. But you didn't answer me. What put you on the track?'

'Ray Brill made enemies easily, but in all his fifty years no-one had hated him enough to kill him. So I asked myself why he had been murdered now. I'd solved the Sefton Park case - '

'What?' Jock was genuinely amazed.

'Oh yes,' said Harry. Despite his tension, he was unable to resist the temptation of a devastating throwaway line. 'Carole's own father strangled her. It's a long story. Another time, perhaps.'

'I doubt if there'll be another time for you and me,' said Jock.

'You may be right. Anyway, I'd learned that Guy Jeffries did murder his own daughter and he was in his grave, safe from retribution in this world at least. The way I saw it, if Ray hadn't murdered Carole, and had no cause to shield anyone else, there must be another reason for his death. Similarly, the motive for that mysterious visit to Miller on the day he died could not be connected with the Sefton Park case. Yet Miller did seem to have stumbled on some sort of secret. I remembered how he seemed almost to have lost interest in the identity of Carole's killer when I met him in the park - which was immediately after he had talked to Ray Brill. I wondered what Ray might have told him.'

'But Ray didn't say anything to you about Warren Hull.'

'No, because you had already warned him to keep his mouth shut. I knew a little about Hull's death, though, and although everyone had written it off as a gay killing of no account which would never be solved, when I asked myself why someone might murder for the sake of self-preservation, it occurred to me that Hull's death might hold the key. Miller had an obsession with perfect crimes. If Ray had spilled a few beans about Hull's death, he might have found that more interesting even than his investigation into the Sefton Park case.'

Jock indicated the record sleeve. 'When did you identify me as Ian?'

'Within the past hour. I'd come round to the view that Ray knew who had killed Hull and had kept quiet for purposes of his own. Suppose the culprit was still around, who might it be? I was still groping in the dark until I saw the record sleeve. When I realised who you were...'

'The pieces of the puzzle all fell into place?' asked Jock with a wry grin.

Harry forced a smile. On the way over here, he had been dreading the prospect of a confrontation with a man he had liked, had been far from clear in his own mind what he hoped to achieve. At last he was beginning to relax a little. He wanted Jock to fill in the gaps of the story and thought he could persuade him to do so. 'I don't believe Ross Macdonald would ever have sunk so far as to use that hackneyed phrase, but you have the right idea.'

'I told myself not to underestimate you, though - don't take this the wrong way - it's easily done.'

'Once it dawned on me how careful you had been not to tell me you were Ian Brill, I found it hard to believe there wasn't a guilty explanation. Most former stars I've ever met still hanker after the limelight and I couldn't quite imagine you as a kind of subterranean Greta Garbo. Even assuming you genuinely wanted to forget about your days as a pop star, why not say something when we talked about the Brill Brothers?'

'I toyed with the idea, but the last thing I wanted was for you to get too close to the truth.'

'Which is why you took pains to keep tabs on my own nosing around.'

'My interest wasn't entirely spurious,' said Jock. 'I did find the Jeffries case intriguing. I agree with Miller: people who get away with murder have a special fascination.'

'I guessed that when I told you I was going to see Ray, you tipped him off. Presumably you'd been in contact recently, as a result of Miller's investigations.'

'You're right, though the night I murdered him was the first time we'd met face to face in over twenty years.'

'Quite a way to renew an acquaintance. Anyway, Ray said something to me that seemed to clinch your involvement. I'd introduced myself simply as a solicitor called Devlin. I don't flatter myself that I'm a household name in Southport. Frankly, I'm scarcely a household name in my own flat.'

'You do yourself an injustice. I've heard other solicitors talk about you even down here, you have a reputation for never letting go. You intrigue me, though. What clue did Ray give?'

'At one point, he called me Mister Harry Devlin. The significance of it didn't strike me at once, but later on I asked myself: how did he know I was called Harry? Miller might have mentioned me to him, but you were a likelier candidate. I told you the previous day that I would be driving up to Southport to see Ray. The odds were that you had tipped him off. No wonder he didn't seem too surprised to see me.'

'Simple as that, eh? And I thought I'd been so careful.'

'I decided to call on Ray to ask him how he knew my name, but of course, you beat me to it.'

'So where do we go from here?'

'Let's talk about that in a little while. First, I'd like to satisfy my own curiosity. Obviously, there's a good deal I don't know.'

'And you seem to be short of evidence, as well,' said Jock, stroking his beard.

'You know as well as I do that when the police take a close look at everything that has taken place, it's a pound to a penny that they'll be able to tie you in with Ray's murder. I see it as a panic measure, am I right?'

'I had no alternative. He'd kept his mouth shut about Warren for thirty years, but I couldn't trust him any longer. He was down on his luck, he knew I had a few pennies put by. He saw me as his pension. I couldn't have that, Harry, I'm sure you understand.'

'How did he know you had killed Hull?'

'I admitted it, of course.' Jock shook his head. 'I was only a boy, remember. A frightened wee boy.'

'What happened?'

'Warren fancied us, of course. He had a reputation for sleeping with his acts, though I didn't know that when he signed us up. In the early days, he had his eyes on Ray, and Ray was crafty enough to hold him off whilst encouraging him to think that his defence might one day slip. To keep him interested in us, that's all. No-one was straighter than Ray, in the sexual sense at least.'

'But in the end Warren turned his attention to you?'

'When we started to hit the big time - or the biggest time we ever hit, at any rate - Ray could afford to be brave and to tell Warren where to get off. The man was no fool, he knew he couldn't risk exposure. So he started to spend more time with me.'

'And you were glad of his attention?'

Jock gave him a sharp glance. 'What makes you say that?'

'I've never thought about it coherently until now, but I suppose I've sensed subconsciously that you may be gay. You're not married, are you?'

'So what?'

Jock had raised his voice and Harry guessed he had touched a nerve. Well, this was no time for tact. 'And I guess you like the company of young boys like Adrian, your saxophonist friend.'

'There's been nothing between Adrian and me,' said Jock fiercely.

'But you wouldn't have said no, had the opportunity arisen, would you?' Harry's tone softened. 'I suppose society was different in the sixties. Gay sex was a vice. You were young and unsure of yourself, easy meat for an experienced predator like Warren Hull.'

'He was a cruel man,' said Jock. Suddenly the fight seemed to have gone out of him and he closed his eyes for a moment as he cast his mind back down the years. 'Selfish and cruel. I was flattered by his overtures, yet frightened at the same time. One night he invited me back to his flat on a pretext. I think I knew what would happen, but I couldn't find it in me to refuse.'

'And?'

'He raped me,' said Jock flatly. 'If I'd dared to hope for anything, it was for romance. I'd left my family behind in Glasgow, come down to Liverpool to make my fortune, changed my name. I found it a lonely place and, once I got to know him, I disliked Ray. You could say I was vulnerable.'

'Not as vulnerable as Warren Hull when he was lying naked on his own bed.'

'No,' admitted Jock, 'but he was a brutal man and my life was in ruins. Certainly, it was never the same again. While he was sleeping, I picked up a lampstand and just lashed out. God, I've never seen so much blood and mess. I watched as the life oozed out of him and laughed hysterically. It took me half an hour to come to my senses, but at last I did so. As I said, my survival instinct is well developed, it has had to be. So I cleaned myself up...'

'I gather it was a frenzied attack,' said Harry, watching carefully for the reaction.

'So the papers said. I suppose it was a case of the famous red mist - another phrase you'll never find in the pages of Ross Macdonald, eh? Afterwards I blotted the whole thing out of my mind. You have no choice, otherwise it's simply too much to bear. I took care to remove any trace of my presence - fingerprints and all that stuff - and then I scurried off home. No-one saw me.'

'Did you have an alibi?'

'Thanks to Ray.'

Harry stared. 'How come?'

'As soon as the news came out and we had a chance to be alone together, he confronted me. He was no fool, he knew that Hull had been chasing me. I soon broke down under his questioning and told him the truth. I begged him for mercy and I'll never forget the moment when he laughed in my face and promised that of course he would say we'd spent the evening together. He kept his word and the police were never any the wiser.'

'Why was he willing to save your neck? You've admitted you were hardly bosom buddies.'

'He pretended he was glad that I'd been a worm who turned. Warren Hull made his flesh creep, he never concealed that. The two of them were perfectly matched, I've often thought, they were both trying to screw each other for everything they could get.'

'And the real reason?'

'Simple. The publicity would have destroyed him. He realised that if I were charged with the murder, the bad press would have dragged him down with me. He reckoned we were successful enough to prosper without Warren, but much as he despised me, he knew that he couldn't risk losing both his manager and me and still hope to keep the hits rolling. So for the sake of the Brill Brothers, he lied through his teeth and I was saved. Only trouble was, after we lost Warren, we soon stopped making the charts.'

'The day you killed him was also the day the music died?'

'You could say so - though Warren was no Buddy Holly.'

'And in the end the Brill Brothers broke up anyway.'

'Yes, I was sick of it all. The phoney glamour, the stupid screaming schoolgirls. And most of all I was sick of Ray. Never mind that he'd given me the alibi, it came to a point when we couldn't stand the sight of each other. I'd done well at school in Scotland before I moved south, and now I had the chance of a job in the shipping business. We were never going to recapture the glory days, so I jumped at it. I found I enjoyed the book-keeping. When you've killed another human being, Harry, I suppose something dies inside you as well. It was enough for me to play around with figures in a ledger. In time I did well, earned promotion, moved to a better position with the Byzantium Line. Where I stayed until they made me redundant.'

'So you finished up here?'

'That's right. And let me tell you, I've loved it. I'm my own boss in my own kingdom. No-one bothers me and I bother no-one. And I enjoy meeting the likes of you.'

'A pity I'm even keener on playing the detective than you.'

'Yes,' said Jock sorrowfully, 'it is.'

'Tell me about Miller. How did he find you?'

'He rang me at home out of the blue, said he thought a chat might be to our mutual advantage. From the moment I heard his voice, I knew he meant trouble. He'd met Ray and pestered him about Carole Jeffries. Ray was pissed and must have said something to suggest he knew someone who had got away with murder. Miller wormed enough information out of him to track me down. There aren't many McCalliogs in the Merseyside phone book. I already knew from you that someone was sniffing round the Sefton Park case.'

'You arranged to call on him?'

'Yes. I rang Ray first to find out what he'd been saying. He was relatively sober and he admitted he'd been indiscreet. His attitude was devil-may-care, as if after all this time nobody would care what had happened to a man like Warren Hull. I felt I must meet Miller, find out what he wanted. I expected a straightforward blackmailer, but Miller was something else, one of the strangest men I ever met. You know, I don't think he was interested in money. What intrigued him was simply the idea of committing a murder and then escaping detection. He seemed to gloat over his knowledge about what I had done, and he was more anxious to discover the details of the crime than to make anything from it.'

'How did he die?'

Jock spoke rapidly, as if despite everything he was still anxious to exonerate himself from blame. 'It was so stupid. My nerves were at breaking point. I'd kept my secret for so long and now this old fool had discovered it. I asked him bluntly what he wanted. He laughed and said he would settle for the pleasure of keeping me guessing about what he proposed to do. In a fury, I grabbed him by the scruff of the neck and before I knew what was happening, he was having a fit, couldn't breathe.'

'He suffered badly from asthma.'

'He broke free but was fighting for air. All at once he lost his balance and hit his head on the side of the fireplace. It was so stupid, I couldn't believe it. For the second time in thirty years I was in another man's home, watching him die.'

'And you did nothing to help?' asked Harry coldly.

Jock spread his arms. 'What could I do? I was in a state of shock and in any event it was soon all over. Tell you the truth, after a couple of minutes I said a little prayer of thanks. Everything seemed to have worked out perfectly.'

'Except for Miller.'

'He was no good, Harry. Like Warren Hull and Ray, he was no loss to the world.'

'I take it you were the one who burgled my office?'

'Stupid, of course, but I panicked. The problem I had was that I just didn't know what was in Cyril Tweats' file. I'd never dreamed it would contain anything damaging to me - why else do you think I let you have it that time? But it began to prey on my mind. I started wondering whether it might contain information I would prefer you not to know. Above all, I didn't know what Ray had said during the police enquiry. He hadn't fingered me for Warren's murder, but he still might have revealed more than I'd have liked. It was important to me that you shouldn't realise that Ian Brill and I were one and the same. As you know, Jim stores spare copies of internal documents down here - including details of your burglar alarm system and how to disable it. When I couldn't find the file in your room that night, I feared the worst. Then lo and behold, you handed it back to me for safekeeping! I needn't have worried after all.'

'And Ray? Another unlucky break?'

'No need to take that tone, Harry. It was obvious I had a problem with Ray. I couldn't be sure what he would say or do - especially if you turned up and started to sweet-talk him. I went to see him in Southport. He'd been drinking, as per usual. He was hostile, in fact he was downright offensive. Kept saying he owed me nothing. I pleaded, I cajoled, but he started to tease me by speculating aloud how much the tabloid press would pay for his story, doubting whether I could outbid them. I couldn't take it any longer. I hit him hard a couple of times; the second blow knocked him unconscious. You wouldn't think it to look at me today, but I boxed at school, won a schoolboy title. Ray may have been bigger than me, but I've downed better men than him.'

'And then you set fire to the flat and tried to make it look as though the blaze had started by accident. Not easy to fool trained investigators, Jock. What were you thinking of?'

'All I knew was that I had to do my best to cover my tracks. Ideally, the police would regard it as an accident. Failing that, I thought the fire would destroy any evidence of my presence in the flat.'

Harry sighed. 'Three deaths in the victims homes. Your *modus operandi* never varied.'

Jock climbed to his feet and stood, hands on hips, looking round the Land of the Dead. The deedboxes, the old files, the detritus from cases long forgotten. 'You're accusing me of a lack of originality? Somehow I feel that's the least of my problems.'

Harry looked him in the eye. 'I'm sorry I've become the greatest of them.'

'Me too,' said Jock. 'I liked you, Harry, I really did.'

A subtle change in his tone alerted Harry and he dodged to one side as the balled-up fist flew towards him. It caught him only a glancing blow, but it was enough to make him stagger. Before he could defend himself, Jock followed up with punches to the stomach and kidneys, sickening blows. He felt himself gagging and, although he flailed with his arms in a vain attempt to save himself, he could not help crumpling to the ground.

As his head hit the concrete floor, the pain made him shout aloud. For a few seconds he was too dazed to be capable of coherent thought. When he managed to raise his head a fraction and blink away the tears, he saw Jock had grasped the handle of the heavy-duty truck he kept parked at the corner of the room. He was lifting on to it an old six-foot filing cabinet.

'Jock, don't be stupid!'

The little clerk steadied his load. He was panting with the effort - and his tension. 'I told you before - my survival instinct is well developed.'

The truck needed oiling. Its wheels screeched as Jock began to manoeuvre it towards where Harry lay. Harry tried to haul himself to his feet. Every bone in his body seemed to be hurting and all his strength had drained away. He scrabbled with his fingers in the dirt, but he could hardly lift his chin off the ground, let alone struggle to his feet. He could see Jock looking at him, concentrating intently on the task in hand. The filing cabinet was wobbling on the lip of the truck. It must be packed with suspensions full of thick old files ready to archive. Better not to think what would happen when Jock dropped it on him.

'I'm sorry about this, Harry, I really am,' gasped Jock.

'Let's talk about it,' said Harry, barely able to make himself heard. 'Surely...'

'No, the time for talking has gone.'

The truck came nearer. Harry could see its vast load looming over him, ready to topple him into darkness.

'Jock!'

The little man spun round. He took one hand off the handle of the trolley and the filing cabinet crashed down on to the ground, the sharp edge of its bottom end only inches from Harry's nose. Dust blew into Harry's face and he shut his eyes for a second, still half-expecting permanent oblivion. But he had recognised the voice and never had he been so glad to hear it.

Kim Lawrence was standing in the entrance to Jock's domain. By her side was Adrian the saxophone enthusiast. Amazement was scrawled over their faces at the sight which greeted them.

With a roar of fury, like some wild animal, Jock ran past them and out of the door, into the maze of passages that made up the Land of the Dead. After a moment's pause, Adrian thundered after him.

Harry found himself looking into Kim's eyes. There were so many things he suddenly wanted to say, but his head and body were aching and words were beyond him.

But not beyond Kim. She strode towards him and stood with folded arms above his prostrate form.

'So,' she said, 'another fine mess you've got yourself into.'

Chapter Twenty-Six

since for the rest of my days, I am condemned to stay in this house,

'I miss him, you know,' said Gloria Hegg.

It was Sunday afternoon, a week after Harry's last visit to the little house in Everton and once again he was sitting in her armchair, drinking her tea and offering her sympathy.

He was not quite sure why he had come back here. Miller's death had not increased his liking for the man and, as the will had never been signed, he had no obligations as executor. Besides, if Miller had not poked his nose into other people's affairs, Ray Brill would still be alive and Jock would still be presiding over the Land of the Dead, his murderous youth no more than a distant memory.

Yet Edwin Smith's name would not have been cleared and the truth about a terrible crime would have remained hidden, as so often it does. Harry felt he owed Miller something at least. Besides, the man still baffled him. He felt he had never been able to understand what made him tick. Why was he so fascinated by cases like the Sefton Park Strangling and the murder of Warren Hull, cases which had never been regarded as classic mysteries? What was the appeal to him of the unsolved crime?

Perhaps by looking through his papers, it might be possible to glean some clues as to what had made Ernest Miller tick. Harry was uncomfortably aware that in the Land of the Dead, his curiosity had nearly cost him dear. This would prove a safer investigation.

He had called Kim to check that he was right in believing that Jock's surname was McCalliog. Although he had not explained his reason for asking, she had been sufficiently intrigued to tell Adrian that they should now start ferrying over to archive a load of files that had cluttered up her office for far too long. In the past few days Harry had sent up many a silent prayer of thanks for that.

Adrian had brought Jock down with a rugby tackle in the passage leading to the outside world, and held him while Kim phoned 999 on her mobile to fetch the police.

Once under arrest, the little archivist had spoken as freely to his interrogators as he had to Harry. But it would be a long time before Kevin Walter, now stricken by paraplegia, would be fit to plead. MOJO were no longer planning to use Kevin's experiences with the South West Lancs Major Enquiry Squad as a case study for their workshops. Harry had also made it clear to Kim that he did not want any public discussion about the Guy Jeffries case, at least while Kathleen was still alive.

'I know she should not have kept quiet,' he said, 'but what purpose would it serve during the last years of her life to turn her into a public outcast? In a way, she was Guy's victim too.'

At first Kim had disagreed. 'But what about Edwin Smith? His name was dragged through the mud; surely he deserves to have his innocence made known?'

'Who would benefit? He's dead, so is the one person who always stood by him. Let it rest, while Kathleen is around. She's suffered punishment enough.'

He would never have the chance to tell Vincent Deysbrook what he had learned. The previous morning, he had rung Jasmine House to see how the old detective was feeling. In their brief acquaintance, he had come to have a grudging respect for the man: the mistakes he had made had at least been honest.

'I'm sorry,' said the deputy matron who took his call, 'Vincent passed away yesterday. It was quite peaceful at the end.'

A merciful release, Harry supposed as he put the receiver down. He had come to the view that when life has absolutely nothing more to offer, it ceases to be worth striving for mere survival.

He had not managed to resist the urge to tell Cyril Tweats of Edwin Smith's innocence. On calling round at the Aigburth villa, he had again been made welcome with tea and biscuits. Having heard Harry out, Cyril had simply smiled his amiable smile and said, 'Well, well, well. Who would have thought it?' Water off a duck's back. Harry had made his excuses and left. He decided he would not be calling there again.

The doorbell rang and Gloria sprang to her feet. 'This will be your friend, I expect.'

Harry followed her to the door and introduced her to Kim. He had thought about inviting Jim Crusoe to have a look with him at Miller's effects, but he could readily imagine the big man's baffled shake of the head. Jim had seemed distracted lately, although Harry could not guess why. Thank God, at least, that he had not pursued the idea of the promotional video filmed by Benny Frederick. When he had suggested to Kim that she might care to accompany him over the weekend, however, she had been quick to say yes.

'Truth is,' she said, 'I'm almost as inquisitive as you. Bear in mind I've never even met Miller and yet he seems to have been such an extraordinary man, fascinated by miscarriage cases. It will be marvellous if MOJO can claim on his estate, after all.'

This had been Jim's idea. He had remembered the small print of the old doctrine of escheat. Since Miller had clearly intended the charity to benefit, the law might permit his wishes to be given effect.

'I find it hard to think of him as a philanthropist, somehow.'

'Face it, you don't have the foggiest what his motives were.'

'For me, that's part of the interest. I'd love to get an insight into his mind, to discover what made him the man he was.'

'And you seriously think you'll find that out simply by going through what he left behind?'

'Unlikely,' Harry admitted, 'but you will come anyway, won't you?'

'Of course.'

Now here she was, looking good in Aran sweater and jeans. Accompanied by Gloria Hegg, they opened up next door and Harry made at once for the study on the first floor which still overflowed with Miller's books and papers. There was an immense amount of junk: old bills, receipts and scribble about household trivia as well as sheet after sheet of foolscap on which Miller had jotted small bits of information about the strangling in Sefton Park. He might not have deduced that Guy was the killer, Harry thought, but had his attention not been distracted by Ray Brill's revelations, he would surely have done so in time.

Presently, he turned again to the filing cabinet he had looked through on his previous visit. As he glanced again at the folder titles noted on the suspension tabs, a thought occurred to him. Miller had set out in his will instructions a list of all his assets. Yet other than saving certificates, there was nothing that one would normally describe as a long-term investment. He slipped out the folder that bore that description and found that it contained a thin lined notebook. A glance at half a dozen lines of the opening page made him catch his breath. He read them again to make sure he was imagining nothing. But there was no doubt that they were Miller's words, written in his characteristically over-ornate script and style. Harry could almost hear them being uttered in that odd, pedantic manner Miller had. And he realised that the long-term investment Miller had made in his own life had been one that explained his preoccupation with unsolved crime.

'Kim!'

She had been downstairs, chatting to Gloria about Miller, but came running up in response to his cry.

'What is it?'

Harry handed her the notebook. 'Look at this.'

She turned to page one and stared at the title. *Confession To Murder*. Good grief, did Miller write this?'

'No question.'

She glanced down the first few paragraphs and whistled. 'I don't believe it!'

'I think you should,' said Harry quietly. 'It's quite short. Would you like to read it aloud to me?'

She cleared her throat and gave him a wry smile. 'Are you sitting comfortably? Then I'll begin.'

Chapter Twenty-Seven

I *killed her many years ago, but I shall never forget the day of her death, when I broke forever with the past and made my murderous dream come true. We always bury our darkest secrets and I feel no sense of guilt at all. I doubt whether people would believe me even if I admitted everything.*

I shall put the facts down on paper so that when my own life is at an end, people can judge my confession to the ultimate crime

In the aftermath of death, I relished the sense of having settled old scores: she was always so provocative. She had only herself to blame: the fatal outcome was inevitable and I had to gamble everything, hoping that luck would be on my side.

People talk about justice, divine retribution. Yet I have concealed a most terrible crime and I may succeed in carrying my secret to the grave. For the record, I do not regret the murder at all, but I have not altogether escaped punishment, since for the rest of my days, I am condemned to stay in this house, where buried beneath the cellar floor lies the bludgeoned body of my wife Marlene.

Excerpt from *The Devil in Disguise*

Prologue

*H*e had dreamed of this.

Her parting words echoed around the cellar. 'Don't go away.'

As if he would. As if he could. Listening to her high heels click-click-click up the stone steps, he smiled to himself. He could have sworn he heard her choke back a grunt of pleasure at the prospect of what lay in store. The door closed behind her: was that a key turning in the lock, or just wishful thinking? He had always wanted to be her prisoner. And tonight his imagination was working overtime.

The steel handcuffs were cutting into his wrists, but for him the sensation was exquisite. At last she had consented to play the game. She seemed different, somehow, as if the fantasy excited her as much as he had ever hoped.

Waiting for her return, he stretched his limbs. She had snapped the other half of each pair of cuffs around the hooks set into the wall a little above head height. He let his mind wander. This was an old room; perhaps eighteenth-century merchants had once tethered their own slaves here. Those poor devils would not have chosen such a fate, but he luxuriated in it. He could move his trunk and legs, feel the warmth of the sheepskin rug against his feet. Presently she would release him and they would make love with wild passion.

Although he was in the heart of Liverpool, he might have been marooned on a Pacific atoll for all that he was aware of the world above ground. It was night-time in the city, but he could hear no voices or traffic noise, nothing but the faint buzz of an unseen fly. The air was damp and musty but he did not care. This was as close to heaven as he was ever likely to come.

The fly landed on his chest and he blew it off. She was taking her time, he thought. Impossible to understand: she had promised to be back within a minute, once she had checked that the front door was locked. They did not want any unexpected callers, not tonight of all nights.

He opened his eyes and tried adjusting to the gloom. An unshaded bulb glowed overhead, but most of the room was in deep shadow. Straight ahead, she had propped the dusty old mirror. All the better to see everything with, she had said. She had written something in lipstick on the splintered surface of the glass and he craned his neck so that he could read it.

YOU KILLED HIM, YOU BASTARD

It was as though a donkey had kicked him in the balls. He blinked once, twice, unable to believe the message in the words. Was his mind playing games of its own? He screwed up his eyes so hard that the muscles hurt and looked again.

YOU KILLED HIM, YOU BASTARD

It couldn't be true. She was teasing him. He sucked the moist air into his lungs and held his breath, telling himself that she was on her way back, that it was all some kind of joke. But in the end he had to exhale.

Slowly, experimentally, he tried to move his wrists. The handcuffs did not give. His skin was beginning to itch. The unseen fly was buzzing in the shadows, as if in mocking reminder that it was free.

Time passed. His breath was coming in short shallow gasps. He did not understand what was happening. Everything had seemed so perfect. Yet now he was limp and cold and afraid. And the heaven he had dreamed of had turned into his own private hell.

Chapter One

A solitary candle lit the darkness, allowing Harry Devlin to see the man in crimson robes. The sickly smell of incense hung in the air. The high priest was standing in front of the altar, his arm raised. As the flame flickered, Harry caught sight of a gleaming blade.

'Blood is the sacred life-force in both man and beast,' a disembodied voice intoned. 'The rite of sacrifice enables gods to live and thus man and nature may survive.'

A small bundle lay trussed up on the altar. The whimper of a child cut through the silence. Harry's stomach lurched and instinctively he took a pace forward. Suddenly he remembered where he was. He halted, feeling foolish. Why did his imagination always run away with him? He was a grown man, a solicitor of the Supreme Court, supposed to be dispassionate and the master of his emotions. Yet he could not help shivering when he felt a touch upon his spine.

'Frightening, isn't it?'

He spun round. A woman was studying him intently, as if he were a specimen in a glass case. His cheeks felt hot and he said awkwardly, 'For a moment, I almost believed...'

'That's what we like to hear, Harry.' She bent her head towards his and added in a whisper, 'You know, the sign outside does make it clear that the exhibition isn't suitable for small children. Parents never cease to amaze me.'

A harassed teenage girl hurried past them, dragging a pushchair. Its occupant's whimper had matured into a wail. Harry always admired the fortitude of those who had children, but he kept quiet, guessing that Frances Silverwood would regard his reaction as another example of the inability of his head to rule his heart.

'Very lifelike,' he said. 'I know a judge who might be the twin of your high priest. Come to think of it, I'm not sure which one is the dummy.'

'Sorry to keep you waiting after I begged you to come over here,' she said, raising her voice to compete with the loudspeaker commentary. 'I had to take a call from my opposite number at the Smithsonian.'

'When they told me you were engaged I thought I'd take a look,' Harry said. He gestured to the sign by the entrance: *Understanding the Supernatural.* 'I wondered if it might give me a clue to the workings of the British legal system.'

'Bad day in court?' she asked over her shoulder as she led him through a door marked *Museum Staff Only*. He followed her down a long corridor so still that the slap of her flat-heeled shoes against the floor tiles sounded unnaturally loud.

He gave a rueful grin. 'The woman I was acting for was found guilty of *not* being a witch.'

She paused in mid-stride. 'You're teasing me.'

'Lawyer's honour. When witchcraft ceased to be a hanging offence, Parliament made it a crime to pretend to use sorcery. So being a *genuine* witch became a defence to the charge. My client was accused of casting a spell on her best friend's unfaithful husband, to make him love her again.'

'Good God. What happened?'

'The magic didn't work. To make matters worst, the friend found my client in bed with her man. There was a fight, the police were called and a prosecutor with time on his hands decided to test out the law on fraudulent mediums.'

'Only in Liverpool.'

Frances laughed, a rich deep sound. On a bad day, Harry thought, she might be mistaken for a witch herself. She was striking rather than beautiful in appearance, with a high forehead and sharp chin. As he had got to know her, he had begun to realise that her

258

abrupt manner was a mask for shyness. He'd grown to like her and to believe it would do her good to laugh a little more often.

They arrived at a door whose sign bore her name and title: *Keeper of Ethnographical Artefacts.* She waved him inside and as he took a seat on a hard plastic chair, his eye caught a ghastly face staring at him from a display cabinet on the wall. It was a shrunken brown head with flowing black locks and its ravaged features had formed into the expression of a soul in torment. Harry's flesh prickled. With an effort he tore his eyes away and focused his gaze on the Native American portrait calendar on the wall behind Frances's desk.

'Sorry to startle you,' she said briskly. 'I should have given you advance warning. I'm very fond of Uncle Joe, but I tend to take him for granted nowadays.'

Trying to make light of it, he said, 'I ought to expect something out of the ordinary in a place like this. But why isn't he out on display?'

'Preservation is a problem with human remains,' she said crisply. 'Many of them were brought over from the colonies in the nineteenth century. We had to inter a number of Uncle Joe's colleagues in the local cemetery when the smell became too much to bear.'

Harry shuddered and glanced again at the shrunken head. Once it had belonged to a human being who lived and breathed. He felt his gorge rising.

Frances said, 'You don't approve?'

'Perhaps I'm too squeamish.'

'He keeps me company,' she said with a shrug.

Forcing a smile, he said, 'He looks even sterner than Luke Dessaur when a trustee turns up late for a meeting.'

To his surprise, she flushed. 'Strange you should say that. Luke is the reason why I asked you to come over here at such short notice.'

'I assumed that it was in connection with the meeting tonight.'

'It is. You see, Luke's told me that he's unable to come. The first time he's ever missed since he became chairman. I'm worried about him, Harry.'

He stared. 'Why's that?'

'I think - he's afraid of something.'

'*Afraid?*'

Harry did not try to hide his incredulity. Could she be joking? Her earnest face gave no hint of it: no smile, no twinkle in the deep-set eyes. She was leaning forward, chin cradled in her hands, elbows touching her overflowing in-tray. Her whole body was rigid and he could sense the tension in her shoulder blades, almost taste the dryness of her lips.

Yet the thought of the chairman of the Kavanaugh Trust experiencing fear was comic in its absurdity. In Luke's presence, Harry always found himself fretting about the shine on his shoes or the length of his hair. Luke was the sort who had a fetish about punctuality and never took the minutes of the last trustees' meeting as read. He was capable of great personal kindness, but Harry had never heard him split an infinitive and suspected that he would rather face torture than surrender the crease in his trousers. What could perturb such a man - other than, perhaps, the prospect of having to act on Harry's advice?

'What exactly is the problem?'

Harry noticed a tear in the corner of Frances's eye. Hot with embarrassment, he studied his palms whilst she dabbed at her face with a tissue.

'I wish I knew. Last week he and I went to a rehearsal of a musical the Trust is subsidising. He seemed preoccupied, but then, he's hardly an extrovert. After a quick drink, I left him in the bar having a chat with the producer. I had to be up early for a train trip to London the next morning. When I arrived back, I gave him a ring at home. He was out, so I left a message on his answering machine. He didn't call back the next day, which puzzled me. It was so unlike him.'

Harry nodded. Luke always returned calls and responded to letters without delay. Something of a paragon. And as a client, therefore, something of a pain as well. Most of the people Harry acted for were consistent only in their incompetence. The previous day he'd been called out to advise a burglar arrested after being spotted by a woman whose house he had robbed the night before. She had recognised him because he was wearing her husband's clothes.

'I called again. Same thing. This time he did ring back. He sounded agitated and I asked if he was all right, but he assured me everything was fine. I thought he might be ill and not looking after himself properly. That night I dialled his home at around ten thirty, but again I could only get the answering machine. The day after, I bumped into him in the street as I was coming back from a meeting at the Albert Dock.'

'How did he seem?'

'His face was like chalk and he'd been gnawing at his fingernails. He looked as though he hadn't slept a wink since I'd last seen him. His hands kept trembling and his manner was twitchy. Suddenly I realised that he wasn't ill. He was worried sick.' She let out a breath. 'I said as much and he bit my head off. Told me not to interfere in his private business, said he could look after himself perfectly well. He'd never felt better. I was dumbstruck.'

'I bet.' Harry began to realise why Frances was concerned. Luke being rude? The Archbishop of Canterbury was more likely to let rip with a string of obscenities.

'After a couple of minutes, he calmed down and apologised. He did admit he had things on his mind, but said I shouldn't trouble myself about them. He would be fine. And that was that. There was nothing more I could do. Luke's lived alone ever since Gwendoline died. And he's proud, too. He wouldn't seek help even if he really needed it.'

'He's no fool.'

'But people don't always behave rationally, do they?' Frances said.

Don't I know it? thought Harry. Yet Luke Dessaur was one person who had always struck him as supremely rational. He had been personnel director for an arts and heritage charity before taking early retirement at fifty, weary of the endless round of redundancies and budget cuts, and devoting himself to the Kavanaugh Trust. 'So what did you do?'

'I called round at his house this lunch-time. I rang his bell and rapped on the door until my knuckles were sore, but there was no answer. Then a woman passed by. His next-door neighbour. She said that if I was hoping to find Luke, I was out of luck. She'd seen him driving off a few minutes earlier. He'd put an overnight case into his car.'

'Observant lady.'

'She's an old gossip with too much time on her hands,' Frances said. 'Though who am I to talk? I suppose you think I'm overreacting.'

'Not at all.'

What he really thought was that Frances's dismay revealed how sweet she was on Luke. He'd suspected it for a while. Looking round her office, he saw no evidence of a private life. No photographs, nothing unconnected with her work, although he knew that in her spare time she was a keen singer. He had heard her once at a private party, singing about the loss of love and loneliness. For his part, Luke had been a widower for years. Maybe she thought it time they both had a change of status.

'When I arrived back from Luke's house, there was a message from him on my voicemail. He asked me to present his apologies to the meeting tonight. He spoke in a jerky way, as if his nerves were in pieces. I called his mobile this time and managed to catch him. Though I guessed that he regretted answering as soon as he heard it was me on the line. It was as if he'd been hoping to hear from someone else.'

'What did you say?'

'I said he needn't try to bluff me. I knew him too well not to realise he was sick with worry. I asked him to talk to me, to trust me with the problem, whatever it was. He didn't bother to deny the truth of what I was saying, but he said there was nothing I could do, nothing anyone could do. He was desperate to get off the line. Finally he said a quick goodbye and put down the phone before I could utter another word.' She groaned, put her head in her hands. 'This must all sound ridiculous to you. Am I being silly?'

'You're bound to be anxious. And confused.' Harry paused. He thought about telling her of his own last conversation with Luke Dessaur, but something held him back. 'What's the explanation for the overnight case? Is there anyone he might be visiting? What about his godson?'

'You know Ashley Whitaker?'

'Yes, I often buy books from him. I first met Luke through Ashley, as it happens - years before Crusoe and Devlin started to act for the Kavanaugh Trust.'

'Luke can't be staying with him. Ashley and his wife are attending a book fair in Canada. I remember Luke mentioning it that night at the theatre.'

'Any other lines of inquiry?'

'You sound like a policeman,' she said. 'I know you have been involved in a number of - unusual cases, but I would hate to think...'

Harry loosened his tie. The room was warmed by twin radiators and poorly ventilated. Perhaps that, and the watchful presence of Uncle Joe, explained why he felt so uncomfortable. 'Luke's behaviour is a mystery.'

'Yes, but it's not...'

Again, she allowed her voice to trail away. Harry could guess the reason. She had meant to say: *it's not a* murder *mystery*. He said gently, 'Anyone else who might be worth contacting?'

She pushed a hand through her thick black hair. 'He's a good man, as you well know, but I wouldn't say that he has many friends. He and Gwendoline lived for each other. Since she died, I think he has led a solitary life. But I would have expected him to let me know if anything was amiss.'

Harry caught the eye of the shrunken head and quickly glanced away again. How could Frances concentrate on her work with that face staring down at her? 'Has he seemed out of sorts before?'

'As you might expect, this business with Vera Blackhurst has appalled him. He is very suspicious of her. He's even said that the Trust's survival might depend on the outcome of her claim. The Trust means a great deal to him - and we are desperate for money. But I can't believe there is any reason for him simply to... well, to act as though he is personally under threat.'

'Have you discussed this with the other trustees?'

'Only with Matthew Cullinan and even with him I was rather circumspect. He oozed charm as usual, but he obviously thought I was making a mountain out of a molehill. Perhaps I am. Even so, I wanted to have a word with you before tonight's meeting. I was sure that you would listen to me patiently. As you have. Sorry to come crying on your shoulder.'

She smiled ruefully and Harry found himself having to fight the urge to give her hand a comforting squeeze.

She wasn't his type, but he had a lot of time for Frances Silverwood.

'I'm sure Luke will be fine,' he said. But he wasn't sure that he really believed it.

She stood up. 'Thank you for hearing me out, Harry. I expect this will probably all blow over and I'll have made a complete fool of myself in Matthew Cullinan's eyes. Worrying over nothing.'

Harry stood up and took a last glance at the shrunken head. It stared back, as if to say: *You know it's right to fear the worst.*

The Making of *Yesterday's Papers*

Writing Yesterday's Papers was a hugely enjoyable experience. It was my fourth book, and – proud though I was of the first three – my aim was to step up to the next rung of the ladder as a crime novelist. One of the pleasures of writing a series of books over a number of years is that you have the chance to soak yourself in the recurring characters and their world. I felt that by now I was really getting to know Harry Devlin. In the early days, inevitably, his life had been dominated by the murder of his estranged wife Liz. Her death would continue to haunt him, but he was also moving on.

Since I was working in Liverpool, and since, like me, Harry had fond memories of the Merseybeat era, I thought it would be fun to write a book drawing on Liverpool's pop music heritage from the days of the Swinging Sixties. This idea led me naturally to a plot involving a "cold case" – long before I wrote The Coffin Trail, the first of the Lake District Mysteries which introduced, in Hannah Scarlett, a detective who leads a team specialising in unsolved crimes from the past.

The popular music of the 1960s holds a special place in my affections; so much of it was fresh and unforgettable that it is hard to surpass. And Liverpool, for several years, seemed to be at the heart of the world of pop culture. It was an exciting time in the city. The Beatles soon claimed iconic status, and the Cavern Club was legendary. I vividly remember the one and only time I saw the Beatles live – at the age of seven. They were not performing on stage, but rather opening a carnival in Northwich, the Cheshire town where I lived – presumably fulfilling a contractual obligation taken on before their breakthrough. My memory is of a colossal crowd in a modest town park that had never seen anything like it – and of the four stars in their purple suits, at constant risk of being engulfed by their adoring fans.

As well as the Beatles, countless other groups and solo singers from Merseyside had recording contracts, and a good many of them featured in the Top 20. But even more disappeared before long without trace. While driving into work in Liverpool one day, as I was planning the book in my head, I stopped at traffic lights in Aigburth. I was listening to a favourite song that I'd heard a hundred times before, "Do You Know the Way to San Jose?" It was written by Bacharach and David, the only songwriters to match Lennon and McCartney for both dominance and brilliance in the era of the Mersey Sound, when many of their hits were covered by artistes from Liverpool. There is a line in the lyric about "all the stars that never were", and as I sat in the queuing traffic, those words sparked an idea which became central to the plot.

The storyline required Harry to dig into the past, and from an early point I decided that the archives of Crusoe and Devlin would play a significant part in the events of the book. By way of research, I decided to explore my own firm's archives. Solicitors have a cautious habit of keeping their files and deeds for many years, and although in recent times many archives have been digitised, this was uncommon at the time I was writing the book. Thousands of files take up a huge amount of space, and as we did not have enough secure rooms in our offices to keep them, we rented not one, but two storage areas elsewhere in Liverpool. I had never had cause to visit these premises previously, but when I was taken on a guided tour by our archivist, I was fascinated.

The fictitious archive in the book is an amalgam of its two real-life counterparts, with a few invented extras thrown in. One of our archives was indeed underground and close to the waterfront – an extraordinary and atmospheric labyrinth. The other was located closer to the city centre, and I was told that part of the building had once been a ballroom. Both places fired my imagination. There is something emotionally, as well as physically, chilling about dank subterranean places that makes them very appealing as settings for scenes in a crime novel. So much so that I later varied the theme, and had Harry venture into Williamson's Tunnels in First Cut Is the Deepest and a disused railway tunnel in Waterloo Sunset.

Harry, like me, is interested in classic true crimes (including the extraordinary Liverpool cases of James Maybrick and William Herbert Wallace), as well as in detective mysteries. So I felt he could not possibly resist the approach made to him by Ernest Miller at the start of the story, despite Miller's unattractive personality. For the subplot featuring Miller, I was influenced by a narrative device used ingeniously by the superb Canadian writer Margaret Millar in one of her best novels, A Stranger in My Grave, which I decided to give a fresh twist. Playing a game with the structure of the story was something new for me as a writer, one of those risks that doesn't always work out – but in this case, I was very happy with the result, and the fact that I was able to deliver a twist in the very last line of the book.

A word about chronology in crime fiction. A couple of issues tend to arise. First, when characters in the present investigate a case of the past, the writer has to handle the story with care, to make sure that the gap in time does not create insuperable problems. Yesterday's Papers concerned a murder in 1964, 30 years before I started work on the book. If I were writing the story today, the material would need to be treated very differently, because so much more time has elapsed, and the people who were around in 1964 are correspondingly older, even if they're still alive. Second, there is the question of how a detective ages over the course of a series. It is a problem that Agatha Christie encountered (but ignored) with the length of Hercule Poirot's career, and that, in common with many others, Ruth Rendell has had to face with Reg Wexford. I was 32 when I first started writing about Harry; suffice to say, he has aged much less rapidly than me! At the time of Harry's last outing, in Waterloo Sunset, I acknowledged the passage of years, while compressing the interval between that book and his early cases. It is fiction, after all…

Few writers feel total satisfaction with their books; there is always something that you think you could have done better. This is certainly true of me, but all the same, I was very happy with Yesterday's Papers. I had wanted to create a complex, multi-layered mystery, and the reviews were extremely gratifying. The Sunday Times was among the newspapers that praised it lavishly, later choosing the book as one of the few mysteries to feature in its collection of "Paperbacks of the Year".

Briefly, if naïvely, I hoped that these accolades would signal a boost in sales. Instead, my paperback publishers (who did not publish me in hardback) decided to concentrate on their own stable of authors, and Yesterday's Papers soon disappeared from the shelves. Happily, when I moved to Hodder and Stoughton, the book enjoyed a fresh incarnation in paperback form. And I'm delighted that a mystery that will always be one of my favourites amongst my own works is now enjoying, thanks to the wonders of digital technology, a new life in a brand-new form.

Martin Edwards: an Appreciation

by Michael Jecks

Both as a crime writer and as a keen exponent of the genre, Martin Edwards has long been sought out by his peers, and is now becoming recognised as a contemporary crime author at the top of his form.

Born in Knutsford, Cheshire, Martin went to school in Northwich before taking a first class honours degree in law at Balliol College, Oxford. From there he went on to join a law firm and is now a highly respected lawyer specializing in employment law. He is the author of Tottel's *Equal Opportunities Handbook*, 4th edition, 2007.

Early in his career, he began writing professional articles and completed his first book at 27, covering the purchase of business computers. His non-fiction work continues with over 1000 articles in newspapers and magazines, and seven books dedicated to the law (two of which were co-authored).

His life of crime began a little later with the Harry Devlin series, set in Liverpool. The first of his series, *All The Lonely People* (1991), was shortlisted for the CWA John Creasey Memorial Dagger for the first work of crime fiction by a new writer. With the advent of his second novel, Martin Edwards was becoming recognised as a writer of imagination and flair. This and subsequent books also referenced song titles from his youth.

The Harry Devlin books demonstrate a great sympathy for Liverpool, past and present, with gritty, realistic stories. 'Liverpool is a city with a tremendous resilience of spirit and character,' he says in *Scene of the Crime,* (2002). Although his protagonist is a self-effacing Scousers with a dry wit, Edwards is not a writer for the faint-hearted. 'His gifts are of the more classical variety - there are points in his novels when I think I'm reading Graham Greene,' wrote Ed Gorman, while *Crime Time* magazine said 'The novels successfully combine the style of the traditional English detective story with a darker noir sensibility.'

More recently Martin Edwards has moved into the Lake District with mystery stories featuring an historian, Daniel Kind, and DCI Hannah Scarlett. The first of these, *The Coffin Trail*, was short listed for the Theakston's Old Peculier Crime Novel of the year 2006.

In this book Martin Edwards made good use of his legal knowledge. DCI Hannah Scarlett is in charge of a cold case review unit, attempting to solve old crimes, and when Daniel Kind moves into a new house, seeking a fresh start in the idyllic setting of the Lake District, he and she are drawn together by the murder of a young woman. The killer, who died before he could be convicted, used to live in Kind's new cottage.

Not only does Edwards manage to demonstrate a detailed knowledge of the law (which he is careful never to force upon the reader), with the Lake District mysteries he has managed to bring the locations to vivid life. He has a skill for acute description which is rare - especially amongst those who are more commonly used to writing about city life.

More recently Edwards has published *Take My Breath Away*, a stand-alone psychological suspense novel, which offers a satiric portrait of an upmarket London law firm eerily reminiscent of Tony Blair's New Labour government.

Utilising his legal experience, he has written articles about actual crimes. *Catching Killers* was an illustrated book describing how police officers work on a homicide case all the way from the crime scene itself to presenting evidence in court.

When the writer Bill Knox died, Edwards was asked by his publisher to help complete his final manuscript, on which Knox had been working until days before his death. Bill Knox's method of writing was to hone each separate section of his books before moving on to the next, so Martin was left with the main thrust of the story, together with some jotted notes and newspaper clippings. From these he managed to complete *The Lazarus Widow* in an unusal departure for him.

More conventionally, Martin Edwards is a prolific writer of short stories. He has published the anthology *Where Do You Find Your Ideas?* which offers a mix of Harry Devlin tales mingled with historical and psychological short stories. His *Test Drive* was short listed for the CWA Short Story Dagger.

Edwards edits the regular CWA anthologies of short stories. These works have included *Green for Danger*, and *I.D. Crimes of Identity*, which included his own unusual and notable story *InDex*. In 2003 he also edited the CWA's *Mysterious Pleasures* anthology, which was a collection of the Golden Dagger winners' short stories to celebrate the CWA's Golden Jubilee.

A founder member of the performance and writing group, Murder Squad, Martin Edwards has found the time to edit their two anthologies.

When not writing and editing, Edwards is an enthusiastic reader and collector of crime fiction. He reviews for magazines, books and websites, and his essays have appeared in many collections.

He is the chairman of the CWA's nominations sub-committee for the Cartier Diamond Dagger Award, the world's most prestigious award for crime writing.

Martin Edwards is one of those rare creatures, a crime-writer's crime-writer. His plotting is as subtle as any, his writing deft and fluid, his characterisation precise, and his descriptions of the locations give the reader the impression that they could almost walk along the land blindfolded. He brings them all to life.

(An earlier version of this article appeared in *British Crime Writing: An Encyclopaedia,* edited by Barry Forshaw)

Meet Martin Edwards

Martin Edwards is an award-winning crime writer whose fifth and most recent Lake District Mystery, featuring DCI Hannah Scarlett and Daniel Kind, is *The Hanging Wood*, published in 2011. Earlier books in the series are *The Coffin Trail* (short-listed for the Theakston's prize for best British crime novel of 2006), *The Cipher Garden*, *The Arsenic Labyrinth* (short-listed for the Lakeland Book of the Year award in 2008) and *The Serpent Pool*.

Martin has written eight novels about lawyer Harry Devlin, the first of which, *All the Lonely People*, was short-listed for the CWA John Creasey Memorial Dagger for the best first crime novel of the year. In addition he has published a stand-alone novel of psychological suspense, *Take My Breath Away*, and a much acclaimed novel featuring Dr Crippen, *Dancing for the Hangman*. The latest Devlin novel, *Waterloo Sunset*, appeared in 2008.

Martin completed Bill Knox's last book, *The Lazarus Widow*, and has published a collection of short stories, *Where Do You Find Your Ideas? and other stories*; 'Test Drive' was short-listed for the CWA Short Story Dagger in 2006, while 'The Bookbinder's Apprentice' won the same Dagger in 2008.

A well-known commentator on crime fiction, he has edited 20 anthologies and published eight non-fiction books, including a study of homicide investigation, *Urge to Kill*. In 2008 he was elected to membership of the prestigious Detection Club. He was subsequently appointed Archivist to the Detection Club, and is also Archivist to the Crime Writers' Association. He received the Red Herring Award for services to the CWA in 2011.

In his spare time Martin is a partner in a national law firm, Weightmans LLP. His website is www.martinedwardsbooks.com and his blog www.doyouwriteunderyourownname.blogspot.com

Also Available from Martin Edwards

All the Lonely People   *Suspicious Minds*   *I Remember You*

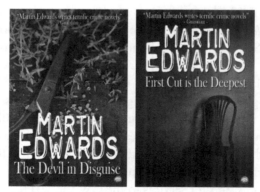

The Devil in Disguise   First Cut is the Deepest